Origins

A NOVELLA

by

Niko Zinovii

Zinovii Art Studio

Santa Monica, California

chalkos

Published by: Zinovii Art Studio
Santa Monica, California
www.zinoviiartstudio.com

ISBN: 978-0-9860685-9-1 (trade paperback)
ISBN: 978-0-9900085-2-1 (ebook: ePub)
ISBN: 978-0-9900085-3-8 (ebook: mobi)
LCCN: 2019919142

Cover concept & design by: Niko Zinovii
Cover art by: Leonardo Ariel Ariza Ardila
Cover art Copyright © 2019 by Niko Zinovii
Chapter symbol art Copyright © 2019 by Niko Zinovii

First Edition, 2019
Printed in the United States of America

Dedication

To the imaginative daydreamer

This novella is also dedicated with special appreciation to
Kenny F. and Michael P.

Contents

Part Four

Opening Note from the Author

This modest novella is based on an original screenplay of the same title written by this author. The novella adheres closely to that script in content and story presentation. The result is a lean literary work, a script adaptation in manuscript format that contains screenplay-like elements.

Niko Zinovii
Santa Monica, CA
16 October 2019

Niko Zinovii

Part One

"Man still bears in his bodily frame the indelible stamp of his lowly origin."—Charles Darwin

I. Anon

L ucy is dead."

Anon opened his lecture with these words, his dignified tone reflecting an unusual humanity, a depth of the soul that was made all the more pronounced by his sonorous voice, which projected a mix of strength and tenderness. "She died more than three and a half million years ago…"

Anon placed a cast of a fossil skull down upon the table before him, turning it to face the auditorium of university students he was lecturing.

"*Australopithecus afarensis,*" Anon identified the cast, drawing inquisitive stares from the students as he did so, for his look, his bearing, was rather arresting. He was classically tall, dark, and handsome, with a countenance that reflected a thoughtful dignity, a genuine decency and morality, heroism coupled to humility and compassion and tolerance. He seemed to reflect all man's nobler qualities absent humankind's vices. And yet there he stood, on display, paradoxically at one in the middling role of a humble, bespectacled, fortyish lecturer of staid, academic learning: Dr. David Anon, PhD, anthropology.

As Anon continued, his voice momentarily weakened, as if he were under some burdensome strain, some unknown oppressive stress. He suddenly looked quite vulnerable, and totally alone. There was something rather tragic about him, the lines of his face hinting at a past of isolation, loneliness, and loss. He seemed a man who clung to hope as he filled a space.

"Apparently, when the first *afarensis* fossil was found, in 1974, a Beatles song, 'Lucy in the Sky with Diamonds,' was playing on the radio. And so, that first skeleton was aptly given her informal name: *Lucy*.

"Lucy was considerably ape-like, her brain only slightly larger than that of today's chimpanzee, but her posture was upright. She walked this world fully bipedal, in a human-like fashion. Like you do. She was your direct ancestor."

Anon paused, momentarily losing himself in thought. When he continued, he did so with a deep, sympathetic, and contemplative appreciation for the subject matter, almost as if he were drawing upon some clairvoyant perception, as opposed to knowledge gleaned from books alone.

"They were fragile creatures," he continued, his baritone voice held controlled. "Surrounded by death. Average life expectancy less than twenty years. They couldn't speak. They couldn't create stone tools. Or use fire. They had no culture. But they did give rise to two unique and distinct lines of hominid evolution."

Anon reached into a nearby box and pulled out a second skull. It was slightly larger than the *afarensis*. It was also more primitive in appearance, markedly more ape-like. Anon placed it down upon the table, angling it off from the first skull.

"*Australopithecus africanus*," Anon named the fossil by genus and species. "Slightly larger than *afarensis*, *africanus* appeared approximately two and a half million years ago."

In Anon's mind's eye he momentarily visualized the past owner of the skull, so intimately connected was he to his lecture.

He imagined the *africanus* surrounded by forest, among a small group of others of its kind. He envisioned the hominid tugging a large root from a freshly dug hole, sniffing it, mouthing it apishly.

Anon pulled out a third skull, aligning it with the others but angling it further off to the left. This skull was even larger, more robust than the second skull, with heavier brow ridges and more pronounced facial prognathism.

"*Australopithecus robustus*," Anon stated. "Ruggedly built and massive-jawed, robustus met extinction one million years ago, ending this line of hominid evolution with a dead end."

Once again Anon briefly envisioned the mentioned hominid's vanished living face from the past. It was significantly more ape-like than *africanus*. In his mind Anon watched the *robustus* pull itself up into a tree, where it slowly rested its heavy head upon a branch and closed its eyes.

Anon motioned to the three skulls and a barren look palled his face. "*Afarensis*, *africanus*, *robustus*, and the end of the *Australopithecus* line. Africa was drying. Its forests were shrinking. This line of hominid, rather than moving out onto the expanding and danger-filled savanna, moved deeper into the forest. Seeking the safety of the trees. But these smaller forests were becoming increasingly crowded, their resources dwindling. Competition between their inhabitants was growing. *Robustus*'s fate was extinction."

Anon paced away from the table slowly, speaking with a tinge of forlorn sadness, as if he were once again privy to unusual insight, beyond the academic.

"Africa was changing. *Australopithecus* simply couldn't survive on the open savanna. They were forced to choose the forest and extinction. Their fate was inevitable, but, fortunately, for you, not altogether inescapable."

Anon stepped back to the table and pointed to a spot located parallel to the second skull but branching off to the right of the first skull.

"Two and a half millions years ago, right here, something extraordinary occurred. These pre-men of Africa, these Australopithecines, the first of them, Lucy, she gave rise not only to *africanus* but also to an entirely new genus. Something unlike anything to have ever walked this world before. In a sense, Lucy was Africa's *Eve*."

Anon reached down into his box and pulled out a fourth skull, positioning the plaster cast in its designated spot upon the table. This skull was human-like.

"*Homo habilis*. Handy man," Anon stated, his voice resonating with the pride of ancestral linkage, of connection. "The first early human. First of the genus *Homo*. *Habilis* possessed a substantially larger brain, rudimentary speech, the beginnings of culture, and the ability to look into a stone and see the tool inside it, not yet chipped free from the surrounding rock. *Habilis* dared to go out onto the savanna. This is your single most important ancestor."

And in Anon's mind's eye he saw this first true early human. Although the hominin's face was still primitive, his eyes held an intelligence and an awareness found nowhere else in the animal kingdom. Bringing down a blood-stained stone in his strong right hand, the *habilis* struck two rocks together, splitting one of them in half, creating a sharp cutting edge.

Jarred back to reality by the imagined blow, Anon reached down into his box and rather quickly pulled out three additional skulls, placing them down in line with *habilis*, one after the other, angling them off to the right so as to make a distinct evolutionary line apart from the *Australopithecus* dead-end line.

Each skull was larger and more human-like than its predecessor. Anon identified the casts promptly, matter-of-factly, as he placed them.

"*Homo erectus*, one point seven million years ago, the first to control fire. Archaic *Homo sapiens*, four hundred thousand years ago, transitional between *erectus* and later forms. And, finally, anatomically modern *Homo sapiens*, one hundred and twenty thousand years ago. You.

"In a somewhat more recent form, during the upper Paleolithic, the familiar although outdated term *Cro-Magnon* is sometimes used to identify the first early modern humans of Europe, named after the cave where their remains were first found, in France.

"There are a number of intermediate stages, interesting side branches, *neanderthalensis*, Denisovan, *floresiensis*, and others, which we'll discuss in future lectures, but today—today I want to keep this simple, to focus here, on the fact that as the *Australopithecus* line naturally evolved into a more brutish form that met eventual extinction as it crept deeper into the forest, the *Homo* branch rose to face new challenges, evolving over the past two and a half million years into today's culturally advanced form. Into you, this world's principle force. All because of what occurred at this point here."

Anon picked up the *habilis* skull, cradling it paternalistically.

"Next time," he continued, "we'll discuss how *habilis* came into existence. But, in observance of recent world events…"

Anon glanced at the newspaper lying nearby. Its headline read "World's First Limited Nuclear Exchange Expands India–Pakistan War."

"… and as today is our first lecture, I'll let you go early. Have a nice afternoon."

Anon stood there quietly amidst the arising clamor, carefully observing the students as they walked off chattering about matters entirely unrelated to his lecture. Apparently what he had just presented had had little if any impact on any of them—except for a pierced and tattooed young man who approached Anon with palpable enthusiasm.

"Wow." The student smiled. "Great lecture, Dr. Anon."

"You appreciated it?" Anon asked with genuine interest.

"Oh yeah, it was great. Awesome skulls."

"Good, good," Anon responded slowly, studying the youth quite seriously. "Did you find the lecture believable?"

"Believable?" the student's smile half dropped. "Like, did I believe it?"

"Yes." Anon nodded. "Did you feel that the archaeological evidence supported the facts? That man evolved, through natural processes, from a bipedal ape-like ancestor?"

"Well, yeah, sure, I guess so. I mean, I didn't really question it."

"You didn't question it?" Anon asked, rather surprised, still studying the student, carefully examining the boy's eyes, his facial expressions.

"Well, no, I mean, you wouldn't be teaching it if it weren't true, right?"

Anon finally sensed the boy's growing unease and in a calculated gesture he somewhat awkwardly placed a reassuring, fatherly hand upon the lad's shoulder. "No, no, of course not. Of course I wouldn't. Why would you ask such a thing?"

The boy stammered a bit, preparing to answer.

"No"—Anon feigned a smile, attempting to put the boy at ease—"it's a rhetorical question. No need to answer."

"Well, I should get going—"

"Do you think the others, your classmates, also took the lecture at face value? I mean, without questioning it?"

"Uh, yeah, I guess so," the student responded as he slowly backed away, heading off, having had enough. "With the skulls and all…"

"Interesting," Anon commented to himself quietly. "That's interesting."

Anon then picked up the *afarensis* skull, the Lucy-type hominid, Africa's Eve, and looked into its dark hollow eye sockets, which stared back at him mutely but hauntingly, as if calling out to him, beckoning to him from across the ages.

"So fragile," Anon mumbled to himself, almost as if in a trance, sympathetically running his fingers over the puncture holes in the back of the cranium, feeling the wounds inflicted by a great cat millions of years ago, back in the remote and unreachable Pliocene; a bygone epoch swallowed forever by the past. "So terribly fragile…"

—Time past:

> Dawn.
>
> At the forest's edge, a dozen or so hominids of the species *afarensis*, Lucy's kind, stirred, moving cautiously through the dense, leafy foliage, foraging for food within the safety of the trees. They were lean, chimpanzee-like, but oddly unfamiliar in appearance, disturbingly surreal, for they stood and walked upright, bipedally, their movements those of pre-men, not apes.
>
> One young female, lured by inquisitiveness, peered through the forest, past the trees, and she slowly and quietly wandered away from the others of her kind.
>
> Stepping out onto the savanna, she looked over Africa of time past: Africa of three million years ago.

11

Fear and curiosity filled her light brown chimp-like eyes, which by way of intellect emitted a glint of pre-humanity.

Following some irresistible, silent calling, the young *afarensis* walked off toward the activity surrounding a nearby water hole. After nearly a hundred unsure steps, she stood at the pool's edge, curiously surveying the animals gathered there: primitive baboons, antelopes, large herbivorous beasts.

Flap. She turned to the sound. A prehistoric vulture momentarily shadowed the sun as it dropped out of the cloudless sky, its talons sinking into the mud. The scavenger at once turned its hungry eyes to the young hominid, and she felt the surrounding animals grow still.

There was an unexpected flash of movement as the prehistoric leopard sprung from the tall grass, racing toward the slowest of all the assembled potential prey: the *afarensis*. The young female shrieked out as she desperately ran off for the safety of the trees, but within seconds the powerful cat pounced upon her, bringing her slight form crashing to the ground under its heavy, predatory weight, and a proto-human scream of horror echoed out over the early-dawn savanna.

Her kind, back in the safety of the trees, stiffened as they all turned to stare out of their forest, out to the savanna and its water hole, to watch the leopard suffocate and kill its prey, silencing the young *afarensis*'s horrid shrieks.

Off in the distance, prehistoric hyenas, ears thrust forward, cackled wildly as they started their mad race across the drying grassland toward the fresh kill.

In response the leopard growled, opened it jaws wide, and sank its canines into the head of its victim. There was the cruelest and most callous popping sound as its teeth punched through bone.

And a shiver ran through the small clan of hominids, who watched mutely, helplessly from afar as the great cat dragged away their family member. There was absolutely nothing they could do to alter the situation. Slowly, fearfully, the early pre-men of Africa retreated, vanishing deeper into the safety of the forest.

In the yellow light of the rising sun the leopard pulled its catch up into a lone knotted and twisted tree. There, undisturbed: teeth tore, large paws pushed and pulled, and the cat began to strip away the hominid's flesh, in order to devour her. The *afarensis*'s decapitated head dropped down out of the tree, white bone painted by smeared crimson, pasted to bits of flesh, tufts of hair.

Bouncing, the head tumbled through the grass until it disappeared into a large sinkhole in the earth. Dropping into subterranean darkness, the skull bounced once, twice, and then slowly rolled to a stop, where it lay unmoving, hauntingly still, in absolute silence—two deep, terrible, gaping holes in its whiteness mutely testifying to the brutal reality of life.

Niko Zinovii

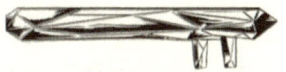

2. Eva

Taking long, rather elegant strides, Eva, slender and blonde, moved purposefully through the sea of oncoming students as she made her way toward the auditorium. Although wearing low-heeled shoes, she carried herself with uncommon European grace and femininity. She turned more than a few heads despite her conservative dress and minimal use of makeup, due to her refinement, but also because of her natural and unpretentious beauty, which seemed to amplify a fragile innocence, coupled to an aloof sensuality.

"I hear he's single and tall, dark, and handsome," an enthusiastic, earthy female faculty member, leaning out into the hall, whispered mischievously, teasingly, to Eva as she passed. "You know, like an old-time movie star."

Eva found the thought interesting but flashed back a soft, relaxed smile fixed to an incredulous look. As she entered the auditorium, however, she felt her smile drop, and suddenly she felt a bit nervous. For standing there before her, quietly placing skulls into a box, was a man whom she instantly felt powerfully drawn to, in a way that she had never before experienced. He was indeed tall, dark, and handsome, just like an old-time movie star. But there was something more; his mere presence—serious, restrained, noble, intelligent— seemed to express so much more in an unordinary, near tangible form.

"Dr. Anon?" she asked, almost shyly.

"Yes?"

She placed her books upon the table and extended a hand. "I'm Dr. Lie. That's Lie, *l, i, e,* as in not to tell the truth, although I always do. Eva Lie. Please call me Eva."

Anon took her offered hand and shook it a bit clumsily. But his touch was warm and pleasant, and Eva found herself momentarily hesitating to let go.

"It's nice to meet you, Eva," Anon responded, looking at her inquisitively. "Your accent, your surname, Lie, is it... Swedish?"

Eva felt her relaxed smile returning and she nodded, pleasantly surprised, her expressive slate-gray eyes widening with anticipation. "And yours, *Anon,* it's quite unusual. Other than the prolific genius Anon of ancient Greece, the name is virtually unknown in any language. So much so, in fact, that I understand it's become a synonym for *unknown.* The Greek Anon, he didn't leave behind any known descendants, so the origin of your surname is—well, I find it quite interesting."

Eva noticed Anon shift uncomfortably in his stance and she noticed something in him: loneliness, an inborn silence, a private pain.

"I teach ancient history," she offered as an explanation, as she sensed Anon erecting a protective veil of professionalism. "Classical antiquity."

"Ah," he nodded, but he remained noticeably on guard. "You're lecturing in here? Next?"

She nodded back and Anon reached for his box.

"Well," he remarked, "let me get this out of your way."

Eva surprised herself by stepping in front of him, blocking his exit. Instantly embarrassed, she stepped back, but not completely. "Actually," she found her voice, "I'm glad

I happened to come down early today, it gives me the opportunity to be one of the first to welcome you to the university. Welcome."

"Oh, thank you," Anon responded hesitantly, his pensive, guarded expression changing little.

"Do you like it so far?" she struggled to make conversation.

"Yes, yes I do."

"That's good. It's said that there's nothing like a good first impression."

"No, I guess not..." Anon admitted, relaxing a bit, looking at her for the first time in a different manner, in a genuinely interested, amorous way.

In that brief moment of pleasant silence, Eva felt a subtle romantic tension arise between them. It made her blush.

"So..." She found herself motioning to his box of skulls. "You teach anthropology? Human evolution?"

"Yes," Anon answered, suddenly staid and concerned. "Did you know that over fifty percent of the populace disbelieves in human evolution?"

"No, I didn't know that."

"Why do you think that is?" he asked earnestly.

"Religion maybe?"

"Do you think there's a conflict? Between religion and science?"

"I'm not sure." Eva hesitated. "Maybe it's that people don't like to think of themselves as... glorified apes."

"Dr. Lie," Anon asked her most seriously, "how do you view evolution?"

"I'm not sure I want to answer that."

"Why?"

"Because," she proceeded cautiously, "you might not like what you hear."

"You do accept Darwin, you do believe in human evolution, don't you?"

"I really don't want to welcome you on a bad note," she answered softly, in more of a plea than a statement, her accent and smile lending tenderness and emphasis to her words. "I mean, if I were to tell you 'not really,' or 'perhaps not,' or 'I'm not sure,' you, being a learned anthropologist, you'd likely react as if I told you that I believed the world was flat. I don't want to start things off badly. Really, I don't."

Anon stood there silent for what seemed a long moment. "I'm sorry," he then apologized. "I didn't mean to make you feel uncomfortable."

The noise and commotion that followed caught Eva by surprise. She had completely forgotten the students, who were now flooding into the auditorium, intruding upon her moment of privacy.

Anon picked up his box of skulls and newspaper. "It was nice meeting you, Eva," he said in a professional, guarded manner, and he walked off.

Eva nodded and stood there in silence, watching him leave, blinking, thinking, a bit confused, upset at the awkwardness of their initial conversation, yet feeling in her heart and in her mind that her life had somehow changed this day completely and forever.

As her students took their seats, she felt her eyes looking to the windows in the back of the auditorium, through which she observed Anon leaving the building, walking off across the large, city-centered campus. It was a lovely New England summer day outside, the grass so very green, trees in full foliage, students everywhere talking, laughing, walking, running to and fro. She noticed Anon nodding politely to passing students and teachers. She imagined him taking in all the new faces.

Little did she suspect that as Anon proceeded onward, he rather quickly retreated within himself, struggling against some inner turmoil. Nodding less, avoiding eye contact, he only grew more and more ill at ease. He actually let out a slight sigh of relief as he escaped the crowd and the wide-open outdoor space of the campus, entering a building through a door labeled "Faculty Offices – History, Sociology, Anthropology."

3. The Crystal

Anon nodded a bit hurriedly yet politely to the receptionist as he passed her on his way to his office, where a university employee was just finishing affixing a nameplate, "Dr. David Anon," to the door.

"Sorry, excuse me," Anon stated rather somberly as he entered his office, carefully pulling the door closed behind himself and locking it. Inside, alone, his anxiety lessened. His eyes briefly roamed over the room's empty walls, and then over his empty desktop, upon which he dropped his box and newspaper.

Leaning back against a wall, he found himself slowly pulling a tired hand down over his face, emotionally fatigued, trying not to think about his private stress.

Yet slowly, ever so slowly, he felt his eyes drop and focus upon the *Australopithecus robustus* skull resting atop the other skulls in his box. It seemed to be staring up at him, challenging him, in a mocking, dead silence.

In his mind Anon heard his own words from the lecture he had just given:

Australopithecus robustus. Ruggedly built and massive-jawed, robustus met extinction one million years ago, ending this line of hominid evolution with a dead end.

He then felt his eyes shift slowly over to the newspaper, to focus on the photo of the mushroom cloud below the headline:

"World's First Limited Nuclear Exchange Expands India–Pakistan War."

The headline slowly faded and became phantom-like, ghostly in Anon's unblinking stare. Through its indistinct words Anon found himself envisioning Indian and Pakistani soldiers positioning themselves, yelling, shooting, firing rockets, engaging in combat on a bleak, war-torn, burning landscape.

And more, he envisioned an entire Indian metropolis in the midst of a panic-stricken evacuation. Its citizens suddenly ceasing their mad activity in response to the blast of a haunting siren that wailed shrilly over the city, lifting all eyes upward, causing voices to whimper...

Anon's perception lifted too, ascending high above the Earth, as if he were undergoing an out-of-body experience. From the heavens so high above he saw below, in his mind's eye, the white-hot nuclear flash. It instantaneously engulfed and replaced the lights of the Indian city. The abominable shape of the rising mushroom cloud silently raged upward through the darkness. Within seconds there was a second such horrid blast, this one over Pakistan.

Anon shook his head, clearing his unfocused gaze. He read the newspaper's secondary headline, farther down the page: "USA Enters China–Taiwan Conflict."

Lifting a trembling hand, he nervously checked his left side, feeling beneath his upper arm. *Yes, I still have it.*

Opening his suit jacket, he looked at the holster hanging there, concealed against his torso. There was something tubular and dark and odd resting within it.

With the utmost care, Anon carefully unholstered the object, lifting it up into the light. It was a blue-black prismatic crystal rod, six-sided, a few inches in diameter, perhaps a foot in length. Two rectangular prongs protruded from one of its ends, making it resemble a large skeleton key. Shimmering in the light, it appeared to be made of a polished, futuristic, diamond-like glass. Crude in shape, however, it did not appear to be man-made, machine-made. It looked more like some type of mineral oddity that one might find growing deep beneath the Earth's surface, in a subterranean cavern.

Holding this skeleton key firmly, Anon simply stared at it as if it were of the most vital importance.

Looking back at the newspaper, he then allowed the headlines to provide him with the strength he required to slowly calm himself, to slowly regain his composure.

Niko Zinovii

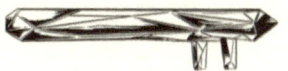

4. The Pale Man

Eva, alone in her office, Google searched for the second time "Dr. David Anon, PhD, anthropology" on her desktop computer.

Again: nothing.

~

Later, as Eva stepped out onto one of the campus's many crisscrossing sidewalks, leaving for the day, she found her expressive friend catching up to her, joining her.

"So, I was right?" Eva's co-worker asked, gossipy. "About the new guy?"

"Yes." Eva smiled softly, admitting it. "You certainly were."

"Oh, Eva, you like him?"

"Am I that transparent?" she asked shyly.

"Well, what did he think of you? Tell me?"

"I'm not sure," Eva answered honestly, wondering about it.

"You didn't talk about Taiwan, did you? You know how politics—"

"No, no politics," Eva interjected, concerned. "But religion somehow came up. And evolution. At times, he seemed so guarded, so stern, and yet I felt such a strong attraction to him. But also… an uncomfortableness—the way he asked certain questions, so seriously."

"You mean he didn't show you any of his laid-back Southern hospitality?"

"Southern hospitality?" Eva asked, confused.

"Yeah, he's supposed to be from North Carolina, born and raised in Charlotte. Moved up here just two weeks ago."

"Are you certain?"

"Yeah, why?"

"He didn't have a Southern accent," Eva answered. "In fact, I thought that— Oh, there he is."

Twenty yards up ahead of them Anon turned onto the city's sidewalk, walking away from them, away from the campus, heading toward a busy intersection and its crosswalk.

Eva's friend smiled. "Well, speak of the devil. Wow, he is good-looking. Tall too. You want to catch up to him?"

"No," Eva answered quickly. "No, slow down. I think we should slow down..."

"Follow him?"

Eva nodded, with a hint of a smile.

While Eva slowed her pace, observing Anon from afar, he stepped up to the crosswalk and stopped. As he did so, directly across the street from him, a dark limousine pulled out of traffic and parked. Anon looked to the limo, rather intensely, as he impatiently waited for the light to change.

Eva's friend poked her. "He's got a limo waiting for him?"

Anon focused on the limousine's darkly tinted driver's side window as it rolled down. It was odd how Anon remained so calm and composed, his face divulging no expression of surprise or fear. Odd because of the bizarre, rather terrifying appearance of the limo's driver.

From Eva's approaching vantage point, all that she could initially see of the driver was a vague, dead-white face, which appeared eerily surreal due to how it contrasted so starkly with the man's black suit and the dark interior of the limousine.

But then the clouds above parted, allowing the sun to shine down upon the driver, lighting the man's sparse, thin black hair, which eerily covered a mostly balding head. Lighting the man's face and dark, lifeless eyes. Eyes without eyelashes or eyebrows, eyes sunken so deeply into their sockets... Eyes set above pale blue lips; eyes framed by an odd, dead-white face pockmarked by patches of razor stubble growing back unevenly within an area of pale naked smoothness.

Eva felt her legs stutter and slow, the hair on the back of her neck rising on end.

The pale man focused on Anon, lifted a large bony hand, and slowly but adroitly shaped his fingers and thumb into a series of different configurations. The hand signals were short and animated, distinctly primitive in appearance, as if they were gestures being made by one aboriginal hunter to another while they silently stalked their prey.

Eva found herself so transfixed, so utterly focused on this pale man, she failed to notice Anon, who, keeping his right arm hanging unmoving at his side so as not to draw attention to himself, responded stealthily: deftly arranging his fingers and thumb into a series of rapid gestures, Anon sent a silent, secretive message back to the waiting limo.

This triggered the limo's rear window to roll down. Within the dark interior, Eva could just make out the limo's heavily shadowed passenger, whose presence was revealed at first only by slanted eyes peering out of the blackness. Eyes emanating nobility yet also pronounced hubris...

Eva watched on as this unusual passenger leaned forward ever so slightly, revealing a face of Caucasian features cast within a deep olive complexion. He looked youthful, vigorous, yet his eyebrows were entirely gray... This man looked at Anon, his stare projecting a calm, formidable intellect.

Anon made eye contact with the man. And they nodded almost imperceptibly to one another.

"The limousine," Eva whispered, captivated, as they slowly walked up to and stood unnoticed right behind Anon, "it is for him…"

"Light's changing," her friend noticed.

The crosswalk sign changed from "DON'T WALK" to "WALK" and Anon immediately stepped off the curb, so intent was he on crossing the street, on reaching the waiting limo.

Eva did not see the car; she only heard the terrible screech of its tires as it skidded to a stop, hitting Anon, knocking him to the street, where his head struck the pavement, hard.

"Oh my God!" Eva cried out and she ran to Anon, kneeling beside him in the street as he lay there flat upon his back, helpless, his eyes blinking in a confused state of shock.

"Call an ambulance!" Eva pleaded, her voice cracking, racked with concern. "Someone call an ambulance! Please!"

Eva glanced over at the limousine to see its mysterious passenger partially open his door, to also go to Anon, but her presence and that of the gathering crowd somehow deterred the man from taking such action. He hesitated, frowned, yanked his door shut, and nodded to his strange pale driver, and the limo drove off.

~

In the ambulance, Anon experienced his vision momentarily coming back into focus, and he found Eva looking down at him, terribly concerned. He felt her put an arm around him to comfort him, and they made meaningful eye contact.

He could hear her clearly as she said his name, but oddly he could barely hear the siren of his transportation, the rest of the world having been somehow muffled in his mind to near silence.

"Dr. Anon?"

Her words echoed in his head. And in his weakening vision everything surrounding her faded to an unsettling, numbing black. Blurring, her face momentarily lost all distinction, before transforming and sharpening into her face from when they had first met in the auditorium earlier that day. In his mind her gentle, accented voice seemed to come from a dream:

"Dr. Anon?"

Before he could attempt to answer, her face distorted and morphed into that of his young, tattooed student:

"Wow, great lecture, Dr. Anon."

Blurring, the young man's face changed back to Eva's.

"Dr. Anon?"

And then back to the student's:

"—great lecture, Dr. Anon."

And back to Eva's:

"Dr. Anon?"

And to the student's:

"—Dr. Anon."

Slowly, the blurred, transforming faces faded, faded, faded, until all became utterly black and all that Anon could hear was the entrancing echoing of his name over and over: "Dr. Anon... Dr. Anon... Dr. Anon..."

Then slowly, ever so slowly, he slipped into a state of absolute silence, absent of thought.

Niko Zinovii

5. A Second Chance

Darkness. Silence. And then, a voice in the dark:

"Dr. Anon?" a doctor asked.

The world slowly brightened and came into focus for Anon. He was quite surprised to find a nurse and a young, Ivy League, butter-haired doctor standing over him. At first he did not know what to make of it. But then he glanced about and saw that he was lying on a hospital bed, in a hospital, wearing a hospital gown. His eyeglasses had been removed—he noticed them resting on the table beside him.

"Well." The doctor smiled. "It's good to see you finally come around. You were beginning to worry us."

Anon reached up to touch the back of his aching head and he saw that his right arm was in a cast from the elbow down. And he found that his head was bandaged.

"No need to be alarmed," the doctor assured him. "Believe it or not, your injuries were surprisingly minor, considering the nature of your accident."

The doctor looked into Anon's eyes with a penlight, observing pupil dilation.

"Other than the broken wrist, you have some badly bruised ribs and a slight concussion. You whacked your head pretty hard on the street. But overall, I'd say you were pretty lucky. Very lucky."

The doctor pulled the penlight away. "How do you feel?"

"I…" Anon answered. "I don't remember being in an accident."

~

"Miss Lie?" the doctor called to Eva as he entered the waiting room, where Eva was sitting rigid, worried.

"Is he going to be all right?" she asked, moving to the doctor.

"Well, we don't know for sure."

"But I thought you said—"

"There's been an unexpected complication."

"What do you mean?"

"Well," the doctor explained, "due to the blow that he received to the back of the head, he's experiencing a state of memory loss."

"Memory loss?"

The doctor gently took hold of Eva by the elbow and led her back to her seat, where he sat beside her. "Post-traumatic amnesia," he clarified. "But it's an unusual case because he's not experiencing total memory loss. He remembers his name, the fact that he's a teacher, and that he's from North Carolina, but nothing else. He remembers everything that he's learned but nothing that he's experienced. Right now he's simply a name without a past. Now, in most cases, memory returns in a few days. But if it doesn't return inside of a week, then, well, he may have serious brain damage."

"Oh God." Eva's voice went weak. "Were you able to contact his family?"

"According to your university he has no family," the doctor replied, thinking. "Would you like to see him?"

"Oh, I don't know—I would like to but I don't really know him. I mean, I only met him this morning."

"This morning?"

She nodded.

"That would make you one of his most recent memories. Could you please come in to see him? Just to say hello. I'd like to see if he recognizes you."

Eva felt uncertain about it, unsure how Anon would react.

"It could help," the doctor added.

"… Okay," she agreed, her emotions racing. "If you think it'll help."

~

Anon sat himself up in bed, feeling disorientated but calm. He wondered why he would feel such a sense of calm, given his situation of having just been in a serious accident, awakening to find himself in a strange hospital. Having completely forgotten his past. Was it normal to feel so calm? So at ease. So emotionally disconnected from… something…

As he struggled with it, he once again noticed his eyeglasses resting nearby. He picked them up, put them on, and instantly found himself quite puzzled. Looking across the room, he removed the glasses and then put them back on. There was no perceptible change in his vision. He brought a hand up in front of his face, looking at it up close, with and without his glasses. No change. He was able to see equally well with or without the spectacles, near or far.

The doctor stepped into the room, leading Eva forward.

"Funny," Anon remarked, perplexed, "I don't seem to need these. The lenses, they must be plain glass."

"Perhaps they were a fashion statement," Eva offered softly, pleasantly, pleased to see Anon, her gentle eyes looking over his cast, his bandaged head.

"David," the doctor asked Anon, "do you recognize your visitor?"

Anon searched his memory.

"This is a colleague of yours," the doctor prompted. "From the university."

"From the university?" Anon asked.

"Yes," the doctor answered. "Where you're teaching."

"Teaching…" Anon repeated the word, straining to remember. He found himself looking into Eva's lovely eyes, at her full lips, her high cheekbones, her soft chin. He found himself quite taken by her youth, her natural beauty, her feminine mannerisms. But he did not recognize her. "I'm sorry… But I don't seem to remember you."

Anon's serious, guarded demeanor from earlier in the day was completely absent, as was his self-erected barrier of professionalism. It no longer existed. Instead, there was only human vulnerability and commonality, layered upon a great decency and a quiet strength. His memory loss seemed to have somehow freed his soul.

"Well then"—Eva stepped over to him with renewed anticipation, offering her hand—"allow me to reintroduce myself. After all, it's not often that one is given a second chance to make a good first impression. My name is Eva Lie. Please, call me Eva."

Anon automatically reached forward with his right hand. Realizing that it was in a cast, he smiled genuinely, warmly, and switched hands, awkwardly shaking with his left.

"Sorry," he apologized. And as he felt her gentle, warm touch, he held on to her hand momentarily, not wanting to let go, finding himself deeply comforted by her, attracted to her. He sensed in her a rare, profound sensitivity. He wondered how he could not remember someone of such inner and outer beauty. It baffled him.

"It's quite all right," she responded, her eyes aglow. "It makes shaking hands much more interesting. David."

"I, um," Anon responded, feeling rather odd, an unsure smile lifting and dropping on his face, "I hear my name, David, and I know it's my name, but for some reason I'm not finding myself comfortable with it. It doesn't feel right. *David*. I know this is going to sound strange but... would you mind calling me by my last name instead?"

"Dr. Anon?" she asked, deflated, yet with hope. "Or just Anon?"

"Just Anon," he answered. "I realize it's a strange request but I'd feel more comfortable if you called me Anon. I don't know why, I just would."

"Well..." She nodded, her calm smile lifting. "Anon it is, then. *Anon*. I like the name."

"Thank you."

"You know," she said, smiling ingenuously, relaxing further, "you seem so much less formal than when we first met this morning—in a good way. You seem more relaxed, more open. More like a real person— Oh, I didn't mean it like that. Please don't take that the wrong way."

Anon's mood dropped. "How can I?" he responded calmly, taking no offence, feeling overcome by his own vulnerability. "I don't remember this morning."

"Anon," Eva could not resist asking, "do you remember the limousine? And the men in it, who were waiting for you?"

Anon struggled to remember, but he could not. His eyes swelled with frustration.

"Well," the doctor stepped in, "it's getting late. I guess we'll leave you now, David—I mean Anon. Let you rest, get a good night's sleep."

"I'll be staying here for the night?" Anon asked.

The doctor nodded.

It was at that moment that Anon noticed his holster. It was

across the room, neatly set atop his folded clothing. Immediately he felt overcome by a powerful, rising state of anxiety, his heart beginning to pound, to race. And more, he felt an overwhelming urge to secure the holster. Before he could give thought to his actions, he found himself stumbling out of bed and rushing over to it.

"What?" the doctor gasped.

Anon grabbed and scooped up the holster, immediately checking to make sure that his unusual key-like oddity was still within it. It was. He felt incredibly relieved, yet he knew not why. He only found himself blindly clutching the holster tightly against his chest, to prevent it from being taken away from him.

"This—" he stammered, "this is mine! It's important. I—I need to keep it near me. Always. Close to me. I can't lose it. Can't risk that!"

"It's okay." The doctor moved to Anon, assuring him in a composed, professional, steady voice. "Calm down. It's your property. You can keep it with you. Nobody's going to try to take it away from you. That's why it's here. In your room. With your belongings. It's yours."

Anon suddenly realized how terribly confused he felt, and also how physically weak he was. He allowed the doctor to guide him back to his bed as Eva watched on, puzzled and concerned.

"Now," the doctor directed Anon, "I want you to get back into bed. Try to relax. Sleep."

Anon nodded and crawled into bed, holding on to his retrieved holster as if his life depended on possessing it. Half exposed, the mysterious blue-black oddity within it sparkled in the room's light.

"Anon..." Eva asked, "what is that?"

Anon felt calmed by her soft voice and his panic subsided appreciably. He looked at the crystal as if seeing it for the very first time, and he tried to remember. "… I don't know… But I remember that… it's important."

He found himself turning to the doctor. "When will I be able to leave?" he asked. "I have to teach."

Eva turned her eyes to the doctor, who did not have an immediate answer.

"It's very important that I teach…" Anon tried to explain. "I remember that. I'm supposed to be teaching."

"The most important thing right now," the doctor responded, "is for you to get some rest. It's a good sign that you're beginning to remember some things, but we don't need to rush this. In a day or two you'll likely have regained your memory completely. Until then, I'd like to keep you here, under observation. Under our care."

Anon looked to Eva, and then back at the doctor. "Yes, all right, I understand."

The doctor nodded, about to turn to leave.

"What day is it?" Anon asked.

"Tuesday," the doctor answered.

"Tuesday." Anon struggled with it. "If I'm feeling better tomorrow, can I teach tomorrow? At the university. I have a class on Wednesday. I remember that."

The doctor thought for a moment. "Perhaps. Placing you back into a familiar environment could prove beneficial. It's often used therapeutically. I'll consider it."

"Thank you," Anon responded, quite relieved. Although he also suddenly felt so very terribly alone as he watched the doctor guiding Eva away.

"Bye," Eva said to him, reluctant to leave but doing so. "It was nice meeting you. Again. Anon."

"Bye…" Anon whispered as they stepped out the door.

Alone, Anon slowly turned his attention to his glass-like key. He strained to remember what it was, completely confounded as to why the object held such emotional power over him. *What is this?*

"… Why can't I remember?"

Origins

Niko Zinovii

Part Two

Niko Zinovii

6. Night Visitor

Night.

An old, black two-door sedan turned into the hospital's nearly vacant parking lot. Despite the dark hour, its headlights were off. The car circled slowly before parking.

Within the sedan, a thick, pale finger pushed down upon the vehicle's ignition button and the engine went silent. Strange that such an old-model automobile would have such a modern ignition switch, allowing for no key to be used.

The tall, gaunt man who stepped out of the car stood there for a moment, silent, motionless. It was the deathly pale man, the limousine driver who had been waiting for Anon at the university. Under the dim, cool light of moon the man's dark, somber suit appeared eerily, unrealistically neat, unnaturally wrinkle free, his pale dead-white face desiccated and inhumanly grim.

Completely devoid of emotion, the man started toward the hospital, his movements deliberate, stiff, sluggish, as if his legs were having some difficulty following the orders given by his brain.

~

Ascending an empty stairwell, the odd, pale man exited onto a particular floor. Slowly and silently, his grim face expressionless, the man started down a corridor, heading toward a distant nurse's station. As he did so, he passed a cart, on top of which lay a coffee cup and spoon. The spoon emitted a lifeless, whispering metallic cry as it slowly and uncannily curled up to lie there deformed, bent upon itself by some seemingly supernatural, invisible force.

~

At the nurse's station, Gloria, pulling a night shift, quietly put away a patient's file as she glanced at her co-worker, Pam, who was paging through a late-edition newspaper, ignoring its headlines on the India–Pakistan War, the Taiwan Conflict, and the ongoing conflicts in the Middle East.

The station's large desktop clock, resting atop the file cabinet, suddenly stopped, its hands frozen in place. Gloria looked at the clock. As she did so, she noticed in its glass face the reflection of an approaching dark-suited man.

"Pam," she asked, "can you take care of him?"

"Take care of who, honey?"

"That man…" Gloria turned around to an empty hall. She glanced back at the clock but the reflection was gone. "I could have sworn…"

"They switch you to nights and you start seeing things?" Pam smiled.

"No, I…" Gloria found it impossible to accept. "I'll be right back."

Placing her heavy key ring upon the countertop, she made her way down the hall, looking for the man she knew she had seen. As she reached the spot where the approaching man had been, she involuntarily clutched herself.

"Oh, so cold," she mumbled aloud, shivering. "How'd it get so cold?"

She then caught a whiff of something very unpleasant.

"Ugh, smells… smells like someone died."

Concerned, she entered the room to her left to investigate.

The moment she disappeared into the room, the pale man stepped back out into the hall, from one of the rooms Gloria had passed. Without hesitation, he continued his silent stalking walk toward the nurse's station.

As Pam turned a page of her newspaper, the bracelet on her left wrist suddenly mysteriously buckled and bent itself out of shape. She just stared at it for a second or two in absolute bewilderment. She then jerked upright and clutched herself as she too felt an uncanny, freezing chill.

"Ohhh…" she murmured.

She then smelled the offensive odor. It made her cough. She looked up and down the hall, but it was empty. She looked for Gloria.

"Gloria?"

Pam found herself bringing a hand to the side of her head, experiencing a sudden, intense headache. She called out louder: "Gloria?"

Out of Pam's line of sight, well behind her, having already passed the station, the strange pale man stepped out of a room and continued his silent walk, moving farther away from her, heading toward the end of the corridor. As he turned the corner, disappearing from sight, Gloria popped back into the hall.

"Did you smell that?" Pam asked. "What was that?"

"I don't know…"

Pam moved to Gloria, guiding her back to the station. "Hey, are you okay?"

"I don't know," Gloria complained. "I suddenly don't feel well."

"Yeah, me neither. Got a splitting headache coming on."

"Pam," Gloria asked, "did you do this to my keys?"

"Do what?"

Gloria moved aside, allowing Pam to see the keys. Lying there atop the counter, all the keys on the ring were bent and twisted, eerily curled up upon themselves.

~

The doorknob to Anon's room trembled and then slowly turned, and the pale man entered. Almost at once the metal utensils resting atop a nearby plate and tray bent and curled up.

Anon shuddered and sat up, clutching himself as he was awakened by the sudden, intense cold and foul smell that accompanied this strange man.

Hearing an odd crackling sound, Anon turned to his night table and watched in amazement as his eyeglasses, resting there, buckled and bent, the lenses cracking as the wire frame curled up upon itself.

Anon then noticed someone standing there in the dark, motionless near the door, a tall figure.

"… Who's there?" Anon whispered.

Anon's visitor unhurriedly moved out of the darkness, toward Anon, stepping into the moonlight. Upon seeing the man's dead-white face, Anon, without his memory, expressed the shock and fear that he had earlier failed to display.

"What do you want? Who are you?" Anon stammered.

The man stepped up to a large metal table. He touched it lightly with his fingertips and it vibrated and moved out of his way, compelled to do so by some unseen, paranormal force.

The man's cold, detached, sunken-in eyes then focused on Anon. He took a few more steps forward and then sluggishly and deliberately sat himself upon a wooden visitor's chair, which did not tremble or shudder or react in any way to his presence.

"Preliminary reports…" the pale man stated in a low, emotionless voice that was bone dry, gravelly deep, his words delivered with forced effort, "indicate that your injuries were minor… They want to know… why are you still here?"

Anon just sat there in shock, not knowing what to make of the situation. He watched on numbly as his visitor tried again:

"… How long will you be convalescing here?"

Anon found his voice this time. "I… I… don't know."

In the silence that followed, Anon could not discern any sign of intent on the man's grim, impassive face.

"… The signature," the pale man finally said. "Do you have the signature? Is it safe?"

Anon stole a quick glance down at his mysterious key-like rod. Subtly, he shifted his body to conceal it entirely with the sheets.

"I—I don't understand," he responded. "I don't know what you want."

And Anon momentarily stopped breathing as he observed his strange visitor's reaction. The man's hollow, unblinking eyes swung phlegmatically left to right, surveying the room.

"… Was it taken from you?"

Anon felt his head begin to ache. He began to feel ill.

"Yes…" he lied again to his visitor.

For the first time Anon saw an emotional reaction from the man, who narrowed his eyes predatorily. It was most unexpected and Anon felt a deep fright creep over him.

"But I know where it is," he quickly added. "I can get it back."

It seemed to take forever for the pale man to respond. Anon felt his fear growing uncomfortably intense as he wondered if he had made the right choice, lying as he had to this macabre being.

"… Will you require assistance?" the man finally asked.

"No…" Anon assured his visitor. "No. I won't require assistance."

Anon then added: "You want this thing? What is it?"

The odd man just stared at Anon. Then, blinking slowly and deliberately, he responded, his words coming out slower than before:

"… My energy… is running low… I… must go now…"

Anon watched on absolutely dumbfounded as the man rose shakily, his movements exceptionally slow and unsteady.

Anon felt his eyes just following his visitor as the man made his way, step by step, over to the door, where he touched the knob lightly. The knob rattled eerily, turning by itself, and the door creaked open.

Before leaving, the man turned back to Anon and breathed out the words:

"… They… will be watching."

And the pale man left, the door closing silently behind him.

Origins

Niko Zinovii

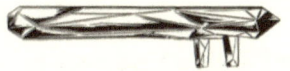

7. A Mutation?

D r. Foster, middle-aged, well dressed, politely held the door open for the younger and brainier-looking Dr. Kaplan as they entered the building in which Anon was giving his lecture. In unison they closed their umbrellas as they started down the corridor together.

"I'm not sure I understand," Foster asked in a calm, professional tone. "Why would they discharge him so soon? Wouldn't his condition prevent him from being capable of teaching?"

"Well," Kaplan answered skeptically, "according to his doctor he should be able to function normally and his returning to work might actually speed up his recovery. The hospital even went and assigned him a nurse; she's with him now, for observation and assistance. They assured me that everything would go smoothly."

"But you're not convinced?"

"No, I'm not," Kaplan stated as they approached the auditorium where Anon could be heard lecturing within. "He didn't seem quite right when I spoke with him this morning. I wanted to get your impression."

Foster nodded to Kaplan as they quietly entered the auditorium, inconspicuously remaining off to the side, standing by its open doors, near where a plain-clothes nurse was seated.

Anon, standing before the hall's podium, his head bandaged more lightly, less conspicuous than it had been in the hospital, noticed the men and paused, looking to them, wondering what they wanted. Foster smiled courteously and motioned for Anon to continue, which he did.

"Many species of fauna and flora alive today," Anon went on, "are essentially identical in appearance to their ancestors and have remained virtually unchanged, except for minimal environmental variation, for millions of years."

Anon felt that his delivery was good, professional, but also that something was wrong. He did not feel as confident as he had thought he would; he felt uncertain, self-doubting. He also felt quite distracted, and still unnerved by the unexpected visit that he had been paid at the hospital last night. He suddenly saw in his mind's eye the grim, dead-white face of his visitor, and he heard in his thoughts the man's bone-dry voice: *They… will be watching.*

The doctors and nurses… They didn't believe me in the hospital, about having a visitor…

I didn't imagine it, he assured himself. *It happened. It was real.*

Anon shook his mind clear, focused his thoughts, and stepped over to the nearby table, upon which rested his casts of fossil skulls, positioned once again to reflect the diverging *Australopithecus* and *Homo* evolutionary lines. He placed a hand upon the cranium of the *afarensis* skull, the Lucy hominid.

"Why is it, then," he continued, "that from *afarensis* to *habilis* there is a rapid and sudden change two and a half million years ago? Remember, Darwin's theory of natural selection calls for continued, minute changes over long expanses of time… The *Australopithecus* line clearly fits this pattern."

Anon motioned to the line of the three *Australopithecus* skulls.

"*Afarensis, africanus, robustus.* The slow, gradual transition is very apparent. Moving back into the forest, these creatures slowly became more and more ape-like until they met extinction. But…"

Pausing, Anon pointed to the line of skulls representing the genus *Homo*.

"But what about *habilis*? Do we see gradual, smooth, continuous evolution in this line? From *habilis* to modern *Homo sapiens*, yes, we do, but what about from *afarensis* to *habilis*? There appears to be a missing link between them… Doesn't there?"

Anon felt himself falter slightly; he sensed that something was deeply troubling him but he did not yet understand what it was. He felt compelled to continue the lecture.

"How can we explain this? This problem of a missing link? How did something so…" Anon paused to pick up the *afarensis* skull. "… ape-like…"

—Time past:

> The young, chimpanzee-like female *afarensis* stood at the water hole's edge, curiously surveying the animals gathered there: primitive baboons, antelopes, and large herbivorous beasts.

"… give rise to something so…" Anon pointed to the *habilis* skull with his other hand. "… human?"

—Time past:

> The first true early human. Although the hominin's face was still primitive, his eyes held an intelligence and an awareness found nowhere else in the animal kingdom. Bringing down a blood-stained stone in his strong right hand, the *habilis* struck two rocks together, splitting one of them in half, creating a sharp cutting edge.

Anon slowly lowered the skull, asking himself aloud, with genuine uncertainty: "How did this happen?"

Out of the corner of his eye, he noticed Foster and Kaplan exchanging glances.

"This is the question that Darwin was unable to answer," Anon went on, choosing to ignore the men. "He couldn't explain it… He couldn't understand it."

Anon suddenly felt his conscience twist, knot up, for he knew that what he was about to say was not the truth but he found himself saying it regardless:

"Punctuated equilibrium. This is what modern science has added to Darwin's theory… a macro-mutation. Every now and then, a species mutates. Creating something very, very different. This is how *habilis* came to be. Two and a half million years ago, an *afarensis* gave birth to something… very different. Because—because of a mutation.

"This is what was missing from Darwin's theory. It's—it's what he didn't understand. What he couldn't explain… Mutation… A mutation?"

Anon looked up as he heard students beginning to whisper to one another.

He then suddenly heard in his mind once again the haunting voice of last night's visitor: *They… will be watching.*

"Who the hell are they?" Anon asked aloud, only to realize after doing so that he had not voiced his question internally. He saw his nurse look at him. He began to feel uncomfortable, a bit panicky, claustrophobic.

"Please, excuse me," he said, trying his best to gather himself as he walked out quickly, moving right past Foster, Kaplan, and his nurse, all of whom followed him out into the hall—where he turned about to face them.

"I—I can't believe I'm teaching that—that lie," he confessed, agitated by the fact that he had done so. "A mutation? Do you really believe that? That you're here because of some freak mutation that happened over two million years ago?"

He noticed Eva coming down the nearby stairs. Their eyes met briefly. He hesitated to go on in front of her. But he felt so perplexed, disorientated. He turned away from them, asking himself:

"Are there species alive today that are in some intermediate, mutated, transitional evolutionary stage? I can't seem to remember…"

"Dr. Anon—" Kaplan called to him.

"Well, I—I don't believe it," Anon declared rather loudly as he turned back around to face them. "I'm not sure why but I just don't. Something deep down in my gut is telling me that it's wrong. That it's a lie. I don't believe it. I don't believe I ever did. Feels good to say that. Wow."

And Anon looked to Eva, who was just staring at him, quite surprised, quietly taking in what he was saying.

"Dr. Anon," Kaplan tried again, concerned about the students who were now leaving the auditorium, lingering there in the hall, staring at Anon. "Remember me, from this morning? I'm Dr. Kaplan, our department chairman."

"Of course I remember you!" Anon almost shouted.

"Please try to calm yourself," the nurse said, and she reached out to place a supportive hand on Anon's upper arm, unintentionally touching him near where he wore his holster beneath his suit jacket.

"No!" Anon yanked away from her in an uncharacteristically violent, desperate manner, clutching at his concealed holster.

Anon found Foster stepping up to him next, the man's manner courteous, respectful, his voice kept low, professional. "Dr. Anon, you probably don't remember me, but I'm Dr. Foster, dean of arts and sciences. I'm afraid I'm going to have to insist on a temporary medical leave of absence, effective immediately. I suggest that with your nurse, you readmit yourself to the hospital to receive proper care. I can assure you that your position here will not in any way be in jeopardy. You're our finest new recruit and we only want you to recover."

"But…" Anon felt a state of confusion settle upon him that he did not understand. "I'm supposed to be here. Teaching."

"And you will be," Foster assured him. "Once you've recovered, fully, we'll restore your teaching status immediately. Dr. Anon, please, I'm only trying to help. I'm acting in your best interest. And the students'."

For the first time Anon became aware of the gathering mob of students. He also noticed the deep concern etched on Eva's face. As he momentarily made eye contact with her, he felt it calm him, ground him somewhat, and he recovered most of his composure.

"I understand." He nodded deferentially to Foster. "Thank you. I apologize for the scene. I'll do what you say."

"Please, this way, Dr. Anon," the nurse offered to guide him away, being careful not to touch him this time. Anon hesitated but then complied, nodding a bit uncomfortably to Eva, who nodded back as they parted company.

Eva stood in place, still and silent, her mild eyes focused solely on Anon as he reluctantly walked off. So intense was her concentration on Anon that all her other senses temporarily disconnected. She became completely oblivious to the crowd of students who, seeing that the show was over, dispersed like a tempestuous storm, navigating around Eva, leaving her alone in a calm eye that formed in the center of the corridor.

In that calmness, Eva's emotions swelled and swept over her. She did not understand what was happening to Anon, but she knew that she wanted to help him, in whatever way she could.

~

Anon felt increasingly uneasy as the nurse walked him down the corridor. He did not understand why, but he felt suspicious of her. He wondered why he should feel such mistrust. *Is it because she touched my holster?*

And Anon thought about the mysterious crystal key that was in his possession. He replayed the pale man's voice in his mind: *The signature… Do you have the signature? Is it safe?*

He called it a signature…

Anon made a conscious attempt to calm himself still further, to enable him to better focus his thoughts. As he did so he reasoned that the crystal key must hold the answer to what he found himself involved in. He concluded that it was paramount that he learn what the key was. Or recover his memory, completely.

"Excuse me," Anon said to the nurse. "I'll just be a few minutes."

And he entered the men's restroom they were about to walk past.

The nurse waited for some time before inching open the restroom's door to call in: "Dr. Anon? Are you all right?"

But there was no response.

"Dr. Anon?" she called again. And again.

Still no answer.

"I'm coming in," she announced, and she did so, only to find the room empty. One of its windows open. Anon gone.

8. Geology

Anon hurriedly walked beneath the covered walkway running along the exterior of the building, encountering the dreary, rainy day that he had forgotten. Realizing that he had left his umbrella back in the auditorium, he considered returning to retrieve it, but then he noticed, not far down the street, stepping out of a parked sedan, the strange man who had visited him last night.

At once Anon felt his heart begin to race. Unconsciously he brought a hand up to his torso to touch his concealed holster, to make sure it was there, safe at his side.

Down the street, the strange pale man sluggishly opened an old-fashioned black umbrella, dipping it to hide his grim face. He was wearing what appeared to be a light coating of makeup and what must have been lipstick. Apparently he, or someone, had made an effort to disguise his unusual appearance, to make him less attention drawing. Despite this precaution, or perhaps because of it, passing students could not help but stare.

Anon found himself by reflex leaping out into the rain and fleeing, in a mild panic. After a dozen or so yards he began thinking and he slowed and glanced back to see the pale man walking stiffly toward the building that he had been lecturing in.

He's looking for me...

Anon read the name of the building directly before him as he ran up to and entered it: Newton Hall.

From within the hall's foyer, Anon peeked outside to watch the pale man enter the building he had left mere moments ago.

Slowly, Anon turned from the window, thinking. He made a conscious effort to slow his breathing. It was then that he noticed the hall's directory. And his eyes focused on a particular listing: GEOLOGY DEPARTMENT.

~

Dr. Edward Shaffner, a lean, amiable bookworm of a man, was alone in his lab, peering through a microscope, when he was disturbed by a light knocking on his door.

"Excuse me…" Anon said as he entered.

"Dr. Anon," Edward responded, smiling, momentarily eyeing the bandage on Anon's head.

"I know you?" Anon asked, surprised.

Edward moved to Anon, shaking his hand in a relaxed, down-to-earth manner. "Edward Shaffner. Ed. We were introduced when you first arrived."

Anon tried to remember the face, but he could not.

"When you toured the university?" Edward attempted to jog his memory.

"Oh, oh yes. Edward," Anon responded, deciding to feign remembrance in order to avoid a complicated explanation. "Sorry, it seems I have a problem remembering names and faces."

"No need to apologize—with all the new faces you've met here I'm surprised you can remember your own name."

Anon forced a smile. "Yes, I'm surprised too."

"So, what can I do for you?" Edward smiled back, good-natured.

"Well, 'Ed,' I was wondering, since we're colleges now, I was hoping that you might be able to help me out with something."

"Sure, what?"

"Well, how can one tell if something is a mineral, found naturally in the Earth, or—or man-made?" Anon asked.

"A visual examination should suffice. But it has to be done by somebody who knows what they're looking at." Edward chuckled. "There are a lot of minerals out there that you'd swear nature could never have produced."

Anon motioned to a nearby display case, which contained a multitude of exotic and strange-looking crystalline minerals.

"Are all those nature-made?" Anon asked.

"Yep. Fluorite, barite, tourmaline, beryl, uvarovite—look at this item of gypsum." Edward opened the case and carefully lifted the item out. It was over two feet long, pearly white, silky, and curved like a tightly curled elephant's tusk. "Almost looks as if it had been carved, doesn't it?"

Anon focused on a green prismatic rod lying in the case. It closely resembled his crystal key in both size and shape, without, of course, the unusual key-like teeth.

"What's that one?" he asked Edward.

"Quartz," Edward answered as he returned the specimen of gypsum.

"Is…" Anon asked as he reached into his concealed holster and pulled out his mysterious key, which he now had wrapped up in a soft cloth, "… this quartz?"

Anon unwrapped the top portion of the key, leaving its unusual prongs concealed.

"Nope… color's wrong," Edward stated as he visually examined the oddity. "Hexagonal prismatic crystals… Horizontally striated…"

Anon felt Edward take his hand to lift the blue-black key up into the light. It sparkled, surprising Edward.

"Wow…" Edward commented. "Index of refraction must be adamantine. Near that of diamond. With this brilliance, optical identification should be immediate but… I have no idea what it is."

"Is it natural?"

"I'm not sure." Edward shrugged. "But all minerals have physical and chemical properties. Some are inherent and reliable. Such as degree of hardness."

Edward attempted to scratch Anon's key with his fingernail but was unsuccessful at marking its surface. He pulled a plastic file out of his shirt pocket and tried that. But the file could not scratch it.

Edward next picked up one of the colorless crystals from within the display case and used it against Anon's oddity. The crystal could not mark it either.

"Harder than quartz?" Edward mumbled, puzzled. He hesitated and then picked up a pale blue crystal, using it, unsuccessfully. "Harder than topaz? It appears that you have something here harder than almost any common substance."

"But… look what happens when you squeeze it," Anon said as he wrapped his left hand around the exposed section of the key, closing his fingers about its circumference. He then squeezed tightly.

"It takes a moment," Anon explained as he held his grip. "I think it has something to do with body heat? Temperature?"

After several silent moments Anon removed his hand to reveal that impressions of his fingers had been left indented into the strange rod, as if it were made of clay.

Baffled, Edward pulled a fingernail down across the key's indented surface, this time easily creating a tiny trench. "Incredible…"

The key's interior then pushed the indentations outward, rapidly returning its surface to its original shape and hardness.

"It always returns to its original shape…" Anon stated.

"But…" Edward was stumped. "Where'd you get this?"

"… I'm afraid I can't tell you that."

"Well," Edward responded, "until this little magic trick, I was about to guess that this was one of nature's mix-ups. A mineralogical imposter—pseudo-morphs, we call them. The Earth rocks the nursery, changes in temperature, pressure, what have you, and sometimes you get adaptation of the mineral inside.

"Like your Darwin's survival of the fittest. But no matter what happens on the inside, the new mineral always retains its original shape. Can't change it by squeezing it. And the way it morphed…"

Anon lowered the crystal key, placing it atop a nearby table. A small Geiger counter resting on the table began to click.

"It's emitting radiation?" Edward asked, surprised.

Anon pulled his crystal away from the instrument.

"Now, that's not an ore and it's not uranium or thorium," Edward stated. "What's going on here?"

"I wish I knew," Anon sighed, disappointed that Edward had been unable to identify the signature. He then noticed Edward possessively focusing his eyes on the key.

"Sometimes," Edward thought it out, "an invading molecule can act as an agent of change. The parting plane of a mineral is related to its atomic structure; a fresh fracture would show its true color. With a sample, I could test it for water infusion, fusibility, magnetism, electrical properties, specific gravity… I'd like to break it."

"Break it?" Anon felt a surge of emotion. "No. No, it—it's not supposed to be broken. Not now. Not yet. Why do I feel that way?"

"What?"

"I—I'd better be going," Anon responded, avoiding the question, suddenly only wanting to leave.

As Anon spun about he found himself facing a tall, stately, elderly professor who was entering the laboratory. Startled, Anon dropped his crystal key. Hitting the floor, it unraveled from its cloth and its unusual prongs became exposed.

Anon was quite surprised to see the recognition that flashed across Edward's face. The older professor appeared to recognize the crystal too.

"I didn't recognize it without seeing the teeth," Edward explained as he picked it up. "How'd you get the museum to lend it to you?"

"Museum?" Anon asked, confused. "What museum?"

"You didn't get this from Chapman?"

"I'm not sure." Anon found himself possessively pulling the key away from Edward. "What is it?"

"John?" Edward looked to the senior professor, John, who was still silently and inquisitively staring at the key.

"It's an incredibly unique mineral anomaly," John answered, "or a fake. Dr. James Chapman, over at the Whitman, claims he dug it up about three years ago. Shortly after announcing the find, he stated it was a fraud and locked it up. Wouldn't let anybody see it. Nobody."

"What are you doing with it?" Edward asked Anon.

Anon thought about the question. "Returning it," he then answered resolutely, and left.

Origins

Niko Zinovii

9. Chapman

Anon, still without an umbrella, was quite wet by the time he very cautiously crossed a busy street to reach the Whitman Museum of Natural History.

Standing down an adjacent street, unseen by Anon, the strange pale man listlessly tilted his dark, antiquated umbrella, angling it to allow himself an unobstructed view of the museum entrance.

~

"Excuse me," Anon asked a mature museum employee as he walked away from the ticket counter, "can you tell me where I can find Dr. James Chapman?"

"Oh," the woman responded, "I think I just saw him in the paleontology exhibit."

"The paleontology exhibit?"

"Yes," she directed Anon, "through that door and all the way back."

"All the way back. Thank you."

"You're welcome."

And Anon headed off in the direction indicated.

~

Anon slowed and looked about curiously as he entered the hall before him, which exhibited a fantastic array of stuffed birds. There were so many different types of birds, it overwhelmed him. *Have I forgotten about birds, due to my amnesia?*

No, there was something more to it, the sheer beauty of birds—he found it momentarily breathtaking. It touched him emotionally. Deeply. Why he did not know.

When will I regain my memory?

After walking the length of the room, he picked back up his pace as he reached his destination, an enormous hall filled with fossils from all ages. But the hall was empty, no Chapman…

Anon found his pace oddly slowing again as he proceeded forward. Mounted on the wall to his left was a large sheet of cracked sedimentary rock upon which there were dozens of fossilized trilobites, frozen in place upon what must have once been an ancient sea floor. The long-extinct armored marine creatures appeared so distantly exotic, so lost in the depths of time, that Anon could not help but stop and stare at their preserved remains.

—Time past:

> Scavenging for sustenance the same trilobites quietly crawled the dim bottom of their shallow Paleozoic sea, in the company of numerous others of their kind, one of which was whisked away as prey, picked off by a shell-covered squid jetting past.
>
> Moving in a tightening school, the remaining trilobites all turned in one direction, taking on positions nearly identical to their fossilized remains on display so far forward in time in the paleontology exhibit at the Whitman Museum.
>
> Unseen by and beyond the comprehension of the trilobites, far above their ancient sea, a stratovolcano roared out its death call, spewing lava, ash, and debris over the surrounding area.

The avalanching layer of ash and solidifying magma sank down from above without mercy, smothering the trilobites, sealing their doom, preserving them to silently, motionlessly march forward through the coming eons of time locked within a chunk of rock.

Continuing down the hall, Anon next encountered a flat slab of sandstone containing impressions of sand grains, oceanic ripples, and dozens of ancient jellyfish the size of dinner plates.

—Time past:

The tropical beach shone a surreal, pale shade of yellow-green, due to the light cast down by the night's full moon, beneath which thousands of giant jellyfish quivered, lying helplessly stranded on the lonely stretch of shoreline.

The earthquake that then came was catastrophic. It lowered the beach over fifty feet, with the sea, sand, and mud instantly rushing in, covering, smothering, burying what would become but a distant, preserved, bygone moment in time.

Anon next focused on a vertical sheet of sedimentary rock containing the partial fossilized remains of a primitive armor-plated fish, caught in the act of swallowing a smaller sea creature.

—Time past:

Thrashing its heavily armored body through the surrounding tropical sea, the same fish turned as it bit into a smaller inhabitant of the deep.

It did not see the larger creature that then flashed by with such unexpected speed, violently ripping it in half, swimming off with its tail section.

Cut in two, the armored fish, its prey still in its mouth, slowly began its long sinking to the bottom, where it eventually landed upon sand and mud, positioned identically to the fossilized "photo" in the Whitman Museum.

Anon shuddered slightly as he stepped away from the sheet of rock, sensing the utter brutality of Earth's ancient ocean realm, captured and displayed so vividly as it was.

And more, the layering of time—it had a powerful, intoxicating effect on him. It reached out to him, it took hold of him, it cast its spell on him. *Why?*

It was his crystal key, the signature that he carried. It was part of the past. The mystery that he found himself immersed in involved the past, man's past.

Anon turned to see a display of a nest of fossilized dinosaur eggs, all of which were crushed, one of the eggs displaying the tiny skeleton of its once-hatching occupant.

—Time past:

Swamp and a thick moss-green carpeting of primordial ferns surrounded the undisturbed nest, its eggs not yet crushed. The shell of one of the eggs quivered as it cracked open, allowing the hatching dinosaur within a peek out at the strange, savage world it was being born into.

Such a terrible sound behind and above the nest...
Such a terrible shadow descending upon the nest...

Anon found himself stepping before the fossilized skull of an Ice Age saber-toothed cat, *Smilodon populator*. He silently gazed at the carnivore's skull, at its incredibly long, curved, saber-shaped canine teeth.

—Time past:

> At the end of the Pleistocene, 11,000 years ago, the great cat growled out as it pounced upon the back of its prey, a large herbivore, bringing the animal crashing to the forest floor.
>
> The cat did not hesitate to sink its claws into the hide of the kicking beast, to secure its position on top of the creature.
>
> Neither did the giant cat hesitate to stab its canines down into its prey, while pulling and tearing at the animal's flesh with its sharp claws. The herbivore thrashed one final time before it became still and mute to the saber-toothed cat's snarling savagery.

It was Chapman's voice that pulled Anon out of the trance that had fallen upon him:

"'I wondered why such perfect fury had been swept away, while man, wide-roaming dark assassin of his own kind, had sprung up in the wake of such perfected instruments as these.' The thoughts of Loren Eiseley, anthropologist and poet."

Anon turned to face Dr. James Chapman, who, graying, bearded, and bespectacled, appeared the stereotypical image of a staid, aging scientist.

"Profound thoughts," Anon remarked.

"I'm James Chapman," Chapman stated, offering his hand to Anon. "I was told you were looking for me."

"Yes." Anon nodded as they shook hands. "My name is Anon. Dr. David Anon. Anthropology. I have something that I believe you'll be interested in."

Anon glanced up and down the exhibit hall to make sure they were alone. They were. Nervously, he pulled out and unwrapped his mysterious crystal key.

"My God…" Chapman mumbled. "There are two of them?"

"Two of them?" Anon felt even more confused.

~

Anon stood silent, motionless in Chapman's book-lined, windowless basement office as Chapman opened and stepped into a large walk-in safe.

"They say that in archaeology," Chapman stated as he moved deeper and deeper into the safe, "you never really find what you set out for. And… and that, well, with the exception of the occasional surprise from Asia, maybe Europe too, most new things are still coming out of Africa."

Anon sensed a nervousness rising in Chapman's voice as the archeologist moved still deeper into his safe.

"I found both these statements to ring true…" Chapman continued, wiping the beads of perspiration from his forehead as he knelt in the back of the safe, where he retrieved a cloth-covered object, hidden away in a dark corner.

Rising slowly, arthritically, Chapman cradled the object as he brought it out of the safe and carefully placed it down upon his desk.

"Three years ago…" he said. "That's when I found it. In Kenya."

Anon watched on with growing anticipation as Chapman unwrapped the thing with wizened, trembling hands. Within the cloth was a blue-black rod nearly identical in size, shape, and composition to his own mysterious crystal key, with the exception that Chapman's find had three large prongs projecting from it instead of two.

Anon reached down and carefully picked up Chapman's key, lifting it into the light. Although it looked considerably older than his two-pronged key, it sparkled just the same. The two men stared at it, transfixed.

—Time past:

Looking up ahead, up high, perhaps at some mountain, a male *Australopithecus afarensis*, with an unusual awareness in his eyes, stumbled and nearly fell as he ran frantically down the muddy bed of a nearly dried up river. Oddly, strung about his neck was a thin cord of twisted, dried weeds and vines from which hung Chapman's three-pronged key.

This *afarensis*, Three Prong, was running for his life. For behind him, chasing after him, was a trio of cackling prehistoric hyenas.

If only Three Prong had been holding the key secure against his chest. But he was not. Bouncing about wildly, it broke loose from its primitive cord and fell to the ground.

It took Three Prong several moments to realize that he had dropped the crystal. When he did realize it, he stopped abruptly and turned around.

Sparkling in the African sunlight, the three-pronged key lay halfway between him and the rapidly approaching hyenas.

Three Prong turned back about to face the direction in which he had been running. He once again looked up ahead, up high. And then, turning back, he chose to try to retrieve Chapman's crystal, risking almost certain death.

Racing toward the dropped key, Three Prong tripped and fell into the mud, the key lying less than a foot away. He thrust out a hairy arm, desperately reaching for it. But it was too late. The hyenas cackled madly as they tore into him.

The largest of the carnivores sank its teeth down into the bone of Three Prong's outstretched arm, crushing it. Another bit into one of his legs. As did the third. And the animals then attempted to pull Three Prong—still alive—off in different directions.

It was the talon of a landing vulture that pressed Chapman's key down into the mud, burying it. And Three Prong let out a strangely sentient, chilling death scream that echoed over the prehistoric landscape.

Anon slowly lowered Chapman's three-pronged key, bringing it down out of the light. As he did so, it reflected less and less brightly. It was rather dark, a near lightless blue-black in color, when Anon finally laid it back down upon its wrapping.

Anon then placed his two-pronged key beside it. There was a long moment of silence between the two men as they simply stared at the crystal oddities, and then at one another.

"I found it," Chapman finally broke his silence, "among the fossilized remains of a torn-apart *afarensis*. Potassium-argon dating set the find at two and a half million years old... You really don't know where yours came from?"

"No. As I told you, I can't remember a thing. Over at the university, they, um, they said it was a mineral anomaly."

"Minerals contain only inorganic elements." Chapman shook his head. "I did a sort of biopsy on this. It contains carbon compounds, oxygen… Typical of living things. And not the result of some invasion of water, mind you, no, this isn't some geological trickster. No, this is clearly different. Unique."

"But if it contains organic compounds," Anon asked, "then why didn't it fossilize?"

Chapman slowly shrugged his shoulders.

"It appears constructed," Chapman then offered, "doesn't it?"

"What? Is it an artifact? Are you suggesting that some hominid made it? Two and a half million years ago?"

Chapman again slowly shrugged his shoulders.

"I don't understand," Anon stated, frustrated, trying to comprehend. "Why didn't you let anyone examine it, study it? Try to determine what it is."

"Shortly after I announced my finding it," Chapman explained, his nervousness reappearing, his voice tinged with uneasiness, "I… I was visited by—by someone. I don't know who he was but he, ah, he threatened me. Said… *they* would kill my wife if I didn't denounce what I had found. They—they kept watching me. I was frightened. Really frightened. It's difficult to explain. I couldn't risk my wife's safety. You see, I felt the threat to be real. And imminent."

"This person who visited you," Anon asked, "did he—was his skin unusually pale?"

Chapman's eyes lit up with fear.

"They—" Chapman gasped. "They know about you?"

"It looks that way," Anon admitted. "But as to who *they* are, I don't have a clue."

"I—I don't want any part of this," Chapman stuttered as he scooped up his three-pronged key, wrapped it up, and moved with it back into his safe. "I don't want this starting all over again. I'm afraid I have to ask you to leave. So please, just take your *mineral anomaly* and go."

"But—"

"Just—just go!" Chapman almost yelled it, but then his voice grew low. "… Please. Just go."

Anon paced as he waited for Chapman to come back out of the safe. When Chapman did, Anon asked: "This… man that came to visit me. He, um, he referred to my crystal as a 'signature.' Do you have any idea what he meant by that?"

"No," Chapman answered honestly. "Look, I'm sorry but I can't get involved."

"I understand," Anon responded, defeated, and he picked up his crystal key, preparing to leave.

"Wait," Chapman stopped him.

And Chapman went back into his safe, returning with a small black box that had been tucked away down near where his three-pronged crystal was hidden. With trembling hands, the archaeologist offered the box to Anon.

"In this box," Chapman explained, "there's a collection of skull fragments. One individual. Not a complete skull, but, well, enough. I found them nearby, in the same stratum as the crystal. They're—they're very… unusual. Maybe the missing piece to the puzzle… I don't know. I never told anyone about this. Kept it to myself. Didn't pursue it. Didn't want to know…"

Anon just stared at Chapman for the longest moment, wanting desperately only to escape from whatever he was involved in, not to step deeper into it.

"Just one question," Anon finally asked. "Why didn't they ever try to take your crystal away from you?"

Chapman for a third time simply shrugged his shoulders.

Letting out a breath in utter disappointment and frustration, Anon summed up his courage, accepted the box, and left.

Origins

Niko Zinovii

10. Pursued

From a distance, unblinking, sunken-in eyes focused on Anon as he emerged from the museum carrying Chapman's black box. As Anon stepped down into the rain and the dimness of the setting sunlight, Eva, carrying a large, bright umbrella, stepped up close to him, covering them both.

The pale man, still standing down the adjacent street, observing, leaned forward, and the "NO PARKING" sign beside him groaned mournfully and bent away from his presence. The man then tilted his grim face rather oddly, as if preparing to eavesdrop on Anon and Eva from an impossible distance.

"Thank you," Anon said, surprised but pleased to see Eva.

"You're welcome."

Momentarily they looked into one another's eyes, only to then shyly glance away, both of them feeling the same strong attraction and romantic tension.

"The way you left..." Eva explained as it began to rain harder, "I wanted to see how you were. I found out you might be here. You're leaving? The museum?"

Anon just nodded, looking again into her eyes, sensing in her such admirable human qualities, seeing in her a unique innocent beauty.

"That nurse is looking all over for you," Eva responded to his penetrating gaze. "Are you going back to the hospital?"

"No," Anon answered, her question pulling him back to face the tension of his present situation. "I don't think so. Not after last night. I guess I'll be going home."

"'After last night?'"

"Oh, never mind that." Anon waved a hand. "I'd rather not try to explain."

Eva nodded, agreeing to let the comment pass. "Are you going home now?" she asked.

"I don't know," Anon answered, suddenly nervous, glancing about. "In a way, I'm afraid to. I don't know what it'll be like. What I'll find. Ah, could we—could we talk someplace else? I don't really feel comfortable standing around out here in the open like this."

"I don't understand."

Anon cracked a nervous smile. "Believe me, neither do I."

It was then that Eva noticed, a distance behind Anon, on the other side of the adjacent street, the pale man, standing beneath his dark umbrella.

"Anon… I think… It is… It's the man who was driving that limo that was waiting for you. Right before your accident."

Anon turned and momentarily froze in fright, before then making a clumsy effort to conceal Chapman's box from sight.

"What?" Eva tried to understand. "What's wrong?"

"I'm not sure…"

"Anon, are you in some type of trouble?"

"I—I have to go now. I'm sorry."

"Anon?"

But Anon forced himself to walk off rapidly. He felt that the pale man represented a danger, and he did not want to subject Eva to whatever that danger might be. He told himself that it was better that he learn what he was involved in by himself. That he should not seek any help.

"Anon?" she called to him, but he did not respond.

She looked back for the pale man, but he was no longer where he had been. It was so odd; it was as if he had simply vanished.

She looked for Anon, but he too had disappeared from sight. Standing there alone in the rain, she felt confused, worried, and thwarted in her desire to help Anon.

~

It was eerie, the sound of the wet, shuffling shoes as the footsteps echoed down the long empty hall of the museum's paleontological exhibit.

~

Chapman, still in his office, slumped forward, fatigued, lost in thought.

Suddenly, the frame of his eyeglasses bent and tightened about his face. He yanked them off, to watch them mysteriously curl up into a ball in his left hand.

Then came the shiver, and the putrid smell, and Chapman stiffened in utter terror.

He sat there frozen by fear as the dark, ominous shadow crept over him. It was not until he was fully covered by its blackness that he forced himself to turn about and face the pale man.

"… What did you give him?" the pale man asked, his deep, bone-dry voice devoid of all emotion.

"I don't know what you're talking about," came Chapman's quick reply.

But the strange man with the dead-white face just stared at Chapman with unblinking, dark, lifeless eyes. Eyes sunken so deeply into their sockets…

"But I didn't give him anything," Chapman avowed. "Nothing. Nothing! I swear. I'll show you the crystal; it's still in the safe. I can—"

"... What was in... the box?" The corpse-like man breathed out his words, curtailing Chapman's lying.

The archeologist reached for his temple, in pain, suddenly feeling unwell.

"... Do not... lie... to me," the pale man warned him.

~

Anon, seated in the back of a taxi, held his wallet open in his lap, glancing down at his driver's license and then out at the buildings they were passing.

"There, that's it, up ahead," Anon informed the cab driver. "You can pull over here. Let me out here."

"Here?"

"Yes, here please. Thank you."

Anon opened the door and stepped down upon the street.

~

A gristly right foot, wearing a shoe, made a disturbing thud as it dropped upon the concrete floor of a dark subbasement. The truncated, grotesque section of lower leg attached to the foot was almost unrecognizable, so burnt to a crisp it was, reduced to greasy white ash. The sizzling of the still-burning flesh and exposed calcined bone sent vapors wafting upward, drifting, swirling, rising toward the smoldering hole in the ceiling directly above.

Above, in Chapman's office, surrounding the hole burnt into the floor, lay the bizarre remains of Chapman's body: a left forearm and hand—still holding his curled-up eyeglasses—a blackened neck and head, and an ashy lump of unidentifiable burnt flesh. It was strange how the floor surrounding the hole and Chapman's remains was undamaged.

Nearby, at Chapman's desk, whitish fingers punched a memorized number into a phone. Slowly, stiffly, the pale man placed the phone's receiver against his ear, holding it there with one hand while pocketing Chapman's three-pronged crystal with the other.

After a few seconds someone answered.

"… Chapman gave him a fossil," the pale man reported into the receiver. "… An important fossil."

~

Within the back of a limousine, the slanted-eyed man ended the call that he had just received on his cell phone. His white eyebrows rose, and the deep olive skin of his exceptionally high forehead—inches higher than a normal man's—furrowed as his hubristically intelligent eyes swelled with concern.

Running a hand through his gray-white hair, he turned to the two other pale men seated beside him. Like the pale man who had just phoned, these men were also dressed in somber, eerily wrinkle-free black suits, and more, they also had the same dead-white skin, sparse straight black hair, pale blue lips, and unblinking, sunken-in, lifeless eyes.

~

Anon, carrying Chapman's box tucked under an arm, flipped open his wallet again, nervously double checking as he approached an attractive four-story brick apartment building. According to his license he lived in apartment 3-B.

He chose the stairs, and he ascended them to the third floor, where he found his apartment. He eyed the lock on the door and then pulled out a key ring with a single key on it.

"I guess this is *the* key…" he whispered to himself.

He inserted the key into the lock. It fit.

~

Anon quite cautiously stepped inside, into the dimness, where he felt something quite odd in his fingers, in the fingers of the hand in which he still held on to his apartment key. He lifted his hand to watch the key slowly curl up before his eyes.

What?

He then shuddered as he felt an icy-cold chill go through him. It was only then that he noticed that seated on the only piece of furniture in the living room was a corpse-like pale man. But it wasn't the pale man who had visited him at the hospital; it was a completely different pale man. One who was bald-headed. The man was still, his chin dropped forward, his sunken-in eyes closed lifelessly.

Anon just stared at the man. Was he asleep? Dead?

Anon winced as he caught a whiff of the man's awful odor. It smelled like death.

Anon noticed that the man's chest was unmoving. The pale man did not appear to be breathing. This gave Anon the courage to cover his nose and slowly approach the man. Summoning up his nerve, Anon extended an index finger and slowly pressed in on the man's odd, wrinkle-free suit. The pale man did not react. Anon pushed in again, this time lower, on the man's stomach.

And the man's mouth dropped open and a breath of stale air forced its way out. Anon fell backward to the floor in fright.

The pale man's bald head lifted slowly, ever so slowly, his lifeless eyes opened, and he inhaled.

"… W… h… a… t?" the man breathed out in a gravelly deep voice, the fragmented word delivered with great effort.

Anon kicked his legs frantically, backpedaling until he found himself pressed up against his apartment's closed door.

"… Wh… ere… have… you… been?" the pale man asked. "… My… en… ergy… is… g… o… n… n… n… n… e…"

And the strange man's deeply set eyes blinked once, twice, and then closed. Once again, he appeared dead, no longer breathing.

Anon, sitting motionless on the floor, attempted to calm himself, telling himself that there was no reason to panic. That he was in no immediate danger.

"… Are you dead now?" Anon asked, hoping that his question would prove itself to be rhetorical.

No response from the dead man.

Rising, Anon rubbed his temples, suddenly feeling unwell.

"… You look dead," Anon commented.

Summoning up his courage, he took a step toward the man. "You certainly smell dead."

He forced himself to take another step, and another.

"Please be dead."

Reaching out, Anon timidly poked the man in the chest. No response. He hesitated and then took the man's pallid wrist in his hand, feeling for a pulse.

"No pulse… So cold."

He dropped the man's lifeless arm.

"What the hell am I involved in?"

Anon just stood there for the longest time, thinking, gathering himself, before he decided to explore the rest of the apartment. Before he worked up the courage to do so.

In the kitchen, which was unfurnished, Anon opened the refrigerator. It was completely empty. *Nothing…*

Anon entered the bedroom, finding the room empty too. He opened the closet. Hanging within were four suits, identical in style to what he was wearing but of different colors.

"… Guess I travel light. Am I on the run?"

Anon peeked inside the bathroom.

"Not even a roll of toilet paper…"

Anon jumped, startled, as his cell phone, which was pocketed somewhere within his suit jacket, began to ring loudly.

He found the right pocket and pulled the phone out. A call from an unknown number… He hesitated, filled with apprehension, but then he decided to answer it.

"Hello?"

There was a moment of silence and then a heavy breathing, followed by the deep, bone-dry voice of the first pale man.

"… Wait where you are… We are coming to collect you."

"… Collect me?" Anon mumbled and dropped the phone to the floor.

"My cell…" he then wondered aloud. "Are they tracking me by it?"

Anon decided to leave the phone there on the floor. Cautiously eyeing the dead bald man, he quietly and quickly moved past him, leaving the apartment, fleeing.

~

As Anon reached the sidewalk he heard the squeal of tires and turned to see a rapidly approaching limousine. He remembered what Eva had told him about a limousine. He also had a flash of memory, of the first pale man driving such a limo. He glanced about, looking for an escape route, and decided on his building's driveway, which he ran down, full of fear.

As he entered the backyard, he glanced back over his shoulder, looking out to the street. Doing so prevented him from seeing the previously unencountered pale man, who stepped out of the darkness directly in front of him. Not until he turned his eyes back forward did he see the man. Startled, he ground to an abrupt stop, almost dropping Chapman's box.

"Huh?"

The strange man lunged to grab Anon, but his movements were unusually slow and Anon found that he was able to avoid being captured.

Anon ran to the high wooden fence marking the property's back boundary. Tucking Chapman's box into his suit jacket he leapt up, catching the top of the fence, his feet kicking and slipping against its boards.

He was almost positioned to flip over the top when he heard his box drop. His pale pursuer was only yards distant, walking stiffly toward him, hands outstretched, zombie-like. But Anon decided it was important enough to chance it and he dropped down to retrieve the box. As he did so he saw stepping off the sidewalk and coming down the driveway a tall, slanted-eyed man accompanied by the pale man who had visited him in the hospital—and two other pale men.

How many of them are there?

Anon watched on as he saw the slanted-eyed man lift a hand to adroitly signal the pale men at his sides, doing so by rapidly shaping his fingers and thumb into a series of different configurations, communicating something to them silently. It stunned Anon that he understood the message: 'Collect him.'

Anon leapt up again, grabbing the fence top, wildly kicking his way upward as pale hands began fumbling over his thrashing legs.

Anon flipped over the top, landing safely on the other side. Immediately, on the opposite side of the fence there was a shockingly loud banging as the nearest pale man began striking his bony fists repeatedly against the wooden fencing like a Frankenstein's Monster run amok.

Anon ran off without looking back, disappearing into the night.

~

Running down a sidewalk, Anon paused to catch his breath, bending over, his hands resting upon his knees.

I understood their signals, their sign language... Anon's

thoughts raced. *Could that be how I learned about them? How I acquired this crystal? Accidentally eavesdropping on their silent communications?*

Anon straightened and he noticed a decorative English-style phone booth outside a pub. He ran over to it.

Squeezing into the booth, he dropped into a squat, pulling the phone book down with him.

"Eva. Eva what?" he asked himself. "Eva... Eva... Lie! Eva Lie!"

He paged through the book rapidly.

"Lie... Lie... Lie..."

"Eva!" he spotted her number. "Eva Lie."

He found change in one of his pockets, inserted it into the payphone, and punched in her number. The line began to ring.

"Come on... Come on..."

"Hello?" he heard Eva answer.

"Eva? It's Anon. I'm sorry. I don't have anyone else to turn to. I don't know anyone else. Not that I can remember. I—I need your help. "

Anon ducked lower within the booth as bright headlights flashed over him. He peeked outside. It was the limousine turning, moving slowly down the street, searching for him.

"Eva... They're after me."

"You are in some kind of trouble, aren't you?" she asked, alarmed.

"Yes, I think so." He peeked outside again, this time catching a glimpse of the original pale man driving the limo, his grim face frighteningly impassive.

"Make that a definite yes. Yes, I'm in trouble. Can I see you, right now, tonight?"

"Yes, of course."

"Thank you, thank you, Eva. Where—how do I get to you?"

Origins

Niko Zinovii

Part Three

Niko Zinovii

11. A Night at Eva's

So, you have no idea who these men are?" Eva asked, sitting on her couch beside Anon, Chapman's black box resting on the nearby coffee table, Anon's two-pronged key and holster lying beside it. "Or what this is?" she asked, referring to his crystal.

"Absolutely no idea," Anon answered, frustrated. "Chapman found the first crystal. I guess I must have found this second one. I just can't remember what it is. But… I feel it has something to do with the past, man's past."

"And their sign language?" she asked.

Anon shrugged—it was all a mystery to him. But he offered a logical guess. "Maybe it's some African hunter-gatherer Bushman signaling that as an anthropologist I was familiar with?"

Eva sat there quietly for a moment, thinking about it all. "Anon," she then said, carefully, "earlier today, I overheard what you said. To Kaplan and Foster. Is it your memory loss, or are you having doubts about human evolution? About what you're teaching?"

"Maybe there are things, facts, that I can't remember," he answered, trying to reason it out. "So, things don't seem to make sense like they used to? Or maybe there's something important missing. Something that I now know, that I found out, but can't remember. Something that changed my view on what I'm teaching. I'm not sure. It's confusing… Why can't I remember?"

Anon became silent and she reached toward him and carefully straightened the bandage on the back of his head. She then compassionately and lovingly stroked his hair, tenderly touching the bruised side of his face. Her gentle touch felt so very soothing to him.

"It'll be all right," she comforted him. "When your memory returns, everything will become clear."

Anon was calmed by her soft voice, and he felt himself begin to relax. But then he noticed his reflection in the mirror on the other side of the room and he jumped up, startled. On his feet, he moved to the mirror, staring at his reflection, touching his own face.

"Eva…"

She moved to his side.

"For a moment," he explained, "I… I—I didn't recognize myself. Not at first… I do now… It startled me…"

She tried to understand. "You're not wearing your glasses," she suggested. "Maybe it's because you're not wearing your eyeglasses."

"No… It… It seems more than that…"

"Anon," Eva responded slowly, deeply concerned, "maybe you should, um, maybe you should let me take you back to the hospital. Until your memory does return."

"No. They'd find me there. Again."

"Anon… These men that you say are following you, I know you said that they threatened this Chapman person, at the museum, but they haven't really threatened you in any way, have they?"

"Eva, there was a dead man in my apartment."

"But the police didn't find a body."

"Because *they* came looking to 'collect' *me* and probably took *him* away instead."

He noticed the odd way she was staring at him. "You don't believe me?" he asked.

"I'm honestly not sure what to believe," she confessed as she reached out, taking his hands in hers. "I do want to believe."

Anon felt himself pulling away from her, pacing away from her, upset, overcome by frustration. "Why is this happening to me? When am I going to remember? When I do remember, will it be too late?

"I feel so... lost. Can you imagine how it would be to feel that you only had a life span of a few days? Trying to remember—it's exhausting. I'm so tired. Numb."

And he grew silent.

"Would you like a drink?" Eva asked.

"Yes," Anon sighed. "Yes, I think I would. Thank you."

"Gin?"

"Sure."

"Water? Ice?"

Anon shook his head.

"Anon," she asked as she walked off, "what happened to your glasses, anyway?"

Anon signed again, his voice strong but then trailing off to a mumble. "Oh, nothing you'd believe. Nothing any sane person would believe..."

Eva hesitated but then stepped into the kitchen, which was open to the living room. She poured two drinks and returned with the glasses and the bottle, handing Anon a glass and placing the gin on the coffee table.

Anon sat back down on the couch beside her, raised his glass, hesitated, and then emptied it in one gulp. He then reached for Chapman's mysterious box but felt Eva's gentle hand stopping him.

"Anon, perhaps if we—if we take a break from all this, step away from it for a little while, think about something else. Talk about something else."

"Like what?"

"I don't know, anything."

Anon poured himself another drink. "Okay," he asked, "what's your favorite color?"

"Blue. You?"

Anon opened his mouth to answer but then stopped short from doing so, almost amused. "I don't remember," he said. "Sorry." And he gulped down his drink.

As he poured another, Eva picked up a book lying nearby. "Look," she said, "this might be interesting."

The book was titled *Dictionary of Subject Quotations*. She began to flip through its pages, reading section headings aloud: "'Knowledge'... 'Laughter'... 'Madness'... 'Man'—Man. That should be good." And she read a quote on man:

"'The only animal that blushes—or needs to.' Mark Twain."

"Clever," Anon remarked. "But I seem to prefer this one, man, 'An ape with possibilities.' Roy C. Andrews. Although this one's even better: 'The cause for women's dislike for one another.'"

Eva laughed lightly and Anon felt his tension slowly dissipating, the alcohol and conversation helping to ease his troubled mind.

"Oh no, " she retorted, "I think this one's much better. Man, 'the second strongest sex in the world.'"

"This one's different." Anon pointed to it.

Eva read it aloud: "'A foundling in the cosmos, abandoned by the forces that created him.'"

And she bobbed her head, not really liking or disliking it.

"No?" Anon responded. "What about this one. 'The greatest miracle and the greatest problem on this earth.'"

Eva shook her head, spotting one that she appreciated more. "'The bad child of the universe.'"

"'Nature's sole mistake,'" Anon read the next one.

"Too pessimistic," she remarked, reading aloud one that was further down the page. "'An earthly animal but worthy of Heaven.' Saint Augustine. Now that's nicer but—"

"But," Anon interrupted, "here's the one that suits us best. 'Mankind is poised midway between the gods and the beasts.' Plotinus. Or, here, even better, more succinct, man: 'Half beast, half angel.'"

"I don't think I like those two," she responded.

"That's because you don't like to think of people as 'glorified apes.' —Hey, I remember that. I remember you telling me that."

Eva smiled and Anon found himself pulled so deeply into her lovely eyes.

"But what I don't understand... is how I couldn't remember you..." he whispered.

And he felt her eyes meeting his, their souls melting into one another.

"Why is it when I see you," she whispered back, "when I'm with you, I feel... The feeling, the attraction is so strong. Since I first saw you..."

Anon leaned in to her, to kiss her. But she gently held him back.

"I've—this is so fast..." she explained. "I've been alone for so very long..."

Anon hesitated but then kissed her, feeling her kissing him back with a release of all her built-up passion. Almost trembling in each other's arms, they embraced as if there were no tomorrow, only this night, and together they sank down upon the couch.

~

Anon quietly slipped out of bed, leaving Eva sleeping silently. Pulling on his pants, he made his way to the living room and sat on the couch, his tired eyes focusing on Chapman's mysterious box.

"The missing piece to the puzzle…" he whispered to himself.

He opened the box. Within it there were a dozen or so fossilized skull fragments of different sizes and shapes. It would likely require a fair amount of work and anatomical knowledge to put them together.

Anon sat back, just staring at the fragments, too tired to begin their assembly, losing himself in sleepy thought.

—*Time past:*

A myriad of scintillating stars twinkled peacefully in the night sky, so high above the red glow of molten rock that was flowing ever so slowly down the slope of a nearby volcanic mountaintop.

Standing together in the tall grass of Africa of two and a half million years ago, a group of four *Australopithecus afarensis* males, all possessing an unusual awareness in their eyes, stood together staring at one another, as if acknowledging some sort of mutually understood kinship, some secret brotherhood.

Each of the hominids wore a blue-black crystal rod hanging loosely around his neck, the teeth of their keys varying in their number of prongs from one to four.

Three Prong, wearing Chapman's key, would later perish under the violent attack of hyenas, but that was still in the future, a time that had not yet come.

Very much alive at this point on time's great arrow, Three Prong looked over his compatriots: One Prong, Two Prong, and Gray Streak—the oldest of them, as was evident from the irregular white stripe running back through the hair on the top of his head. Gray Streak's crystal had four prongs, its teeth seeming to symbolize their number in unity.

Parting company, the quartet of hominids dispersed, each key holder moving off in a different direction.

~

Wading through the tall grass, Gray Streak made his way to a nearby river, where, on the opposite bank, the hulking shapes of ancient elephants, lighted by moonlight, slowly shifted and turned in the stillness of the night.

Gray Streak did not have to walk far before he encountered a small group of *afarensis* creatures. Walking up to one of the females, he touched her affectionately, and she looked at him with caring eyes, less aware than his. He then looked up at the stars. She did not.

And the night dimmed as a great cloud began to slowly drift across the moon.

~

Outside Eva's condominium, the cloud passing before the moon darkened the night, making it easier for the bald pale man—who had "died" in Anon's apartment but was somehow once again alive—to conceal himself as he stared up at the windows of Eva's condo.

Lowering his lifeless, unblinking eyes, the strange man lingered for a while before stiffly walking off, disappearing into the night.

~

Anon, asleep on Eva's couch, found himself lost in a dream. In his dream world he could hear the daytime sounds of moving automobiles and chattering people, but only as barely audible, muffled background noise.

The darkness of Anon's dream then blew away like frightened smoke, and Anon watched himself, in his dream, walking across the university campus. The buildings, landscape, and students were all oddly blurred. Only the immediate foreground was clear, in focus.

Anon suddenly felt insecure, guilt-ridden, nervous. The passing students and faculty were all staring at him as if he were on display.

He felt his heart pounding as he quickened his pace. But the people started to follow him, pointing at him with long accusing fingers.

Unable to escape his pursuers, Anon turned to the street. Waiting on its other side was the dark limousine. Anon looked up at the traffic light. He would have to wait for it to change before he could cross.

Driving the limo was the pale man. Anon felt a shiver run through his mind as he made eye contact with the man. Those lifeless, sunken eyes frightened Anon.

The rear window of the limo rolled down to reveal the slanted-eyed man.

Suddenly, there was deafening silence. And the limo driver pointed at Anon.

"… Deceive," the pale man ordered Anon. "… Lie."

The strange corpse-like man then grinned, horrifically, nightmarishly.

"… Teach."

The traffic signal changed from yellow to red, the crosswalk sign changing from "DON'T WALK" to "WALK."

Anon started toward the limousine, the slanted-eyed man waving him over.

Tires screeched horribly. *A car! It is going to hit me!*

Anon lurched upright, jarred awake by the ringing of the telephone. It rang again, and again, and the answering machine engaged the incoming call, playing Eva's recorded voice: "Hello. I'm unable to take your call right now, so please leave a message after the tone."

The device beeped. There was silence on the other line, someone breathing, listening. Then the caller hung up.

"Eva?" Anon called for her.

No response. Anon got to his feet to look for her.

"Eva?"

Suddenly, the condominium's doorknob began to rattle. It started to turn. Anon froze, staring at the rattling, oddly turning knob.

The door then burst open and Eva entered with a newspaper tucked under an arm.

"Sorry, I didn't mean to startle you," she apologized, seeing that Anon appeared shaken. "The lock sticks, need to jiggle it."

Anon stood there in silence, trembling slightly, slowly regaining his composure as she walked up to him, looking at him in a very special way, giving him a good-morning kiss.

"What's wrong?" she asked.

"Where were you?" he responded stiffly, feeling suspicious.

"Just downstairs. To get the paper. Why?"

"Oh… Just jumpy, I guess," he answered, shaking away his feelings of distrust. "I'm sorry."

Eva placed the paper upon the kitchen countertop. The front-page headline read "Pakistan Threatens Further Deployment of Nuclear Arsenal."

Anon felt himself pulled to the paper, his attention fully absorbed by the headline. It meant something to him, but he did not understand what. He felt the deepest emotional and intellectual concern flood over him. He sat down.

"What?" Eva asked.

"I don't know," he answered. "I suddenly don't feel well. Headache—maybe the gin from last night?"

And Anon found himself thinking about the stuffed birds in the museum exhibit. Somehow his mind was linking birds to the newspaper's headlines of war. *But it makes no sense. What could birds possibly have to do with any of this?*

"Anon, I was thinking—how do you feel about hypnosis?"

"Hypnosis?"

"Yes," Eva explained. "I was thinking it might be a way to help you regain your memory. It's how a friend of mine quite smoking."

Anon nodded slowly, considering the suggestion as he opened the paper. But then his thoughts froze.

"Eva… Did you see this?"

She moved to him as he read the headline aloud: "'Nobel Laureate Killed by Unexplained Fire…'"

With a trembling hand he touched the photograph that accompanied the headline. It was of Dr. James Chapman.

"Dr. Chapman…" Eva read aloud the archeologist's name.

"Now do you believe me? They killed him. Made it look like an accident. My god, they killed him because he talked to me. Because he had a crystal, like I do."

Eva was speechless. She looked over to Anon's crystal and holster, which were still resting beside Chapman's box. Before she could speak, the phone rang, and she jumped.

"Somebody called when you went out," Anon informed her. "Didn't leave a message."

The answering machine kicked in as they stared at the phone: "Hello. I'm unable to take your call right now, so please leave a message after the tone."

Like before, the beep was followed by a moment of silence, and then breathing. But this time also by the bone-dry voice of the original pale man:

"… Anon… They now understand your condition… But they need you to cooperate… Failure to cooperate… may result in additional incinerations… Stay… where you are… Both you… and Dr. Eva Lie."

The caller hung up.

"Incinerations?" Anon said in a low voice. "Like Chapman… killed by an unexplained fire."

"The police?" Eva asked.

Anon shook his head. "No. What would we tell them? We still don't know what this is about. We don't even know who these people are."

"But we have the call recorded. The threat." And she played it back:

"Hello. I'm unable to take your call right now, so please leave a message after the tone."

Then there was the beep. Followed by hissing static.

"… His voice—it didn't record?" Eva could not understand it. It frightened her, deeply.

"No recording," Anon said. "Just like there was no body in my apartment. Now do you believe me? We've got to get out of here. Before they come to *collect* us."

"But to where?" she asked, moving close to Anon.

Anon thought it out. "I have to regain my memory, right?"

She nodded.

"Hypnosis?"

She nodded again, in agreement. "Yes, hypnosis."

12. Forbidden Knowledge

Seated alone in the psychiatrist's office, Anon tried to relax. The brown leather couch was deep and comfortable, the room dark and cozy, book-lined. But he still felt on edge, his mind replaying everything that had happened to him since he had awoken in the hospital without his memory. Could hypnosis work? He hoped so. Unable to learn anything revealing about his crystal key, he was down to the one remaining option: he needed to remember his past in order to understand what he was involved in.

He could hear Eva's voice, and he glanced across the room through its open door to see her standing in the waiting room, talking with the doctor. Anon could not hear her clearly but it sounded as if she was thanking the doctor again for seeing them on such short notice.

The presence of the large, brown Doberman pinscher at the doctor's side made Anon feel secure, protected. The doctor's appearance added to this sense of safety. Tall, gray haired, with a parental face adorned by a neatly trimmed goatee, the doctor represented a wise, learned authority figure in Anon's mind.

Anon watched as the doctor reached back and pulled the door to his office partially closed, to talk to Eva in private.

"Do you know if the hospital tested him for collagen diseases?" the doctor asked, his voice intelligent, calm, and soothing. "Or amyloidosis? Sarcoidosis?"

"I'm not sure," Eva answered, adjusting her hold on Chapman's black box. "I really don't know."

"What about alcoholism? Does he use tranquilizers or barbiturates?"

"No, I don't think so… All I know for sure is that they treated his injuries and told me that he was suffering from post-traumatic amnesia."

"Because of the injury to his head?"

"Yes."

"So, the diagnosis was based solely on the injuries that he sustained from the accident?"

"Yes." Eva nodded. "I guess so."

The psychiatrist turned about to peek in at Anon. "He seems to be healthy. Alert."

"I don't understand," Eva remarked, feeling her concern rising.

"Well," the doctor explained, "receiving a blow to the head isn't the only way to become amnesic. Certain diseases and toxic agents can also cause amnesia. And post-traumatic amnesia is not the only type of amnesia. There are also purely psychiatric forms. Repression amnesia, hysterical amnesia. Maybe it was the trauma of the accident and not the visible, physical injury that induced the condition. Before he lost his memory, do you know, was he feeling guilty, frightened?"

Eva thought about it, but she was unsure. "I don't know, maybe. Why?"

"Well, the mind has a number of ways of protecting itself. A person's psychoneurotic motivation to dissociate himself from what he views as an intolerable situation in his personal life can result in the repression of painful or guilt-ridden memories. This sometimes occurs when a person feels that he must for some reason suppress many of his natural impulses and feelings. In some cases, individuals have even been known to assume new identities in which they can act out their suppressed feelings."

Eva wanted to make certain she understood. "So, you're saying that Anon's memory loss might not be due to his physical injury... but to some suppressed feelings of guilt or fear?"

"It's possible."

"Do you think you can help him?"

"Possibly," the doctor answered. "Why don't you take a seat. It'll be a little while. Oh, and pet Sigmund. Petting a dog has been proven to relax people. Even if it's a Doberman."

Eva smiled unsurely, eyeing the Doberman as she sat, watching the dog moving up close to her, focusing on her. Hesitantly, she reached out and touched the dog gently, pleasantly surprised to see the animal react affectionately.

~

"Well, Dr. Anon," the doctor asked as he closed the door and pulled the window blinds down, darkening the room further, "are you feeling somewhat more relaxed now?"

"A little."

"Good. Now, before we begin, I'd like to point out to you that, although hypnosis is a very useful exploratory tool, there really isn't any way to predict in advance if anything useful will actually come of this."

Anon nodded in acceptance of the statement. "I was thinking," he asked, "what if I can't be hypnotized?"

The psychiatrist smiled slightly as he took a seat near Anon. "I don't think we'll have to worry about that. Although the degree of suggestibility varies greatly from person to person, most people can be hypnotized. The key is placing your trust in me. Do you think you can do that?"

"Yes," Anon answered truthfully.

"Good. Now, most individuals feel cold when reliving experiences, so I'd like you to wrap that blanket around yourself."

Anon noticed a folded blanket resting nearby. He took it and followed the doctor's directions.

"Now," instructed the doctor, "please place your feet comfortably upon the floor and drop your hands into your lap."

Anon did so.

"Keeping your head level, I want you to raise only your eyes and focus them upon an imaginary spot on the ceiling."

"I thought…" Anon paused. "Aren't you going to swing something back and forth and tell me to stare at it?"

For the second time the doctor smiled slightly. "The Chevreul pendulum. I realize that it's become synonymous with hypnotism but it's rarely used today as an induction method."

"Oh."

"Do you have your imaginary spot?"

Anon looked to the ceiling. "Yes."

"Good. Stare at it. Stare at it and concentrate only on my voice. I want you to begin to take slow, deep breaths."

Anon did so.

"With each breath you will feel more and more relaxed. Your face will relax. Your arms will relax. Your hands will relax. Your legs will relax. All the tension will leave your body."

Relaxing, Anon continued his slow, deep breathing.

"Now breath normally," the doctor instructed Anon, "concentrating only on my voice."

Breathing normally, Anon felt his eyelids growing heavy.

"Your eyes feel as if they want to close," the doctor coaxed him. "Let them close."

Blinking slowly, Anon allowed his eyes to close.

"Good. Let your head fall forward."

Anon did.

"Now, I want you to imagine a descending staircase in the darkness of your mind. A deep, dark staircase. Soon, you will be descending these stairs. With each step that you take, you will fall deeper and deeper into a hypnotic state. You will count each step aloud as you take it. Start down the stairs."

Anon was silent for a second or two, and then he found himself counting: "One... Two... Three... Four... Five... S... s... sss..."

And Anon fell silent.

"You are now in a deep hypnotic state," the doctor stated. "The only voice that you hear is mine. When you awaken, you will not remember any of this. Do you understand?"

"... I... understand..." Anon answered.

"Good." The doctor touched the record button on a large digital recorder. "Dr. Anon, together we will now open your memory and examine your past. But first, I have a question for you. Before your accident, were you experiencing feelings of guilt? Of fear?"

Anon did not respond immediately. But he did: "... Yes... Guilt... Fear..."

~

Eva felt safe with the Doberman lying at her feet. But she found herself just staring at the door to the psychiatrist's office, wondering how the hypnosis session was going.

Sighing, she thought about Chapman's box, and she opened it, looking in at the skull fragments. Carefully, she began to sift through them, looking for matching pieces. It was more difficult than she had imagined but she found three pieces that fit together. Holding them in place, she stared at them inquisitively.

"If only you could talk..." she whispered.

—Time past:

Lightning flashed in the distance, announcing the storm that was rolling in, its forewarning drums of thunder sounding its arrival.

A number of *Australopithecus afarensis* hominids scattered and ran for cover, disappearing into a grove of trees.

On an exposed flat rock, surrounded by a sea of tall waving grass, Gray Streak comforted his *afarensis* mate as she lay back, in pain, about to give birth.

A great spider-webbing bolt of lightning brightened the sky over them as the storm grew nearer. But it was too late to seek shelter. The *afarensis* would need to give birth where she lay, out in the open. She shrieked in fright. But Gray Streak placed a caring palm on the side of her face, calming her.

She cried out as she strained.

A head appeared. Gray Streak gently pulled the newborn out into the world. A boy. Strangely, the boy was not covered with anywhere near the amount of hair that his parents were, and, more noticeably, his forehead was much higher in proportion to his face. The child looked more human-like than *afarensis*-like. Like how one might imagine a H*omo habilis* infant to appear. A mutation?

Gray Streak's mate moaned; her labor was not over. A second head emerged. A girl. Also *Homo habilis* in look… Lightning exploded across the sky, thunder crackled, and it began to rain, the falling droplets baptizing the newborns. The children were new, different than what had come before them.

Gray Streak lifted a primitive, hair-covered hand, touched the four-pronged crystal hanging about his neck, and he smiled— uncharacteristic of an *afarensis*. Looking heavenward, he then closed his eyes in deep satisfaction, content for the moment to simply feel the rain on his face.

Eva, her eyes closed, had fallen asleep in her chair. The psychiatrist's office door was still shut. The hypnosis session had gone on for far longer than expected.

Within the office, Anon was still in a deep, hypnotic state.

The doctor, noticeably disturbed, his face beaded with perspiration, reached out with a trembling hand and touched the stop button on his recorder.

"Anon…" the doctor said, his voice reflecting his shaken appearance, "I—I want you to, um, walk back up your staircase now… counting backward from five to one… with each step that you ascend."

It took a while for Anon to respond, but he did: "… Five…"

~

Eva awoke and rose to her feet as the doctor led Anon into the waiting room. At once she noticed how completely drained Anon appeared and she went to him, to physically support him, to keep him on his feet.

She turned to the doctor. "Did the hypnosis work?" she asked. But then she noticed how shaken the man appeared. He looked nervous, frightened.

"Please…" the doctor responded. "Take a seat. Um… Give me a few moments alone, in privacy. To, um, review the session. I'll, um… I'll be out shortly."

Eva watched as the doctor stepped back into his office, glancing back at Anon oddly before closing the door.

"Anon…" she asked, "what happened?"

"I don't know…" Anon answered, very weak, groggy, out of it. "I don't remember anything… after he… put me under."

~

The doctor paused to pull out his keys and lock his heavy office door behind him before moving to a small liquor cabinet where he poured himself a drink, which he gulped down.

As the doctor lowered his glass, a billowing curtain caught his eye, and he saw that one of the room's large windows was now open, displaying the fire escape outside.

He shivered and turned his nose away, coughing at the stench. It was then that he noticed the bald pale man standing motionless in the shadows near the window.

"Oh no…" the doctor mumbled.

The unusual man stepped forward stiffly, pulling out a large, futuristic handgun.

"… Where is Anon?" the man asked, his dead-white face impassive.

The doctor glanced at the door to his waiting room. The pale man looked at the door, and then his lifeless eyes slowly surveyed his surroundings, looking at the couch and then at the digital recorder.

"… You treated Anon?" the man's grating voice dropped low, near a whisper.

The doctor reached for his temple, feeling ill.

"… You treated him?" repeated the intruder.

"Y-yes, I did," the doctor admitted.

"… You entered Anon's mind?" the pale man's voice dropped even lower.

The psychiatrist nodded.

The man's voice dropped lower still: "... You know about... *them*?"

The psychiatrist hesitated and then nodded.

Immediately the pale man expressed his only reaction thus far, a harrowing narrowing of his eyes, a predatorial squint. Simultaneously, he lifted his unusual handgun. The hole at the end of the weapon's barrel wound open automatically, widening to an incredible diameter of over a foot across.

"... That knowledge is forbidden," the corpse-like man stated with finality.

The doctor stepped to his desk and quickly lifted the receiver of his phone and punched in 911.

Stepping forward slowly and deliberately, the pale man lightly touched his fingertips against a metal file cabinet. Vibrating, it rumbled out of the way, giving the strange man an unobstructed path to the doctor.

~

Eva stepped aside as the psychiatrist's dog, Sigmund, brushed past her to go to the closed office door, growling, baring its teeth.

~

The pale man aimed his nightmarish weapon at the doctor as the 911 call was answered.

"Nine-one-one emergency, operator twenty-one, please state the nature of your emergency."

The interior of the weapon's barrel ignited and glowed a fiery yellow-orange.

"Five seventeen Baldwin..." the doctor said numbly into the receiver. "It's going to kill me..."

~

The Doberman started to bark and scratch at the door.

"Why's he acting like that?" Eva wondered.

~

Stiffly, the pale man stepped up to the phone, ignoring the sizzling, frying sound that was coming from somewhere down on the floor.

"A unit is en route and will be there shortly," came the voice from the receiver.

The pale man turned toward the door that led to the waiting room. The Doberman, on the other side, was barking louder, its hard nails scratching madly.

"Repeat, a unit is en route and will be there at any moment."

The pale man made a decision and then placed a palm firmly down upon the doctor's recording machine, and it buckled and bent in upon itself.

Leaving the device utterly destroyed, the man stepped through the open window and out onto the fire escape. From there he pulled the window closed. He then motioned with a single finger and the window's metal lock, on the other side of the glass, as if by magic, twisted closed, locking the window from the inside.

~

The Doberman whimpered and shuffled backward, reacting fearfully to the eerie light blue smoke that wafted into the waiting room from beneath the door.

"Smells... like electricity..." Anon remarked groggily.

Eva tried the door. "It's locked."

She turned her head, alarmed, as she heard the wail of approaching police sirens.

~

Eva continued to physically support Anon as she simultaneously leaned into him, turning her eyes away from the large, ashy, greasy lump of burnt flesh and calcined bones that lay on the floor in the center of the psychiatrist's office.

Surrounding the pile were unburnt body parts: a left arm, a right hand, a right leg from the knee down, and half of a semi-smoldering skull.

"Spontaneous human combustion," a tall, rapidly talking fire marshal provided his opinion to Anon and Eva while observing the other firemen, policemen, and medical technicians who were busily moving about the office. "That's what it's called. SHC for short. There've been about two hundred reported cases."

Eva felt Sigmund lean against her legs and she welcomed the dog's presence.

She glanced at the technicians, who were shoveling the psychiatrist's burnt remains into a body bag as the marshal continued: "Nobody understands it, but sometimes a person just ignites. Just like that. *Woof!* Up in smoke. There's never any apparent source of flame but the person's always fried to a crisp. It's something that seems to start in the torso. Limbs are usually left intact.

"It's weird. And to have two cases in the same week is even weirder. Human flesh isn't easy to ignite, you know. It takes a hell of a lot of heat. Just think what it would take to make a T-bone steak disintegrate in a pan. And look…" He waved an open hand, motioning about the office. "No damage to the surrounding furniture. Only the burnt spot on the carpet."

"Do you think…" Eva asked the marshal, glancing at Anon, "could it have been murder?"

"Murder?" the man answered. "How? He was in the room alone. The room locked from the inside."

"But," Eva pushed her point, "it's just that, well, it's so hard to believe, that a person can just burn up like that."

She leaned closer to Anon to allow the technicians to leave, wheeling the body bag past them.

"Yep..." the marshal agreed. "I know what you mean. Makes you wonder if it can happen to you. Incineration. And it's not something you can hide from if it's gonna happen. People've been burnt like this in bed, in the shower, believe it or not, in planes, on trains. Hell, this can get you anywhere. "

"... Anywhere?" Anon asked, still quite groggy, unsteady on his feet, having not yet fully recovered from the hypnosis session.

"Anywhere," the marshal emphasized.

Eva looked at Anon. She could see that he was thinking the same thing. They had to try to get away, hide somewhere.

"Excuse us," she said to the marshal as she led Anon away, with Sigmund, the Doberman, now ownerless, following them.

Origins

Niko Zinovii

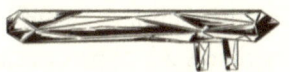

13. Flight

In Eva's car they sped off, heading away from the city, Eva driving, Anon riding passenger, Sigmund in the back seat.

"So," Eva sought confirmation, "we hide out until your memory returns? And we head north?"

Anon nodded. "Feels safer that way, north. I'm not sure why, it just does. It feels like the right direction to travel."

Sigmund whined, and Anon reached back to stroke the dog, his touch quickly calming the animal.

"Maybe we shouldn't have taken him," Anon remarked.

"I'm glad we did," Eva responded. "I feel safer having him with us."

Anon noticed how tightly she was gripping the steering wheel.

"Would you like me to drive?" he asked.

"Thanks, no, I'm—I'm all right."

"Are you sure?"

She nodded. "So, how far should we go?"

"I don't know," Anon answered, thinking about it. "I guess until we're too tired to go on, until we need to stop. Eva, I'm sorry I dragged you into this. It wasn't my intention…"

"You needed somebody," she responded, quickly and genuinely. "I wanted to be that somebody. To be there for you."

"Eva, last night…" Anon said as he caringly reached over and buckled her seat belt. "I want you to know that it was very special for me. As if… as if it gave my life meaning, as if it was the purpose of my being, to meet you, to be with you."

Eva glanced at him tenderly, calming. "That skull in Chapman's box," she then said. "I was thinking that maybe you should put it together. There's a roll of tape in the glove compartment."

"Sounds like a good idea."

Eva turned onto a country road and the car was swallowed by the shadows cast by the setting sun.

~

Dusk:

Anon had taped several small, intricate skull fragments into place, adding to the three that Eva had temporarily pieced together earlier.

He next picked up one of the larger fragments, examined it, and fitted it into what he had assembled thus far.

From the back seat, Sigmund stared warily at the fossil.

—Time past:

> A group of *afarensis* families had gathered together in the tall grass. Digging up roots, eating gathered fruits, and grooming one another, they were silently and peacefully going about their simple daily activities.
>
> Gray Streak, his mate, and their two unusual children, older now, joined the group. Being older, the two *Homo habilis* youngsters differed strikingly from those around them, being much more human-like.
>
> The boy broke a stick and shaped it into a digging tool. Gray Streak eyed his son with pride. But the children drew uneasy stares from the others, who recognized the boy and girl as what they were: different.

Two of the largest *afarensis* males approached Gray Streak's family, observing. Their observation, however, soon turned aggressive. Baring teeth, they began to grunt at the family. Others soon joined in, kicking dirt, throwing small sticks, and screeching at the different children.

Hairy arms swung violently at Gray Streak and his family, hitting them over and over. Huddled together, they stumbled off, driven away, ostracized.

Having taped the fragment securely into place, Anon found another piece that fit.

—Time past:

A nearby volcano, glowing softly against the night sky, was gently spewing molten rock and cinder over the African savanna.

Gray Streak and his mate, carrying their unique children, started across the field of soft dark ash that was being laid down by the ongoing eruption.

As they walked, Gray Streak's son played with the four-pronged crystal dangling from his father's neck.

Gray Streak turned his eyes heavenward, staring up at the millions of twinkling stars. Slowly, he took hold of his mate's hand, holding it affectionately as they walked. She did not appear to fully understand the meaning of the gesture but it felt good and she accepted it.

Together, the outcast family walked toward the horizon, leaving their footprints behind in the volcanic ash.

Eva's car rumbled over dark mud, leaving tire tracks over a stretch of the road that had recently been washed over.

Anon fit another piece of the fossil puzzle into place.

—*Time past:*

Gray Streak's son, now in his early teen years, dug into the mud with a branch that he had shaped into a shovel. His twin sister, nearby, shaped a branch into a digging tool of her own.

Gray Streak and his mate relaxed as they watched their children. Their mother's eyes swelled with curiosity but lacked understanding, while their father's expression denoted acknowledgement and satisfaction.

The *habilis* boy unearthed a buried nest of turtle eggs and he started to pull them out, one by one. His sister moved in closer, watching. The soil in the hole was moist and it stuck to the boy's palms.

The *habilis* girl moved still closer, casting her shadow down over the hole. Her brother pressed a palm upon her forehead to gently push her back, to remove her shadow. He was surprised to see that he had left a print of his hand, in mud, pasted upon her forehead.

He created a handprint on his own forehead. His sister smiled and they begin to paste handprints over each other's bodies.

Their mother displayed no understanding or appreciation of their discovery of art. Gray Streak did. His crystal rod sparkled in the bright sunlight.

The two *habilis* children laughed and ran to the river's edge, washing their hands clean. It was there that they noticed their reflections on the water and stared at them for several important moments.

The *habilis* boy then, for the first time, attempted to speak. His words come slowly:

"Ka... Tama... Ka... Tama..."

His sister attempted an imitation:

"Ka... Ka... Tama... Ka."

The boy stuck a hand into the water, rippling its surface, observing the undulating, concentric rings.

Gray Streak nodded approvingly toward his children: tools, art, and language. Culture.

Anon stared at the assembled fragments. A face was forming. It looked quite odd. The eyes appeared as if they would turn out to be unusually large.

"... Large cranium," Anon remarked. "Unusually large..."

Sigmund, growling low at the partially assembled fossil, retreated into the furthest reaches of the back seat.

"Sun's almost down," Eva said. "I guess we'll stop at the first place we see."

"Mm-hmm." Anon picked up another skull fragment, turning it about, visually analyzing it. He was about to try to place it but he suddenly stopped as he noticed something odd to the east, out on the darkening horizon. It seemed to be a falling star. But this "star" turned away from impacting into the earth, and it began to flash directly toward them at an incredible rate of speed, growing in both brightness and size.

Anon watched on in disbelief, his mouth agape, as it grew nearer and nearer, quickly taking on the surreal shape of a classic flying saucer, with a large lump in its center surrounded by what seemed to be portholes. Its otherwise featureless surface was shiny, the color of polished aluminum, with the glow of ionized gas completely surrounded its hull.

"… Eva…" Anon whispered almost mutely as the saucer flashed toward them at an extremely low altitude.

She turned to him with a soft smile, totally unaware of the approaching craft.

SWOOOSH!

The entire car rocked madly as the saucer zoomed directly over it, and Eva momentarily lost control of the automobile.

Anon, having ducked by reflex, peeked up over the dash to witness the saucer disappearing over the opposite horizon.

"Oh wow…" he muttered, almost inaudibly. "I never expected that…"

Eva regained control of the car and immediately looked up to see what it was that had passed over them, but it was too late, it was gone, she saw nothing.

"What? What was that? A plane?"

Anon shook his head and silently mouthed the word "no."

"Where'd it go?" Eva asked.

"Eva…" Anon found his voice. "I think we're in real, real trouble."

"What?"

"Real serious, serious trouble," he added.

"What are you talking about?" Eva's voice dropped, frightened.

Sigmund barked from the back seat. In the rearview mirror, Eva noticed a rapidly approaching dark sedan.

"Oh no…" she said.

"Oh no what?"

"They found us," she clarified, motioning over her shoulder with a toss of her chin.

Anon spun about to see the approaching sedan that was now directly behind them and moving toward them at an increasingly unrealistic speed. Anon was quite shaken to see that the bald pale man was driving the car. The man had somehow risen from the dead.

"Faster," Anon nervously instructed Eva. "Drive faster."

Eva floored it.

BANG!

The sedan rammed into them from behind.

"Faster!" Anon yelled.

"It won't go any faster!"

Anon looked back again. The dead-white, corpse-like face of the pale man was frighteningly rigid, his eyes lifeless, unblinking, trance-like. Anon could not discern what intentions the strange man had in mind.

BANG! The sedan struck them again.

Sigmund fell to the floor.

Anon saw that the sedan was about to hit them yet again. And that Eva had the gas pedal pushed flush to the floor.

BANG! This time the front of the sedan became entangled with and locked to the rear of Eva's automobile.

Anon and Eva sank back into their seats due to the continued forced acceleration. Directly ahead of them the road divided, forking around a high outcrop of rock.

"Oh no," Anon mumbled.

Eva stomped both feet down on the brake as hard as she could.

The tires of her car locked and skidded, but their automobile continued rocketing straight ahead at a nightmarish speed, pushed forward by the sedan.

Anon reached out and jerked the steering wheel to the right. And Eva's car broke free and swerved off, twisting, turning, skidding down the road, while their pursuer continued to barrel straight ahead.

If Anon had been able to see the face of the pale man, he would have noticed that even as the sedan was about to strike the rock outcrop, the man's countenance remained completely impassive.

The sound was deafening as the sedan hit the outcropping. Ricocheting off the rock, the car flipped and rolled over and over, tumbling past Eva's car, which had skidded to a stop.

Anon watched the sedan noisily roll past them and tumble off the road, where it flipped over, smacking against a stand of trees.

Eva's car coughed and its engine died, leaving Anon and Eva in an atmosphere of surreal near silence, the only sound seeming to be the still-spinning tires of the overturned sedan.

For the longest moment Anon and Eva just sat there in a state of shock, glancing at one other and at the crashed sedan.

It was Sigmund's barking that finally snapped them out of it. Without saying a word, they disembarked and followed the Doberman toward the upside-down sedan.

At the edge of the road they stopped, looking down at the wreck. And they heard Sigmund growl.

The driver's-side door kicked open and the pale man flopped out. Moving slowly and deliberately, the strange man somehow rose to his feet, unsteady. He stood there silent for a moment, before he lost all his strength and dropped into a seated position, his bald head slumping forward.

"Is he… dead?" Eva whispered.

"No, I don't think so. This is the same one that 'died' in my apartment."

Sigmund trotted down to the motionless pale man. Nearing him, the Doberman stopped abruptly, shivering, the fur on its back standing on end. Sniffing the air, the dog began barking loudly, unwilling to go any farther.

"What do we do?" Eva asked. "My car—do you think it'll start?"

Anon looked at her car, up into the darkening sky, and then down at the mysterious pale man.

"I think we need some answers," he said, determined.

And he started down to the wreck. Eva hesitated, unsure, but then followed.

Anon stepped up to Sigmund's side and he too shivered. Eva reacted identically.

"What's that smell?" Eva asked. "And that cold... So cold."

"I'm not sure, but I think it's part of him."

Eva stepped closer and her bracelets and rings suddenly and mysteriously twisted and buckled, painfully. "Ow!"

It was then that the open car door groaned and bent away from the pale man.

"I think that's part of him too," Anon remarked.

Anon picked up a broken branch and moved closer to the "dead" man.

"I don't think he's really alive," he said. "Not like us, anyway. I think... I think he's some sort of living robot."

Anon prepared to poke the man with the stick.

"A living robot?" Eva could not believe it.

Anon poked the man in the stomach. The man's mouth dropped open and a breath of air gurgled its way out. Then slowly, very slowly, the man's dead eyes opened halfway. Eva jumped, about to run off.

"No," Anon stopped her from doing so. "I think it's okay."

The pale man, sitting there motionless, just stared back at them with his half-open eyes.

"When you say a living robot," Eva asked, "do you mean like... like a Frankenstein's Monster?"

Anon nodded unsurely and grabbed the man's wrist.

"So…" Eva struggled with it. "He—he's made up of parts of dead bodies?"

"No, just a single body, reanimated. Sort of like a big rechargeable battery, I imagine. No pulse."

"But his eyes are open. He—he's looking at us."

"Yes…" Anon agreed, a thought striking him. "I wonder if they're looking at us too. Through those eyes."

Anon summed up his courage and poked the man again.

"Who are they?" Anon asked. "Where are they?"

After a silent moment the man's eyes widened and he spoke:

"Bro… ken… Hill… They… are at… Bro… k… en… H… ill…"

"Broken Hill?" Anon asked. "Near or far?"

The pale man did not answer.

"Is it near or far?" Anon repeated.

"… N…. e… a… r… r… r…. r… r…"

The man's eyes slowly closed.

The sedan's open door groaned and the automobile's metal body crumpled as if an invisible wave of force were rolling over it. Eva's jewelry broke off and fell to the ground. The sign up on the road groaned and bent completely over, its top touching the asphalt.

"I guess they're always leaking energy," Anon surmised. "What was left in him must have just… well, been released. Shot out. Inefficient."

Anon used his branch to push open the pale man's suit jacket and then his dull white shirt. Beneath the man's shirt he was wearing a strange, very wide metal band about his torso.

"I wonder if that belt produces an electrical, electromagnetic field?" Anon speculated aloud. "But it would have to be very strong… and constant… producing some type of electromagnetic migration effect? To bend metal… But wouldn't it attract rather than repel? I don't know…"

Anon stepped back to Eva's side.

"Do you have a map?" he asked her.

"Why?"

"I think we should try to find out what this is all about."

"By going to Broken Hill?"

Anon nodded, looking back at the pale man. As he did so he noticed an odd bulge in the upper portion of the man's wrinkle-free jacket.

He stepped back down to the man. With his stick he pushed the jacket open further, revealing the strange weapon holstered at the man's side. It was the unusual gun that had been used to kill the psychiatrist.

"Eva," Anon appealed to her, "they found us. They'll find us again." He reached down and took the gun. "Maybe it's time we find them. If we can learn what we're up against, well, then we'll know what to do. We'll have a fighting chance. I don't think we can really run from them. I don't think we can actually get away from them.

"The way they found us... the way this man was brought back to life... the power behind them, behind resurrection... it—it's godlike. The technological magic of an unearthly science."

"What was it that flew over us?" Eva asked.

Anon looked most seriously into her eyes. "A flying saucer. Believe it or not."

They were both silent as they walked back to her car. Anon tried the ignition key. It took several attempts but the car did start.

"Oh, thank God," Eva said, relived. She then attempted to open an app on her cell phone. "No signal. No connection. Battery low." So she rummaged through her glove compartment and handed Anon a map, which he spread open.

"Broken Hill... Broken Hill... Found it."

Eva looked at his pointing finger. "That's out in the middle of nowhere," she observed. "And... it—it's a cemetery. It's labeled a cemetery."

Anon folded up the map and moved close to her. "We have to go," he told her calmly. "To find out what this is about. It's our only chance."

Anon watched Eva nod her head slowly and climb into the driver's seat.

~

It was dark by the time their car transitioned from a paved road to one of gravel, somewhere deep in the country, no streetlights, trees everywhere.

Eva glanced at the unusual gun Anon had taken from the pale man, which was lying between them.

"Are you sure this is the right way?" she asked.

"According to the map it is."

"How much farther?" she asked, glancing at the gas gauge. They were down to a quarter of a tank.

"Three, four miles, maybe less— What's this?"

Several vehicles were strewn haphazardly about the road directly before them, their hoods and doors open: a United States mail jeep, an old pick-up truck, and a tow truck. All abandoned.

Eva's car suddenly died, and they rolled to a stop near the other vehicles. Their automobile's headlights then dimmed and went out, leaving them in the dark.

"What happened?" Eva asked.

"I don't know."

She tried to restart the car. Nothing. Anon pressed on the horn. Nothing.

"It seems the battery's dead," he said.

"It was a new battery..."

Anon got out of the car, letting Sigmund out as well. Eva also disembarked.

"Do you think their batteries died too?" Eva asked, pointing to the other vehicles.

"It would seem so..." Anon guessed as he took the map, Chapman's box, and the pale man's unusual gun from the car.

"So, what now?" Eva asked.

"Walk, I guess."

"To the cemetery?"

"To the cemetery."

Anon handed the gun to Eva as a bribe. She took it. She also called Sigmund close to her and they started off, heading toward Broken Hill Cemetery.

Niko Zinovii

Part Four

Niko Zinovii

14. Kugelblitz

Anon, following the gravel road, led Eva up a rather steep hill, Sigmund traveling at their side.

As they moved past a dark grove of trees, Anon noticed an old farmhouse just up ahead, on their right. All the windows of its first floor were boarded up. The place looked abandoned.

"Do you think anyone lives there?" Eva asked.

"No lights…" Anon noted as he lengthened his stride, heading toward the house.

As they reached the front of the farmhouse, they encountered an old, beat-up tractor, sitting in the middle of the road. Its hood was up and its large tires were wedged by huge clogs of wood. Although the tractor was pointed up the hill, the blocks were oddly positioned in front of its tires, rather than behind them. Up the road the nearby hilltop was glowing a strange electric blue…

"Abandoned?" Eva wondered about the tractor.

"Let's see if anyone's here…" Anon responded.

Together they walked up to the front door. Anon was about to knock when Sigmund began to growl. Behind them, someone stepped out of the darkness and cocked a gun.

"Turn 'round real slow like," instructed a loud, hick-country voice. "And don't move one damn inch. And hold that there pooch!"

They turned about to face a tall, big-boned, paunchy farmer who was holding a double-barreled shotgun, pointed at them. He looked to be about fifty years old. Oddly, he had no eyebrows or eyelashes... and the hair on the front of his head appeared to have been burnt down to almost nothing. He looked ill, pale. A large nail hung from his neck, dangling from a long, dirty string.

The farmer noticed the unusual gun Eva was holding.

"Hey," the farmer exclaimed, surprised. "You got one a their guns."

Anon watched as the man cautiously stepped toward them, holding out the nail hanging about his neck while sniffing the air.

"Aw." The farmer grinned ear to ear. "You're okay, aren'cha? You're normal people, city folk?"

Anon was unsure what to make of the man. Missing his eyebrows and eyelashes, he bore some resemblance to the pale men.

"Um, yes, we're from the city," Anon answered, reserved.

"How are the cities?" the man asked, his voice full of concern. "Are they okay? Or did they black them out too?"

Anon and Eva glanced at each other.

"I'm afraid we don't understand," Anon stated.

"So, the cities are okay? And here all along we thought it was an all-out invasion. Guess it's only happenin' out here. You come out by car?"

"Engine died a couple miles down the road," Anon replied.

"A couple miles?" The farmer scratched his head.

Anon nodded.

"So, it goes for a couple miles..." the farmer continued. "Well, least now I know how far the damn thing stretches."

"Thing?" Anon sought clarification.

"The blackout. Come on, let's get inside where it's safe."

Anon placed a cautious hand on Eva, stopping her from accepting the invitation.

"Oh, shoot." The farmer smiled widely again, turning his gun away. "You think I'm one of them zombies, don'cha? Heck, look."

And he touched the nail hanging about his neck.

"If it don't bend, then he's a friend." He laughed at his rhyme but then became silent when he saw Anon's and Eva's unchanged worried expressions.

"What?" the farmer responded. "Can't you see I'm normal, like you? Hell, you ain't a-shiverin', are ya? And I don't smell like no dirty beetle, do I?"

"But," Anon said, "your eyebrows, your face."

"Oh, don't mind that," the farmer explained. "Happened last night. They almost got me with their goddamn kugelblitz."

"Kugelblitz?" Anon had never heard the word before.

"That's what my grandpa called it way back in W-W-one. Ball lightnin'. That's how they get ya. Don't you know nothin'? Ain't you seen—"

Sigmund barked loudly. The farmer raised his shotgun, instantly alert and ready. He spotted something out on the dark, starlit horizon.

"Oh lordy," he exclaimed, "here they come again!"

Anon turned to see a bright shooting "star" abruptly pull out of its nosedive and begin to race toward them. Growing larger and brighter, it rapidly took on the shape of the flying saucer he had seen earlier.

A circular hole wound open on the saucer's otherwise featureless underside, and spheres of glowing hot plasma began to drop down over the countryside, as if the craft were initiating a bombing run.

Four of the fireballs descended toward the farmhouse. They were an intense red in color, beach-ball sized, and aflame, burning as brightly as thousand-watt light bulbs.

"Fast! Inside!" the farmer yelled and he charged into the house, wildly waving his arms about over his head. "Frank! Hey Frank! We got incoming!"

"We'd better follow him," Anon suggested, and they quickly did so.

The descending fireballs darted about oddly, haphazardly changing directions as they dropped. Nearing the ground, one ricocheted off a telephone pole, scorching it in the process. Exuding a bluish mist, it then started to roll down the pole's single power line, tumbling toward the farmhouse. The heavy-duty plastic encasing the line melted beneath it, sending up inky black smoke while dripping down dark plastic goo.

A second orb landed by chance upon a fence. Dancing along the fence top, it too made its way toward the farmhouse, turning the wooden posts beneath it to ash.

Bouncing off the ground, the third ball started wobbling toward a boarded-up window as the fourth quietly floated down toward the farmhouse's roof and open chimney.

~

Inside, the farmer yelled again for Frank, and Frank, a lean, weathered fifty-year-old, jumped into the living room from the kitchen. Immediately he pointed his shotgun at Anon and Eva.

"No! They're okay!" the farmer shouted quickly.

"So then what the hell's all the yellin' about?" Frank demanded.

"They're a-shellin' again! We gotta get down inta the cellar!"

"What?" Frank protested. "And leave the prisoner? Hell no! I'm stayin' up here. He ain't gettin' away on us again. No way! No way!"

"But ya can't stay up here," the farmer yelled back. "You'll get fried!"

A fiery ball pushed itself into the farmhouse, squeezing between and burning through the boards crisscrossing one of its window frames.

"I told you to overlap them boards when you nailed them up!" the farmer yelled at Frank.

Entering the living room, the fireball rolled up a wall and started tumbling across the ceiling.

Simultaneously, another plasma orb came bouncing out of the fireplace. This one wobbled toward the farmer. The man immediately fired his shotgun, hitting the thing dead on. Spinning about, the fireball crackled and then imploded and disappeared with the sound of a thunderclap.

"Gotcha!" the farmer exclaimed.

The ball rolling across the ceiling throbbed before it dropped down and wobbled toward Frank, who ran off, yelling. The sphere flashed after Frank with an uncanny burst of speed but it missed the man as he leapt to the floor. Whooshing over him, it bounced into an old iron stove. There was a thunderous explosion as the flaming orb blew the stove apart, sending bits of metal flying off in all directions.

"Frank, stay down!" the farmer yelled.

Sigmund barked wildly as the remaining two fireballs entered the farmhouse. Crackling, one of them bounced into the room, the other came in burning, rolling up a wall.

The bouncing orb pulsated once before turning to the farmer.

"Oh, damn," the farmer cursed, seeing the kugelblitz flashing toward him. "Every man for himself!"

Anon watched the farmer run off as the remaining orb slowly dropped down off the burnt wall and spun about to face him and Eva, hovering right before them, burning hot, trembling eerily.

"We'd better run…" Anon said and he pulled Eva away, leaving Sigmund there, barking at the fireball.

The plasma sphere seemed unmindful of the dog. Throbbing, it wobbled past the animal and gave chase to Anon, who led Eva into the dining room, pulling the door closed behind them.

"It'll likely burn through the door…" Anon stated. "Come on." And he pulled her off toward a hall in the back of the room.

The plasma became pencil thin before squeezing through the keyhole of the dining-room door. Emerging from the scorched hole, it amazingly resumed its spherical shape. Pulsating, it began to search the room for Anon and Eva.

~

The farmer yanked open the door directly before him and he leaped forward, tumbling head over heals down the cellar stairs. The pursuing fireball came bouncing down the wooden steps, scorching each one it touched. When it reached the bottom, it rose into the dank air, hovering, sizzling, exuding a bluish mist.

The farmer frantically scampered off across the dirt floor, yelling loudly, wildly. Somehow he made it up the stone steps leading to the outside, where he cackled out a laugh and slammed the cellar's storm doors shut.

The ball banged against the metal doors, imploding with a crackle, flicking out in silence, like a lamp turning off. But it then reappeared, materializing out of nowhere several feet distant, only to then explode with a violent crackle of thunder.

"Ha!" the famer gloated. He then immediately looked up into the starlit sky and spotted the saucer off in the distance. It was continuing to move away, dropping its balls of lightning down over the countryside.

~

Anon found that he had led Eva into the kitchen. He quickly spun about, looking behind them. There was no sign of the last kugelblitz...

The kitchen's back door suddenly burst open and the farmer rushed in, his shotgun held ready. He jumped over to the refrigerator, which was oddly tied closed by an entanglement of thick ropes, and then he turned to Anon and Eva.

"Where's Frank?" he asked.

Eva was the first to notice the light blue smoke that was drifting into the room, coming from beneath the closed door that led to the living room. It was identical to the smoke that had seeped into the psychiatrist's waiting room.

"Oh..." she uttered.

The farmer rushed past her and yanked open the door. The Doberman, Sigmund, leapt into the kitchen, past the farmer, moving to Eva's side. Then, stepping into the doorway came Frank, who just stood right there before them, blue smoke emanating from a dark, circular spot burnt through the front of his shirt, in the center of his chest.

"Frank?" the farmer moaned.

Frank stumbled into the kitchen, dazed.

"I—I don't feel so good," he groaned. "My chest... It—it's burning."

Anon felt Eva grip him tightly as right before their eyes Frank's torso ignited from within, the man's body burning red hot but with an absence of flames.

Frank tried to scream but he was unable to make a sound.

He dropped to his knees, helpless.

"Frank!" the farmer yelled and he ran to the sink, furiously pushing and pulling the handle of the water pump. "Hold on, Frank! I'll put ya out! Hold on!"

But Frank collapsed completely, his body caving in upon itself, his figure quickly becoming reduced to a lifeless lump of smelly soot.

The farmer pushed by Anon and Eva with a bucket of water but all that remained of his friend was a right hand and forearm and a smoldering left leg.

"Oh…" the farmer groaned. "Oh goddamn. They got ya, Frank… They got ya."

"Excuse me…" Anon asked, finding his voice after a long moment of dead silence. "But who are *they*?"

"Who are *they*?" the farmer grumbled. "Sons of bitches, that's who they are. Sons of bitches."

The farmer stepped over to the refrigerator. Besides being tied shut, it was strangely perforated by numerous jagged silver-dollar-sized holes that had been drilled or knocked into it.

"I… I wasn't sure if it was dead this time," the farmer explained, "so we locked it up in here."

The man started untying a large knot in the ropes.

"It?" Anon asked.

"Yep, it. So hold that gun ready, son."

Anon picked up the farmer's shotgun and did so, hesitantly.

"Anon?" Eva whispered, frightened.

Anon nodded to her, uncertain but trying to assure her that it was okay.

The ropes slackened and fell to the floor.

"Okay," the farmer snorted, "you heard of little green men? Well, two weeks ago, I caught me this big green man."

And he yanked open the refrigerator door.

"Oh…" Eva mouthed the word, her voice barely audible.

Squished inside, stuffed in sideways, in a fetal position, sat a strange extraterrestrial being, who appeared to be dead. The creature wore a form-fitting flight suit, which was torn and shredded. The suit resembled a type of uniform. A wide, metal collar encircled the suit's neckline, perhaps for a helmet attachment, although there was no helmet present.

"No, no," Anon said to Sigmund, who had started growling, barking. "It's… okay… I think."

As Anon held Sigmund back, he took a cautious step toward the refrigerator, to look in at the creature more closely.

The alien's large, fetal head had such pronounced cheekbones… and its face was completely dominated by an enormous pair of wrap-around mongoloid eyes, which were tightly closed. The creature had no real ears or nose that Anon could see, only small holes where these features should have been, and its mouth was simply a narrow slit, with no lips.

Its body was lean, hairless, bony strong yet fragile looking, with long arms and eight-fingered hands. Oddest of all was the thing's rough skin, which was wrinkled and lime in color, resembling, in a strange way, putty, appearing as if it could be molded by mere touch.

"So this is one of *them*…" Anon whispered.

Niko Zinovii

15. The Final Piece

Back near Eva's abandoned car, the original pale man turned to his master, the tall, olive-skinned, slanted-eyed man, who was standing quietly before their limousine in the company of the other three pale men.

The bald pale man, having been recovered from the wreck, was sitting, motionless, in the back of the limousine. The limo, unlike the surrounding vehicles, had power, its engine humming vibrantly, eerily, beneath its hood.

"... Yes..." the pale man reported. "... They are here."

~

The farmer grunted as he pulled the knot in the ropes tight, securing the refrigerator.

Anon dumped the last shovelful of Frank's remains into a large sack. Wiping the perspiration from his brow, he watched Eva gather herself and take a seat, placing Chapman's black box upon the table beside her. Lifting her unusual alien gun, she pointed it uneasily at the closed refrigerator.

"If... if it is alive," she asked, fearful, pulling Sigmund closer to her side, "isn't it going to suffocate in there?"

"That's what them there air holes are for," the farmer answered. "But after what they just did ta Frank, I got a good mind ta go an' plug 'em up."

The man picked up his shotgun and stepped over to Anon while continuing to talk to Eva. "So, you just keep that fancy gun of yours a-pointed right at that door. It tries to get out... kill it."

Anon handed the sack containing Frank's remains to the farmer.

"Bring the shovel," the farmer instructed Anon, before telling Eva, "We'll be right back."

"You going to be all right?" Anon asked Eva, placing a caring hand on her shoulder.

She nodded apprehensively, and they exchanged a tender glance.

Anon nodded back hesitantly, picked up the shovel, and followed the farmer away from the house. As they walked, he noticed the farmer's eyes searching the sky.

"Hate ta leave her alone in there like that," the farmer confessed, "but I just want ta bury Frank right away. What's left of him, anyway. Better this way than to let them turn him into one of their zombies. That's how they do it, you know. They raise up the dead. I think..."

"From Broken Hill Cemetery?" Anon asked.

"Yep. From the ol' Broken Hill graveyard."

"It's that glow over the hill, isn't it?"

"Yep, it's glowin' with spirit light."

Anon stopped as the farmer pointed off to a very large, perfect circle of dead grass that had been flattened down to the ground in a uniform, swirling counterclockwise direction. The grass surrounding this crop circle was tall, green and normal.

"There," the farmer stated. "That's where I seen 'em land. Shoot, at first I thought they was gonna mutilate my cattle. Like they talk about in them videos and magazines. But they didn't touch 'em. That's when I figured it must be an invasion."

"How come you didn't contact the authorities?"

"No signal for a cell since they landed. House phone don't

work none. No power for two weeks now. The green bastards cut us off. We thought it was all over, like I said. Guess it's just here."

The farmer briskly handed Anon the shotgun. Taking the shovel, he started digging.

"Is there any way to reach the police by foot?" Anon asked.

"No use goin' for help," the farmer explained. "Neighbors tried that. Found 'em burned to a crisp 'bout half a mile from here. That's when they almost got me. A goddamn kugelblitz blew up right over my head. Set my hair on fire, burnt my eyebrows off, hell, threw me ten feet through the air and knocked off both my shoes! Nope. Believe me, you don't wanna go trampin' around out there."

Anon glanced at the sack holding Frank's remains. "I see your point."

~

Eva found her attention drifting from the refrigerator to Chapman's black box. She still believed that the fossil within perhaps held a key to better understanding the bewildering situation that she and Anon found themselves in.

The ropes around the refrigerator appeared tight, secure. Slowly, quietly, cautiously, she placed her alien gun down upon the table and opened Chapman's box, carefully removing the partially assembled fossil and the fragile remaining fragments.

She began to fit the loose pieces into place by trial and error, and piece by piece the skull began to take further shape. As it did, she could now see that the back of the skull was terribly fractured, spiderwebbed with fissures, as if something had impacted upon it with great force.

Soon there was only one large piece left, which she turned and fitted into place. This final piece made a tremendous difference. The fossil was not of a hominid.

This had not been obvious before this final piece had been fitted because Chapman's box did not contain a complete fossil but an incomplete one, consisting of only the surviving fossilized pieces that Chapman had managed to recover. Most of the pieces that made up the cranium were missing, casting the illusion that the find was of an unusual hominid when in actuality it was of an extraterrestrial creature identical to the alien locked in the farmer's refrigerator.

—Time past:

> Africa, two and a half million years ago: A lime-green extraterrestrial turned toward an *afarensis* hominid.

"Oh my God…" Eva picked up her alien gun and ran for the kitchen's back door.

Sigmund rose, about to follow her, but suddenly the dog stopped and turned to the refrigerator, as if it had been called by name.

Slowly, Sigmund moved to and obediently sat down before the refrigerator, calmly, quietly, as if obeying commands that only it could hear.

The ropes securing the refrigerator groaned and stretched as its door was forcefully pushed open a few inches. Within, enormous coal-black eyes opened and looked out at the Doberman. And Sigmund appeared to fall further into a trance. Slowly the dog took into its mouth one of the ropes tying the refrigerator door closed and began to bite on it, chew it, vigorously.

~

"Anon!" Eva cried out as she ran toward Anon and the farmer, who were still burying Frank's remains.

"What's she doing outside?" the farmer asked, irritated.

"Anon, the fossil," she yelled. "It's one of them. One of the aliens. They were here before. In the past! And—and now they're back."

She stopped before them, breathing heavily.

"What're you doing out here?" the farmer demanded.

"That's what this is all about," she said to Anon. "Don't you see? They didn't kill Chapman because he had a crystal. They killed him because he gave you that fossil."

"Gimme my gun!" The farmer yanked his shotgun out of Anon's hands and started back toward the house. "Hell's bells! Never trust a woman!"

"And the psychiatrist," Eva continued. "They killed him because he learned what you can't remember."

Anon reached into his holster and partially pulled out his crystal, looking at it. "So, they're not after me because of this signature. They're after me because I know about them. I somehow know what they're doing here. Somehow, I discovered their presence, here on Earth. I must have been in the wrong place... at the wrong time. And so they're after me."

~

In the kitchen, Sigmund pulled forcefully and the chewed-apart ropes slackened and dropped loosely to the floor, falling into a knotted heap.

And the refrigerator door creaked open.

~

The farmer ran up to open the kitchen's back door but it flew open in his face, knocking him backward. As he fell to the ground the escaping alien leapt over him, hunched over, cricket-like.

KA-BOOM! Both barrels of the farmer's shotgun went off aimlessly up into the air as the man hit the ground, landing flat on his back.

The alien paused for a second, experiencing difficulty breathing, its semi-naked chest quivering like a panting dog's. Then it fled, hopping, running. Its movements stiff but purposeful, it headed uphill, toward the glow coming from the other side of the hill.

"Shoot it! Shoot it!" the farmer yelled as he struggled to his feet, reloading. "Don't let it get away!"

Anon watched in surprise as Eva lifted and pointed her unusual gun at the fleeing alien. The weapon's barrel wound open with a whirr to over a foot in diameter, its inner barrel instantly igniting a bright, hot yellow-orange.

"No, wait!" Anon yelled to stop her.

But it was too late—she had already pulled the trigger.

WHAM! A fiery kugelblitz rifled out of the weapon, zipping toward the escaping extraterrestrial.

But then, the strangest thing happened. For some reason, the fiery orb stopped dead in its tracks just before hitting the alien. Spinning about, it wobbled and then started to wander around the yard, looking for a new target.

"Oh crap," the farmer mumbled and he scampered back into the house.

The fiery ball turned away from the disappearing farmer and toward Anon and Eva.

"Oh no..." Anon remarked.

The kugelblitz exuded a bluish mist and then flashed straight toward them at great speed.

"Run!" Anon yelled.

Eva dropped her weapon and they fled. Anon glanced back. The sphere was much too fast. It would soon overtake them. He ducked, pulling Eva down with him, and they rolled through the grass as the thing roared over them, crackling, thundering.

"Come on!" the farmer yelled to them from the open kitchen door. "Get inside! Run!"

"To the house?" Eva asked.

Anon nodded and they ran for the door.

Behind them, the kugelblitz stopped and wobbled oddly as it slowly turned to the farmhouse. Bouncing forward, it then haphazardly darted left to right as it gave delayed pursuit.

"Come on!" the farmer shouted. "You can make it!"

They were almost to the door when Eva tripped and fell. Anon quickly pulled her to her feet but the fiery ball was almost upon them.

He flung Eva to the farmer, who grabbed her, yanking her inside, where they both fell to the floor.

Outside, Anon looked back to see where the kugelblitz was as it roared toward him, about to hit him square in the chest—like how Frank had got it.

Sigmund burst from the house, running toward Anon, barking wildly.

The kugelblitz stopped dead, mere inches from Anon, just hovering there before him, wobbling weakly. Anon stared at it, astonished, perspiration beading his face, his suit blackening, smoking from the intense heat.

Slowly, ever so slowly, the fiery orb turned toward Sigmund, seeming to have acquired a new target. Wobbling, it jerked left to right as it inched away from Anon. Then, moving off toward the Doberman, it simply imploded, disappearing with the sound of crackling thunder.

Anon staggered toward the farmhouse, Sigmund at his side.

"What happened?" Eva asked as she rose and ran to him, hugging him, so relieved that he had somehow survived the kugelblitz that she had released.

"I—I don't know," Anon answered, confused. "I think—did Sigmund interrupt it? Was it defective? Maybe because I have this signature? Is that what it's for, for protection?"

"There he goes," the farmer stated, pointing off to the strange, bounding silhouette that was making its way up the hillside. It looked so eerie, highlighted by spirit light as it was. With a hop, it disappeared over the hilltop.

"It's going up to Broken Hill," Anon observed.

The farmer stamped his foot down in anger. "Ah crap! He's gonna go an' tell 'em all where we are. That we're hidin' out down here. Goddamn! It's gonna be raining ball lightning tonight. We gotta go an' get him, else we're good as dead. We've got no choice."

Anon saw Eva look to him, worried.

"Come on," the farmer yelled, and he ran off toward the gravel road in the front of his farmhouse.

Origins

16. Broken Hill

The farmer kicked out the blocks that were wedged in front of the old tractor's rear tires. The tractor groaned as if straining to move forward, up the hill.

The farmer then abruptly ran to the front of the tractor, where Anon, Eva, and Sigmund were standing.

"Get on in and hold them brakes down hard," the farmer instructed Anon.

Anon glanced into the open hood. "But there's no battery—"

"Just go an' do it," the farmer insisted.

Anon helped Eva into the tractor, and he pressed both feet down upon the brake. "Okay," he said to the farmer.

The farmer slammed the hood shut and kicked out the block that was wedged in front of one of the front tires. The tractor twisted in the road, groaning, straining to lurch forward.

"What?" Anon did not understand what was happening.

The farmer ran up to them, about to hand his shotgun in to Eva, but he quickly had second thoughts. Giving her a dirty look, he instead tossed the gun into the back of the vehicle.

He then ran around them and kicked out the last block. The tractor groaned loudly and started sliding forward, uphill. The farmer jumped inside.

"Ha," the farmer laughed. "Okay, let go of them brakes."

Anon did so and the tractor lurched forward, its large wheels spinning: five miles per hour, ten miles per hour, fifteen, twenty miles per hour. Anon and Eva looked to the farmer for an explanation.

"Don't ask, 'cause I don't know how it works. It just does." The farmer grinned ear to ear.

The tractor jerked slightly to the right. Anon looked down to see its giant rear tires splashing through a stream that was flowing along the side of the road.

"The stream…" Anon could not believe it. "The water's running uphill…"

Eva looked. "How can that be?"

Anon shrugged. *Some kind of gravity anomaly?*

As they rolled toward the top of the hill, the surrounding foliage began to change. Tree limbs curved and bent in an eerie way, as if attracted by some unseen supernatural force to what lay on the other side of the hill.

A layer of green mold then appeared, thin at first but thickening to a smothering blanket as they approach the hill's top. The surrounding trees and fence posts were draped with it.

As they reached the hilltop, Anon noticed dark objects littering the ground: dead birds and the hollowed-out shells of dried-up insects.

The bird carcasses made Anon think again about the exhibits at the Whitman Museum. About the extinct trilobites, armored fish, the hatchling dinosaur, the saber toothed cat. And his mind contrasted these fossil images with the extant stuffed birds.

In his mind's eye then flashed the imagined sight of a white-hot nuclear explosion over India and the abominable shape of its raging mushroom cloud; then newspaper headlines of the bombings, of war and conflict.

It still doesn't make any sense…

As Anon let the thoughts go, the tractor jerked and shuddered a few times as it was yanked over the hilltop.

~

Anon saw as they came over the hill that before them was a long, descending, steep slope and then, down below, Broken Hill Cemetery. The graveyard was spotted by strangely leaning tombstones, open graves, and low-hanging patches of luminous electrical activity in the form of ground-hugging clouds of paranormal fog, glowing a frightening yet beautiful electric blue. The surrounding hills were all aglow with this ominous spirit light.

The tractor began to pick up speed, being pulled faster and faster toward the center of the cemetery.

Anon pressed down on the brake. The huge tires locked but the tractor continued forward, downward, its non-spinning tires digging trenches into the gravel road, which ended at the foot of the cemetery.

"Jump!" the farmer yelled and he leapt from the tractor.

Anon took hold of Eva's hand and they did the same, followed by Sigmund.

Anon and Eva rolled over and over before they came to a stop. Sitting up, Anon watched as the tractor, continuing to accelerate, twisted upon itself as it reached the bottom of the hill, bending in half.

Sliding over tombstones, the tractor slammed into an old caretaker's house, which itself was squished up against a nearby hillside, as if sent there by some invisible mudslide.

Rising to his feet, Anon was astonished to find himself leaning forward at an unnatural, gravity-warped angle, tilting toward the cemetery's center. He saw that Eva, the farmer, and even Sigmund were all experiencing the same incredible effect. It seemed impossible that they were not falling flat on their faces.

Anon noticed the farmer straining to lift and hold on to his shotgun. Apparently a mysterious pull was being exerted on the metal of the weapon, like the force that had attracted their heavy tractor over the hill and down to Broken Hill Cemetery. Cocking his gun, the farmer lifted his chin and lumbered forward, determined.

Anon nodded to Eva, and they followed, taking uncoordinated, unsure steps.

~

"I've been here before…" Anon stated as they reached the cemetery.

"This must be where you found your crystal," Eva suggested. "Learned about them."

"Maybe…" Anon felt unsure.

Anon and Eva followed the farmer through the cemetery. Many of the graves had been disturbed, dug up.

They cautiously walked into one of the low-lying patches of luminous electrical fog. It engulfed them, wrapping them in clinging, electric-blue garments.

"St. Elmo's fire," the farmer said. "That's what this is. St. Elmo's fire."

Anon raised a hand above his head. His fingertips sparkled and glowed a luminous blue. Eva ran a hand over her hair, which glittered.

"This must be some type of electromagnetic hotspot," Anon surmised. "A large-scale discharge of terrestrial electricity into the atmosphere."

"But how can all this be possible?" Eva asked as she glanced down at her legs, continuing to experience difficulty walking, leaning so far forward.

"I don't know…" Anon responded. "The Earth is a gigantic electrical machine, but this…"

"There he is!" the farmer yelled.

BLAM! The farmer fired his shotgun. Ten yards up ahead a dark figure fell to the ground.

"Gotcha, you son of a bitch!"

They all headed toward the fallen body.

As they neared it, they found themselves straightening in their stances until they were standing normally, the gravity anomaly no longer in effect at the center of the cemetery.

As they stepped up to the body they all felt the same sudden chill, they all smelled the same reeking odor. The farmer's nail, hanging around his neck, bent and curled up. Lying at their feet, motionless, was the pale man who had chased Anon down his apartment driveway.

"He's dead?" Eva asked, unsure.

Anon shrugged.

The farmer kicked the pale man over, flopping him onto his back. There was a large wound in his chest but there was no blood and the man's eyes were open, blinking slowly.

The man tried to speak but he only managed to exhale stale air. Slowly, his eyes closed, and the farmer's nail knotted up and his gun's barrel groaned, bending slightly.

"First time I ever killed someone who was already dead," the farmer remarked.

Anon knelt beside the downed pale man, tapping him forcefully. His dead eyes opened.

"You—you're from here?" Anon asked, determined. "From Broken Hill? They dug you up?"

"No... o... o... o..." came the answer.

"But then what are they doing out here?" Anon inquired. "The open graves?"

"Arch... ae... ology...."

"Archaeology?" Anon now felt quite confused. "But where are you from?"

"... The... P... a... s... t..."

"The past?"

"... Y... e... s... s... s... s... Ke... pt... al... ive... to... ser... v... e..."

The pale man's lifeless eyes began to close.

"Wait," Anon insisted. "What about them. Where are they from? What are they doing here?"

But the man's eyes closed completely and he became lifeless. He truly appeared to have actually died.

Origins

Niko Zinovii

17. The Elders

Sigmund growled and the fur on the dog's back stood on end.

Before Anon could determine what Sigmund was reacting to they all shivered intensely, assaulted by a shockingly powerful icy chill—far stronger than any they had experience before. And the stench—it was overpowering.

Groaning loudly, the barrel of the farmer's shotgun curled up, twisting itself into a useless knot of dark metal.

Anon felt Eva lean into him as the tall, gaunt shadows appeared and crept over them like living things of the night. Slowly, reluctantly, the trio turned about to witness the original pale man and five others like him stepping out of the darkness behind them, spreading out to encircle them, to entrap them.

Anon felt goose bumps tingle over him as he recognized the bald pale man standing among the others, recharged, "alive" again.

"What do you want of me?" Anon demanded shakily, staring fearfully yet defiantly into their grim, dead-white faces.

The original pale man looked down at his shot comrade. Slowly, his dead-white face wrinkled up. He was angry and it was terrifying. Moving stiffly yet swiftly, the man drew a kugelblitz pistol from his shoulder holster and pointed it at the farmer. The gun's barrel immediately wound open to a diameter in excess of twelve inches, its interior igniting a fiery orange-yellow.

"No! Stop," a voice ordered.

Anon sighed in relief as the pale man obediently lowered his weapon.

It was then that the owner of the voice, the mysterious slanted-eyed man stepped out of the darkness. Anon recognized that it was the same man from his apartment driveway, from his dream. Anon thought how different the man looked: such an unnaturally high forehead, Asiatic eyes set within olive-skinned Caucasian features; a man appearing young and vital, yet his eyebrows and his head of hair were both so strikingly white.

The Doberman left Eva's side to meekly approach the man, who took a moment to affectionately pet the dog before looking down at the pale man shot by the farmer, expressing a moment of genuine grief. He then focused a potent combination of arrogance and compassion on Anon's little group.

"You still bear the stamp of your lowly origin," the man stated calmly yet with deep emotion, his tone hubristically noble, compassionate yet reprimanding. "Too much *ape* in your blood."

Something large then moved in the darkness behind the man. Bent forward, the escaped alien emerged from the night. The slanted-eyed man immediately took one of the extraterrestrial's long bony arms, steadying the creature, who was taking short, labored breaths.

Sigmund moved to the alien's side, affectionately licking one of its eight-fingered hands.

Anon stood there in absolute silence as the extraterrestrial stepped closer to them. Its large wrap-around eyes were entrancing, like living pools, reflecting a noble alien mind of benevolent wisdom. Although in regard to intellect the alien appeared as distant from humans as humans were from apes, an overwhelming kinship of the soul was palpable.

As Anon became lost in those huge, alien eyes, he understood that there was nothing to fear. He glanced to Eva and saw that her fear had also completely vanished.

"You were here before, in our past, weren't you?" Eva asked the extraterrestrial.

"Long ago," the strange slanted-eyed man answered for the alien, "your ancestors were confronted with regression. Extinction. But your kind displayed promise. And so they helped. This is their way.

"And now they're here once again. To again prevent your extinction. You haven't really changed. Only in your destructive ability. You once used stones to kill… And now, nuclear bombs. Over 15,000 nuclear warheads spread over this planet?"

Anon felt the silence of shame descend upon him. Ashamed to be human.

"To them, you were apes only yesterday," the man continued. "They believe you require more time. And further assistance to mature. They're here to help once more."

Anon felt Eva leave his side, stepping forward. "But… if they're here to help…" she began, unable to understand, "then why are you killing people?"

"Once unleashed," the slanted-eyed man responded, "these pallid automatons can prove challenging to control. Even in this artificially reanimated state, Cro-Magnons have a proclivity for aggression."

"Cro-Magnons?" Eva asked. "As in cavemen?"

The man did not nod, but something in his eyes reflected confirmation.

And Anon thought of their hand signaling: an Ice Age hunter-gatherer Cro-Magnon sign language, likely used during the hunt.

"The first early humans of Europe," Anon said. "The Paleolithic cave painters, of thirty thousand years ago…

'kept alive to serve.' The extraterrestrials, they've been visiting Earth repeatedly, haven't they? Monitoring us…"

Anon noticed a hint of affirmation appear on the face of the slanted-eyed man.

"And killing…" Eva added.

"*They* don't want to kill," the man explained, his voice low, composed, yet deeply emotional. "But, like all living creatures, they feel the need to protect themselves. Their interests. These ancient, hibernating benefactors, these amazing collectors and keepers of lost knowledge, these elders of the universe, to protect the secrecy of their existence, the secrecy of their mission, to prevent any opposition to their cause, yes, they will condone killing. In order to help your entire kind."

"To help us?" Anon asked. "How? How did they help us? How are they helping us?"

Anon felt his eyes lift to the bright disturbance before them as the flying saucer from earlier made its appearance, slowly rising from behind the other side of a nearby hill. Unhurriedly, it glided silently toward them, hovering over the graveyard.

Anon then saw the slanted-eyed man look respectfully and affectionately at him.

"Anon…" the man said softly. "It's time to break your signature."

Anon glanced to Eva, confused.

"… What?" Anon asked the man.

"Your signature," the man stated calmly.

Anon found himself pulling his crystal key out of his holster, looking at it.

"Yes, break it," the man instructed Anon.

"No—Anon, don't," Eva cautioned Anon. "Don't trust him."

"If you don't trust me," the man responded evenly, "ask yourself, Anon, what do you genuinely want to do? What are your innermost feelings telling you to do?"

Anon stepped away from Eva and the farmer, and guided entirely by instinct, he took his crystal rod in his two hands and strained to break it.

"Anon, no!" Eva shouted, about to go to Anon. But she found herself restrained by one of the pale men, who, reacting to a Cro-Magnon hand signal from the slanted-eyed man, grabbed her by the shoulders, holding her in place.

Anon felt the crystal become soft in his grip, as he had demonstrated to Edward at the university's geology laboratory.

From the saucer, a radiant transparent tube—an elevator of sorts—descended to the ground. Two lime-colored aliens with giant wrap-around eyes stepped out of this elevator. They were garbed in flight uniforms similar to the escaped alien's, except that both of these creatures were also wearing giant, fully transparent helmets over their large, fetal heads.

Anon strained harder, and the key snapped in half. At once something astounding occurred: a transparent cone of cloud-like, crystalline material crackled into existence around Anon, imprisoning him.

"Oh damn," the farmer swore. "They got him, like a firefly in a jar."

Anon heard Eva screaming his name from outside the cone, but he was suddenly intensely interested in observing the luminous blue-green mist that drifted up out of the broken signature. Oddly it did not disperse as a gas normally would; instead it remained more or less concentrated.

Anon found himself, in an unexpected instant of pure impulse, plunging his face into the strange glowing gas, inhaling it deeply.

"Why did I do that?" he then asked himself, utterly confused.

He watched as Eva broke free and ran up to his cone of entrapment. He noticed the slanted-eyed man signaling for the pale men to leave her be.

"Anon!" she yelled, banging her open palms upon the cloud-like material, which although it appeared as insubstantial as fog had solidity to it, and it kept her out.

Captive inside the cone, Anon suddenly went numb, stiff, frozen in place.

From outside, Eva noticed something peculiar: the grass and wild dandelions and weeds at Anon's feet began to grow and die and bloom and whither at a rate akin to what an observer of time-lapse photography might witness. She backed away from the mysterious cone.

"Time, it—it's passing more quickly inside that thing," she observed. "Oh… Anon…" She turned to the slanted-eyed man, in tears. "Why did you trap him like that? What are you doing to him?"

"Watch," was his calm response.

And then it happened. Anon began to change. He began to rapidly transform, into one of *them*. Time was indeed passing far more swiftly inside the cone and in a matter of moments to the outside observers Anon the human was no more, replaced by Anon the extraterrestrial.

Eva ran to the slanted-eyed man, beating upon his chest with her fists, crying. "What did you do to him? Why did you do that? Why did you change him into that—that thing!"

The man took her clenched fists and gently, using the minimal amount of necessary force, lowered her arms. "It was time for Anon to shed his disguise," he explained to her.

"Disguise?" Eva choked, her emotions spiking, her thoughts chaotically disordered.

The man caringly turned her about to face Anon.

The cone crackled and vanished, leaving a powdery residue on the ground in a ring encircling Anon, who stood there as an extraterrestrial.

"Oh, Anon…" was all Eva could manage.

Anon could manage no words. He was in utter shock. Looking over his lime-colored, wrinkled body, he finally remembered who he truly was as his alien identity flooded into his expanding mind.

"He didn't know," the slanted-eyed man comforted Eva. "He had become one of you. Temporarily. In order to complete his mission. The accident, the memory loss, it was unexpected. For a short time, he truly was one of you. They thought they had lost him. And they are so very few in number."

As Anon experienced his thoughts becoming different and labyrinthine, he saw it all in his mind's eye in the flash of but a single moment. It explained how he understood their hand signaling—he was one of their landing party. His cover identity: a teacher, a university professor. It was why he felt the need to teach. Why he felt guilty—because he had been teaching a falsehood. Why he felt so ill at ease, being an alien in a strange land surrounded by so many humans. Why he had in his possession the transformation crystal. Why the kugelblitz would not harm him. Why he—

"Anon." Eva stepped up to him, her eyes full of tears. "… Anon… I—I loved you."

A smothering feeling came over Anon as he began to experience difficulty breathing due to Earth's atmosphere being incompatible with his alien physiology, but he fought against the rising panic and tried to speak: "—I…—loved—you…—Eva."

Anon stopped, surprised and frightened by the sound of his own unearthly, vibratory, stilted voice, his mind not having yet fully adjusted to his transformation. But then he looked

into her beautiful, soulful eyes and felt calmed. "—I—love…
—you…—still…"

He felt his soul being so painfully torn asunder, ripped in
one dimension by his love for Eva, in another by the
rediscovery of his true identity, and the shock of it, coupled to
the disjointedness of his mind struggling to adjust to his
expanding, alien intellect.

One of the two extraterrestrials from the saucer
approached Anon. Anon noticed the distinctive red birthmark
on one side of the alien's face. Anon recognized him. He knew
him. Anon allowed the creature, Red Mark, to gently take him
by the arm, to guide him toward the saucer.

"I'm sorry," the slanted-eyed man said to Eva, "but Anon
must go now."

Eva nodded hesitantly, her emotions swelling beyond belief.
She watched on in silence as Red Mark walked Anon toward
the saucer's elevator.

Unable to continue standing, she momentarily collapsed
into the farmer's arms. As she regained some of her strength,
she just stood there, leaning into the farmer. She noticed the
original pale man turning to the slanted-eyed man and silently
signaling something.

"No," the slanted-eyed man stated aloud, decisively. "Let
them live. There's been too much killing."

He then turned to the other pale men. "It's… your *time*
now," he said compassionately yet firmly.

The resurrected Cro-Magnon men obediently picked up their
shot kinsman and orderly assembled into a tight group before
their master, who signaled something to the original pale man—
who obeyed by stepping a good distance away from the others.

"Faithful yet…" the slanted-eyed man remarked in a feeling
yet controlled tone. "The present is not for the likes of you."

Hesitantly, he drew out a long, tubular alien pistol.

"You belong to the past," he pronounced with sympathetic regret, waving his long pistol left to right to left, peacefully spraying the pale men with a diaphanous otherworldly vapor, which silently and unceremoniously disintegrated the biological robots, clothing and all, into harmless piles of dust.

"Do not grieve for them," the man said in response to Eva's look. "They had their time. In this state, they were never truly alive."

Something caught Eva's eye. It was the spared pale man, the original pale man. She thought that she had noticed a flicker of disturbance on his dead-white face, in his sunken-in eyes, but it was gone almost in an instant. An emotion that flickered out of existence? A forbidden thought that was purposefully hidden?

Eva turned to the saucer's elevator, where she saw Anon look back at her as he stepped into the device. And their eyes met.

"… How did all this happen?" she mumbled wearily to herself. "Why?"

Anon kept his huge eyes on Eva as he spoke in his native, alien tongue to the two aliens who had retrieved him. "No," he protested. "I want to stay."

"You know you cannot," Red Mark responded, compassionately yet firmly.

"I *need* to stay," Anon stated. "I *love*—"

"This is not our world." Red Mark's giant eyes filled with sympathy and understanding. "Remember Atha?"

Anon nodded, grieving.

"Always remember Atha…" Red Mark cautioned Anon as they started to ascend, slowly floating up toward the saucer, lifted skyward by a seemingly magical technology.

Back on the ground, the farmer turned to the slanted-eyed man. "Aren't you a-going with them?" he asked timidly.

"No. My place is here. It's now my time."

Eva looked at the man's unusually high forehead and suddenly she understood. "The way they helped us in the past... The way they're helping us now... You're..."

The slanted-eyed man nodded.

"And Anon's mission, I'm... I'm..."

Again he nodded.

"Oh, no... please no..." She began to cry again, this time silently, only tears.

"What?" the farmer asked, confused. "I don't get it."

"I—I'm pregnant..." she answered. "Glorified apes. 'Half beast... half angel.' That's what we are. That's all we really are..."

The saucer's elevator retracted and the craft silently lifted high up into the sky, traveling straight up for some time before then gliding off horizontally, looking like a slow-moving star drifting unhurriedly toward the horizon.

With the saucer's departure, the supernatural spirit light of Broken Hill dimmed and slowly vanished and the cemetery returned to normal.

"Long ago," the slanted-eyed man said softly, watching the slowly departing saucer, "when Earth was young, they destroyed their own planet. War. Only these few survived. They've since genetically eliminated all aggressive traits from within themselves. They've rid themselves of all their inborn vices, allowing nobility to reign. But they are so few in number. And only male.

"They adopted Earth, your kind, and the other known worlds. In order to live on in some way... by proxy. And to prevent others from suffering their fate."

And he turned to Eva. "You've been blessed." And he then said her name aloud, as he turned and left with the surviving pale man. "'Eva…' A variant of *Eve*. How appropriate."

Niko Zinovii

18. Habilis

At the farmhouse, in the kitchen, on the table, the assembled although incomplete fossilized alien skull lay in utter silence, the spiderwebbing fracture on the back of it a complete mystery.

—Time past:

Africa of two and a half million years ago: The hooves of the prehistoric herbivores thundered as the animals scattered, fleeing in all directions, as the flying saucer that would later appear at Broken Hill Cemetery in the far-distant future slowly descended straight through the atmosphere to stop thirty feet or so above the flat African savanna.

The blue corona discharge from the bottom of the craft arced, making its way to the ground below, where it ignited an electromagnetic hotspot, sparking into existence a low-lying luminous electrical fog, which glowed a frighteningly beautiful electric blue.

Hovering noiselessly above the electrical discharge, the saucer just hung there in the daytime sky like a beacon, the sun gleaming brilliantly off its highly polished metallic exterior.

Nearby, in the tall grass, a small group of two *afarensis* families pointed excitedly and fearfully up at the saucer. The children of the group, all *habilis* boys and girls, sought the safety of their parents, especially of their fathers, One Prong and Two Prong, who unconsciously lifted trembling hands to touch the signature crystals dangling about their necks.

One Prong at once started to walk toward the saucer as if responding to a long-awaited calling, but he stopped abruptly as he noticed Two Prong hesitating to follow, unwilling to leave his family.

He walked back to Two Prong and compassionately yet forcefully took his comrade by one of his lean, hair-covered arms, to pull him away. But Two Prong resisted, reaching out to lovingly touch his *afarensis* mate, and his children.

One Prong leaned very close to Two Prong and whispered to him for some time. By the end of the whispering, Two Prong had regained most of his composure and, with reluctance but acceptance, he allowed One Prong to guide him away. And walking off toward the saucer, the two left their hominid families behind.

~

The male *afarensis*, Three Prong, with Chapman's three-pronged crystal dangling about his neck, lowered his battered, cupped hands into what little was left of a river to get a drink. As he did so he noticed a strange reflection upon the surface of the water and his eyes bolted upward, where, in the sky, he saw the distant flying saucer, radiantly hovering in place.

Immediately he ran off down the riverbed toward the saucer, looking up at it, relieved, exultant.

A cackling rifled through the air and Three Prong heard them before he could see them. Somewhere beyond his view, a trio of prehistoric hyenas raced over a small hilltop and leapt down into the mud of the riverbed.

It was when Three Prong heard their paws tearing up the wet earth that he glanced back to see the cackling hyenas giving chase. And he ran for his life.

Glancing up at the saucer, Three Prong stumbled and nearly fell as he continued his frantic race down the muddy bed of the drying river.

If only Three Prong had held the key secure against his chest. But he did not. Bouncing about wildly, it broke loose from its primitive cord and dropped to the ground.

It took him several moments to realize that he had lost the crystal. When he did realize it, he stopped abruptly and turned around.

Sparkling in the African sunlight, the three-pronged key lay halfway between him and the rapidly approaching hyenas.

Three Prong spun about to once again look up at the saucer. And then, turning back, he chose to try to retrieve his signature, risking almost certain death.

Racing toward the dropped crystal, he stumbled and fell into the mud, the key lying less than a foot away. He thrust out a hairy arm, desperately reaching for it. If he could grab it he could activate its protective transformation cone. But it was too late. The hyenas cackled madly as they tore into him.

The largest of the carnivores sank its teeth down into the bone of his outstretched arm, crushing it. Another bit into one of his legs, as did the third. And the animals then attempted to pull him in different directions.

It was the talon of a landing vulture that pressed Three Prong's key down into the mud, burying it, where it would lie preserved for Chapman to discover in the far-distant future.

The hyenas continued to tear into Three Prong, and he let out a sentient, chilling death scream that echoed over the prehistoric landscape.

~

Gray Streak cautiously led his *afarensis* mate and daughter out of a small clump of trees, drawn by the sound of stampeding hooves. And he noticed the saucer.

He turned to his *afarensis* mate, looking at her with loving eyes. He then looked back at the hovering saucer. He noticed the *afarensis* forms of One Prong and Two Prong moving toward the saucer's descending elevator, within which the shape of a single lime-colored alien floated down toward the grassland, which danced with luminous blue light.

Gray Streak yanked upon his crystal, snapping the primitive cord that held it secured about his neck.

He squeezed the signature, breaking it in two. At once a transparent cone of cloud-like, crystalline material crackled into existence around him, protecting him.

Inside the shielding cone, where godlike alien technology affected the passage of time, making it pass much more rapidly than on the surrounding African savanna, Gray Streak inhaled the luminous, blue-green mist that rose from his activated signature.

And it began to happen. Billions of inhaled nanobots went to work, and Gray Streak began to change. He began to rapidly transform, and in a matter of moments—Africa time—he stood there no longer as an *afarensis* hominid but in his true extraterrestrial form.

The cone crackled and vanished, and Gray Streak, the alien, slowly turned toward his mate, and to his daughter, suddenly overcome with emotion, with love, not wanting to abandon his new family. With outstretched arms he stepped toward them by impulse. The *habilis* girl screamed out, hysterical.

Gray Streak stopped, attempting to calm her.

"—Eve…" He forced her name out, experiencing difficulty breathing in Earth's atmosphere.

It was then, at that moment, that Gray Streak's *habilis* son emerged from the trees to witness a lime-green monster approaching his sister. He picked up a large rock.

WACK! The young *habilis* struck his alien father from behind, shattering the back of his skull. And Gray Streak toppled forward.

A distance away, out in the luminous fog of the tall grass, as they stepped into the saucer's elevator, One Prong and Two Prong witnessed Gray Streak falling to the ground, dead.

"Atha…" Two Prong uttered in grief, in their alien language, through hominid vocal cords not meant to produce speech.

One Prong slowly turned to Two Prong, his *afarensis* face catching the strong African sun, the light deepening the redness of the distinctive birthmark that distinguished one side of his face.

"Atha is no more…" One Prong, Red Mark, said in their alien tongue. "Always remember, Anon, we do not belong here."

Two Prong, Anon, felt the comforting eight-fingered hand of the alien within the elevator settle upon his slender, hair-covered *afarensis* shoulder. And Anon looked into the creature's large wrap-around eyes, and then at its familiar lime-colored face, seeking comfort in the visage of one of his own kind.

Anon then felt the pull of the Earth disappear, and he started to float upward.

Down below, Gray Streak's *habilis* son stood over his father's alien corpse. The boy's eyes lifted as the saucer started to leisurely rise vertically, up, up, up toward a dizzying height.

The luminous, electric-blue fog vanished as if it had never been, and the animals flooded back onto the vacated area of savanna, the herbivores wary of the predators stalking in through the tall grass.

The *habilis* boy eyed the carnivores, and then he looked at the bloodstained rock he still held. His eyes swelled with an intelligence, an awareness found nowhere else in the animal kingdom, and he saw something inside that stone. He picked up a second rock. Bringing down the blood-stained stone in his strong right hand, the *habilis* struck the two rocks together, splitting one of them in two, creating a sharp cutting edge. And the first true human entered into the world.

~

The interior of the saucer, humming with otherworldly power, was dominated by one enormous hollow, surrounded by over two dozen vertical, coffin-like, frost-covered chambers that lined most of the circumference of the craft's circular inner wall.

In the center of the cavernous hollow, a single alien, wearing an elaborate helmet, flew the craft by amplified thought. Fewer than two dozen others were present, all male. Several of the beings were quietly performing various instrumental tasks, but nearly all the others were silently making their way to their individual ice coffins. Climbing into the frosted booths, the aliens were independently sealing themselves into deep cryogenic freeze.

In silence Anon followed Red Mark into the saucer's central hollow. There, he watched on mutely as Red Mark walked over to a circular depression on the floor and activated his signature by breaking it. The device's protective cone formed about him, in alignment with the circle sunk into the floor, and Red Mark began to rapidly transform into his true non-hominid alien morphology.

Two of their landing party had survived their mission on Earth. Two had been lost. If only Three

Prong had been able to activate his protective transformation cone before the hyenas had reached him. If only Atha (Gray Streak) had waited to transform, or had not hesitated in leaving.

Anon thought of his *afarensis* mate, and of his *habilis* children. Feeling heartbroken, grief stricken, he wandered off to the saucer's huge rear viewing portal as he awaited his turn at the transformation station. Leaning against the portal's transparency, he peered down at Africa.

Suddenly there was a living whirlpool of beatific life encircling the saucer—a migratory flock of hundreds and hundreds of birds, spiraling upward in the updraft generated by the rising alien craft, following the strangeness of its presence up into the heavens.

Flight had never evolved on Anon's home planet. There had been no birds, no such wondrous things of the sky.

Anon found the unexpected majesty of the sight breathtaking, emotionally overwhelming, ethereal, celebratory. It made him feel that their intervention had accomplished something wonderful.

He would never forget his *afarensis* mate or the unique children he had fathered on this alien world. He would also never forget Earth's birds.

The land shrunk away from the rapidly rising craft. Clouds soon obscured Anon's view, and then the curvature of the planet became visible.

As the saucer flew off into the vast emptiness and blackness of outer space, Anon dutifully made his way to the transformation station to shed his *afarensis* disguise and identity, willingly submitting to the moment, leaving his emotions of heartbreak at the portal, taking with him his feelings of wonderment, celebratory accomplishment, and placid triumph.

~

Far, far below, on Earth, on ancient Africa's expanding grasslands, a small band of fatherless *Homo habilis* youths united and ventured out onto the savanna, to make it theirs.

Homo habilis. Handy man. The first early human. First of the genus *Homo*, *habilis* possessed a substantially larger brain, rudimentary speech, the beginnings of culture, and the ability to look into a stone and see the tool inside it, not yet chipped free from the surrounding rock. *Habilis* dared to go out onto the savanna and become man's single most important ancestor.

Epilogue

Gliding over New England farmland, the saucer departing from Broken Hill continued to slowly, unhurriedly slip off toward the horizon.

~

Within the saucer's central hollow, several alien beings moved to and assisted the farmer's former captive, placing him into a crystalline chamber for medical treatment, to heal his injuries, to repair his damaged multiple lungs.

Anon, obediently following Red Mark, glanced about, observing his fellow beings who were preparing to enter cryogenic deep freeze, to hibernate, in order to sleep away their coming epoch-long journey between distant star systems. As he witnessed his compatriots crawling into their ice coffins, he shivered.

They were the only survivors of their lost world, reduced to cosmic castaways, hibernating benefactors of other civilizations. By circumstance and adaptive choice they were now paternal, living to father other species. It was what they now did, having so long ago lost their own world to their own unanticipated destructiveness.

Guilt ridden, they had come to believe it to be their penance, their responsibility, to intervene on other planets, to help others along evolutionarily. Also... to spread their seed. They had progeny on Earth, and elsewhere. But this did not reverse their plight...

The memory center of Anon's labyrinthine mind pulsed and he glimpsed, vividly, in his mind's eye their wonderful home world before its destruction. Heavenly ringed and luminously mooned, their blissful planet had been the marvel of the galaxy: sparkling elevators had risen up from the surface of their world to the artificial platforms anchored to their majestic, colorful rings. He remembered how the gleaming, synthetic polar shells of their extreme hemispheres had once throbbed as they absorbed the countless warm photons arriving from their distant and ancient red dwarf sun.

Theirs was a world as beautiful as it was old. They were the elders of this galaxy. But... the forgotten brutish primitive from which they had so long ago arisen still dwelt somewhere deep within them... and they destroyed glory.

It was a flash in Anon's expansive memory, the obliteration of his home world. This solitary saucer alone having escaped the incredible annihilation...

Anon felt his large brain pulse again as he imagined the white-hot nuclear explosions that had recently taken place on Earth. He considered the potential extinction event now facing man of Earth. How different it was from the changing environment that had confronted *afarensis*. It was now man's own brutish, savage hand that placed him so precariously balanced upon the knife's edge.

Was it the blackness of the night or something else? Anon did not know. But he did not feel, within his still transitioning mind, the celebratory catharsis that he had hoped for. He only felt heartbreak—terrible, devastating emotional loss. Where was the splendor of the birds this time?

And as Anon had done two and a half million Earth years ago—although in his mind Africa of the distant past was but a recent event, a living segment of his mostly hibernating existence—he wandered over to the craft's huge rear portal. Standing before it, he imagined for a moment seeing Eva's soft face reflected off the transparency.

And in his vast, alien mind, he heard Red Mark's somber words: *This is not our world. Always remember Atha...*

His thoughts then flooded with his remembrance of Eva's soft voice crying: *I—I loved you.*

And Anon heard pulsating in his memory his own words: *—I—love...—you...—still...*

Eva's visage faded from his mind, replaced by the remembered breathtaking imagery of living, beatific birds. And Anon thought of their ethereal beauty, and of their wondrous freedom of flight...

The idea came to Anon slowly. At first he was surprised by the thought. But then he found himself accepting it, with all of his heart.

Skulking off, crouched, cricket-like, he stealthily obtained from a nearby station an apple-sized crystal sphere, blue-black in color. With the crystal in his possession, he quietly moved to one of the spherical pods sunk deeply into the craft's aft hull.

Emitting a silent invisible stream of mental energy, he defiantly opened one of the pods with the power of his mind. At once he stepped into it. It closed behind him and silently jettisoned itself away from the saucer.

~

The small pod sped through the glow of the ionized gas surrounding the saucer's hull as it flashed away, glimmering in the night sky high above the New England countryside.

~

Far below, on a gravel road, the slanted-eyed man, leading the sole surviving pale man back toward their limousine, stopped abruptly as he noticed, off in the distance, the escape pod shining brilliantly as it dropped toward Earth.

At first the man's face was quite severe. But slowly the glint of yielding interest lit in his eyes.

~

The pod floated down from the sky daintily, like a snowflake, and it landed so very lightly in a farmer's cornfield. There, in the field, the pod burst into light and dissolved, creating a crop circle with Anon, the extraterrestrial, kneeling in its center.

Staggering away from the flattened corn, Anon dropped to his knees amongst the tall stalks, panting, finding it difficult to breathe even with his four lungs. With his eight-fingered hands he squeezed the crystal sphere he had taken from the saucer. It burst, igniting into existence a protective transformation cone about him.

Within the cone, Anon the alien transformed back into Anon the human.

The cone then crackled and vanished, leaving behind it upon the ground a two-pronged crystal signature, which Anon took possession of.

Rising, Anon looked up into the sky, worried, his eyes searching the distant horizon. He spotted the saucer, shining like a star, gliding off into the night. It appeared to be slowing, stopping… Reversing?

Anon staggered off, running through the corn.

~

Stumbling out upon a dark country road, Anon waved his arms above his head, flagging down an approaching pickup truck. The truck stopped and Anon shuffled over to the driver's opened window.

"I—I need your help," Anon pleaded. "Can you take me to the nearest town? I need to find someone."

Origins

Niko Zinovii

A Note from the Author

This author hopes the reader was entertained by this novella, which was based on an original, feature-length spec screenplay of the same title, *Origins*, imagined and written by this author in 1992.

For those interested in how a script differs from a manuscript, the second draft of the screenplay *Origins* follows this author's note.

Novelizing a screenplay written twenty-seven years ago was an interesting and challenging experience. In the writing of this novella, this author made some minor alterations and added some new elements to the story but was mindful to adhere very closely to the original script, in artistic deference to the young, optimistic screenplay writer he had once been so very long ago.

This author thus asks the reader not to view this novella as a measurement of the growth of an artist but rather as an artist reaching back in time and connecting with an earlier self. This is not a story that this author would write today as a new piece, nor would it be written in the manner in which it was first crafted. This author thus conjured up elements of his past self while limiting his present self, the aim being to produce, in writing style, story content, and presentation, a nice complement to the original screenplay that his younger self would have found satisfying.

This author does, however, believe this novella is an improvement on the original story. The reader may wish to compare the two, novella vs. screenplay, and come to his own conclusion.

This author has labeled *Origins* as science fiction, as opposed to fantasy. The reasoning behind this involves the definitions of science fiction and fantasy as offered in the past by Arthur C. Clarke and Isaac Asimov.

Arthur C. Clarke once defined the genres as follows: Science fiction is what is possible and can be; fantasy is what is inherently impossible and can never be. Asimov agreed with Clark's basic definition, once stating: "Science fiction, given its grounding in science, is possible; fantasy, which has no grounding in reality, is not."

Yet, one of Clarke's three laws states:

"Any sufficiently advanced technology is indistinguishable from magic."

This would appear to present a conflict, as it opens a gray area between science fiction (what is possible) and the magic of fantasy.

Isaac Asimov addressed the difference between science fiction and fantasy as partially resting with the author. Asimov once gave the example of an author writing a story about a man who had an encounter with a miniature demon who possessed magical powers. Asimov pointed out that if the author had simply left the story at that, the story would clearly be of the fantasy genre. But if the author took the time to explain the demon as being an extraterrestrial and its seemingly magical powers as being the product of an advanced alien technology, then, as long as the fundamental laws of science were adhered to, the story would be classified as science fiction.

This author thus classifies *Origins* as a piece of science fiction, although he recognizes it could be argued that the story is really a fantasy with a science fiction feel, as the aspects of the tale that lie in the area of Clarke's third law may not adhere to the laws of an advanced science.

Incidentally, the species *Australopithecus robustus* is also known as *Paranthropus robustus*.

This author would like to end by stating that this story was written to entertain. The idea of extraterrestrial intervention in humankind's evolution is entirely fictitious. This author recognizes that the evidence supporting human evolution by natural means is scientifically convincing and unproblematic.

Niko Zinovii
Santa Monica, California
16 October 2019

niko@zinoviiartstudio.com

www.zinoviiartstudio.com

Niko Zinovii

A Note on the Screenplay

The screenplay that follows is reproduced in its entirety and unaltered, with only slight adjustments made to its original format in order to provide greater ease of reading; specifically, script page numbers and scene numbers have been eliminated, as have all the uses of "(CONTINUED)" and "CONTINUED:" and "MORE" that delineate the continuation of scenes and dialogue across ordinal pages.

As this book is of a smaller size than a standard 8 ½" x 11" screenplay, each page of script no longer represents one minute of screen time. (The *Origins* screenplay in its original 8 ½" x 11" size is 148 pages in length.)

Readers will notice, due to how this story ends, that although the script was written for a feature film, its ending was designed to potentially spin off a television series.

The screenplay *Origins* was pitched to agents, production companies, and studios as "a strange, mystery-driven story with a feel somewhere between *Close Encounters* and *The Bourne Identity*." The script was not sold, and so no film or television series was ever produced.

If *Origins* is ever in the future to be made into a feature film, this author suggests that it be done with a yet-to-be-written new draft of the script that incorporates the new strengths of the novella.

Niko Zinovii

FADE IN:

EXT. KENYA - DAY

Short bushy trees and scattered clumps
of dry grass dot the bleak, arid
landscape. The sun above is a hot ball
of fire.

AFRICAN MEN, using picks and shovels,
are digging at an archaeological site; a
cave excavation consisting of a
labyrinth of exposed and interconnected
sinkholes.

ARCHAEOLOGISTS are busy observing,
measuring, and taking copious notes.

The **FILM'S TITLE "ORIGINS"** appears upon
the screen, disappearing soon after.
CREDITS BEGIN.

Whack... Whack... Whack... The picks of
the diggers repeatedly chop down into
the dry earth.

Nearby, shovels dig deeper and deeper,
the dirt dumped into large wire mesh
boxes that are being shaken by **WORKERS**
who are sifting through the soil,
collecting anything unusual,i.e.,
fossils, artifacts.

After many pounds of rocky earth a
fossilized ape-like skull appears,
causing great excitement. An **OLD
ARCHAEOLOGIST** removes the fossil,
carefully, turning it about, discovering
two rather odd round holes in the back
of the skull.

Smiling, the archaeologist then lifts
the find high above his head, displaying
it to his rapidly approaching, clamorous
colleagues. The rising fossil eclipses
the sun and everything **GOES DARK** as
CREDITS END.

The following quote appears on the black
screen:

> Man still bears in
> his bodily frame the
> indelible stamp of
> his lowly origin.
> — *Charles Darwin*

After this is read by the audience, the
words fossilize and break apart,
crumbling upon one another. Turning to
dust, what remains is blown away,
leaving the screen dark.

FADE IN:

EXT. AFRICAN SAVANNA - DAY (EARLY)

Color is faded - Distant past is viewed

A large **SABER TOOTHED CAT** is facing the rising sun, the yellow orb mirrored in the carnivore's dark eyes.

The surrounding savanna is slowly coming to life. Ancient **BABOONS** stir and prehistoric **ANTELOPES** disperse from the safety of their tightly gathered herds.

EXT. EDGE OF FOREST - DAY (EARLY)

Color is faded - Distant past is viewed

A dozen or so **HOMINIDS** are moving through the foliage, searching for food within the safety of the leafy trees.

These creatures are dark, short, and lean. Their bodies are hairy and they look very chimpanzee-like but they are walking upright. And their movments are more like those of a man's than an animal's.

What are these strange creatures? Are they human or animal? The answer, of

course, is that they are neither. They
are man's earliest bipedal ancestors:
Australopithicus afarensis.

We are looking at the dawn of human
prehistory. The scene is absorbing and
strangely, slightly disturbing.
Disturbing to see that these simple,
earthy primates are our Adam and Eve. It
makes us aware of our frailty and of our
smallness.

A **YOUNG FEMALE** wanders away from the
others, stepping out onto the savanna.

EXT. AFRICAN SAVANNA - DAY (EARLY)

Color is faded - Distant past is viewed

The young female looks out over Africa
of time past. Fear and curiosity fill
her chimp-like eyes, which, by way of
intelligence, emit a palpable glint of
humanity.

There is a large water hole less than
one hundred yards distant. Ancestral
BABOONS, **ANTELOPES**, and assorted
HERBIVORES are gathered about the
precious pool.

The young hominid walks toward the water

hole, sniffing the air.

EXT. EDGE OF FOREST - DAY (EARLY)

Color is faded - Distant past is viewed

The other hominids, continuing to forage, are unaware of the young female's departure.

EXT. AFRICAN SAVANNA - DAY (EARLY)

Color is faded - Distant past is viewed

The young female steps up to the water hole, surveying the gathered animals. Curiosity.

Flap. An ancestral **VULTURE** drops out of the cloudless sky, landing near the water's edge, where its talons sink into the mud. The scavenger immediately turns its hungry eyes to the young hominid and the surrounding animals suddenly become silent and still. Confusion.

A prehistoric **LEOPARD** springs out of the tall grass, racing toward the slowest of all assembled potential prey, the bipedal hominid. The young female takes off, running back toward the safety of the trees, but within seconds, the

leopard pounces upon her, bringing her
crashing to the ground.

An ape-like proto-humanish scream of
horror echoes over the savanna.

EXT. EDGE OF FOREST - DAY (EARLY)

<u>Color is faded - Distant past is viewed</u>

The hominid family stiffens, looking
toward the distant water hole.

EXT. AFRICAN SAVANNA - DAY (EARLY)

<u>Color is faded - Distant past is viewed</u>

The leopard kills its prey, silencing
her horrid screams.

A pack of primordial **HYENAS**, ears thrust
forward, raceacross the savanna, toward
the fresh kill.

EXT. EDGE OF FOREST - DAY (EARLY)

<u>Color is faded - Distant past is viewed</u>

The group of hominids remains
motionless, staring out at the savanna.

EXT. AFRICAN SAVANNA - DAY (EARLY)

Color is faded - Distant past is viewed

The leopard opens its jaws wide and
sinks its teeth into the dead hominid's
head. There is a bone popping sound as
its canines punch through the skull. The
leopard runs off, dragging away the
hominid by her head.

EXT. EDGE OF FOREST - DAY (EARLY)

Color is faded - Distant past is viewed

The small hominid clan bears witness to
the killer cat dragging away their
family member. Slowly, fearfully, they
pull deeper into the forest.

EDGE OF SAVANNA - DAY (EARLY)

Color is faded - Distant past is viewed

The leopard pulls its catch up into a
tree and begins to strip away the
hominid's flesh, devouring her. Teeth
tear, large paws push and pull and the
hominid's head drops down out of the
tree, white bone painted by smeared
blood, bits of flesh, and tuffs of hair.
Bouncing upon the ground, the head rolls

through the grass and drops down into a large hole in the earth.

INT. CAVE - DAY (EARLY)

Color is faded - Distant past is viewed

The head lands with a thud, the back of the skull displaying the two deep holes inflicted by the leopard's lower canines.

INT. UNIVERSITY LECTURE AUDITORIUM - DAY

A plaster cast of the same skull is placed down upon a table, positioned identical as the skull from the cave; the puncture holes serving as the identifying marks.

> **ANON** (O.S.)
> Australopithecus
> afarensis.
>> (MORE)

DR. DAVID ANON is giving a lecture in a university auditorium filled by **STUDENTS**. Anon is in his 40s, attractive, intelligent; resonating a calm dignity. Although confident, he is a bit wary, on alert, almost vulnerable, under some unknown stress. His decorous

demeanor conceals all else beneath a
blanket of professionalism. He wears
eyeglasses.

>   ANON (CONTINUED)
>   Often referred to as
>   "Lucy."
>   (A beat)
>   Dating back to more than
>   three and a half million
>   years ago, afarensis was
>   considerably ape-like.
>   Its brain was only
>   slightly larger than that
>   of today's chimpanzee but
>   its posture was upright.
>   It walked this world in a
>   bipedal,human-like
>   fashion.

Anon momentarily loses himself in
thought. Continuing, he speaks with an
unusual first hand knowledge and deep
sympathetic appreciation of the subject.

>   ANON (CONTINUED)
>   ... They were fragile
>   creatures. Surrounded by
>   death. Average life
>   expectancy... less than
>   20 years.
>   (A beat)

> They could not speak nor
> could they create stone
> tools. But they did give
> rise to two unique and
> distinct lines of hominid
> evolution.

Anon reaches into a large box and pulls
out a second skull. It is slightly
larger than the first and more
primitive, more ape-like. Anon slowly
turns the skull, positioning it to face
the students.

EXT. EDGE OF FOREST BY LAKE - DAY

<u>Color is faded - Distant past is viewed</u>

A **HOMINID** slowly turns its head, moving
identical to Anon's turning skull. This
hominid is larger and more apish than
the hominid killed by the leopard.

Surrounded by forest, the hominid is
among a small group of **OTHERS** of its
kind. It pulls a large root from a
freshly dug hole, sniffing it, mouthing
it.

INT. UNIVERSITY LECTURE AUDITORIUM - DAY

Anon places the second skull down in

line with the first skull but angled off
to the left.

> **ANON**
> Australopithecus
> africanus. Slightly
> larger than afarensis,
> africanus appears
> approximately two and a
> half million years ago.

Anon reaches back into the box, pulling
out a third skull. It is a bit larger
and noticeably more robust than the
second skull. Anon lifts it up,
providing the students a better view.

EXT. MOUNTAIN FOREST - DAY

Color is faded - Distant past is viewed

A **ROBUST HOMINID**'s face appears as the
creature pulls itself up onto the low
branch of a tree. Ruggedly built and
massively jawed, this hominid is even
more ape-like than africanus. Relaxing,
it lays its chin down upon the tree
branch and closes its eyes.

INT. UNIVERSITY LECTURE AUDITORIUM - DAY

Anon lays the third skull down upon the

table in line with the other skulls but
angled further off to the left.

                  ANON
        Australopithecus
        robustus. Ruggedly built
        and massive-jawed,
        robustus met extinction
        one million years ago,
        ending this line of
        hominid evolution with a
        dead end.

Anon pauses, motioning to the three
skulls before continuing.

                  ANON
        Afarensis, africanus,
        robustus, and the end of
        the Australopithecus
        line. You see, as I said
        earlier, Africa was
        drying. Its forests
        shrinking. This line of
        hominid, rather than
        moving out onto the
        expanding and danger
        filled savanna, moved
        deeper into the forest,
        seeking the safety of the
        trees. These smaller
        forests, however, were

> becoming increasingly
> crowded. Competition
> between its inhabitants
> was growing. Robustus'
> fate was extinction.

Anon paces away from the table, once
again speaking as if he were privy to
special first hand knowledge on the
subject.

> **ANON** (CONTINUED)
> Africa was changing.
> Australopithecus couldn't
> survive on the savanna.
> They were forced to
> choose the forest and
> extinction. Their fate
> was inevitable, but,
> fortunately for you, not
> altogether inescapable.

Anon steps back to the table and points
to an empty spot located parallel to the
africanus skull but forking to the
right, branching off from the first
skull, the afarensis skull.

> **ANON**
> Two point five million
> years ago, right here,
> something extraordinary

> occurred. Afarensis gave
> rise to a new genus.
> Something unlike anything
> that had ever walked
> Earth before. Africa's
> first "Eve."

Anon reaches into the box and pulls out
a fourth skull. It is human-like.

EXT. SAVANNA - DAY

Color is faded - Distant past is viewed

The first true **EARLY HUMAN**. Although his
face is still primitive, his eyes hold
an intelligence and an awareness
seen nowhere else in the animal kingdom.
Bringing down a strong right hand, he
strikes two rocks together, creating a
sharp cutting edge. The broken off
section of stone thuds to the ground.
(One of the rocks is stained by blood.)

INT. UNIVERSITY LECTURE AUDITORIUM - DAY

Anon thuds the plaster cast down into
its designated spot on the table.

> **ANON**
> Homo habilis. Handy man.
> First of the genus Homo,

> habilis possessed a
> substantially larger
> brain, rudimentary
> speech, the beginning of
> culture, and the ability
> to look into a stone and
> see the tool inside it.
> Habilis dared to go out
> onto the savanna. This is
> your single most
> important ancestor.

Anon reaches back into his box, quickly
pulling out three skulls, one after the
other, placing them down in line with
habilis, angling them off to the right
so as to make a distinct line from the
Australopithecus line. Each skull is
larger and more human-like than the one
preceding it.

> **ANON**
> (As he places the first)
> Homo erectus, one point
> seven million years ago.
> The first to control
> fire.
> (As he places the second)
> Archaic Homo sapiens,
> 400,000 years ago.
> Transitional between
> erectus and later forms.

    (As he places the third)
And, finally,
anatomically modern Homo
sapiens, 120,000 years
ago. You.
    (A beat)
There are a number of
intermediate stages,
interesting side
branches,
Neanderthalensis,
Floresiennsis, which
we'll discuss in future
lectures, but today, I
wanted to focus on the
fact that just as the
Australopithecus line
evolved into a more
brutish form that met
extinction as it crept
back into the forest, the
Homo line rose to face
new challenges and
evolved into the
culturally advanced form,
which has, over the past
two and a half million
years, rose to its
present position of
planetary dominance.
    (A beat)
All because of what

occurred at this point
here.

Anon picks up the habilis skull,
unconsciously cradling it in a
paternalistic manner.

>   **ANON**
> Next time we'll discuss
> how habilis came into
> existence. But today,
> I'll let you go a few
> minutes early.Have a nice
> afternoon.

There is a clamor as the students head
out, chattering about entirely unrelated
subject matter. Anon hears this and
becomes concerned, disturbed.

As Anon begins to put away his skulls a
pierced and tattooed young man, a
FRESHMAN, steps up to the table.

>   **FRESHMAN**
> Wow, great lecture
> Dr. Anon.

>   **ANON**
> You enjoyed it?

FRESHMAN
Oh, yeah, I thought it
was real interesting.
Awesome skulls.

As Anon responds, he studies the youth,
unintentionally making the boy feel a
bit uneasy.

ANON
Good, good. Did you find
the lecture, believable?

FRESHMAN
Believable? Like, did I
believe it?

ANON
Yes, did you feel that
the archaeological
evidence supported the
facts? That man evolved,
through natural
processes, from a bipedal
ape-like ancestor?

FRESHMAN
Well, yeah, sure, I guess
so. I mean, I didn't
really question it.

ANON
You didn't question it?

FRESHMAN
Well, no, I mean, you wouldn't be teaching it if it weren't true, right?

ANON
— No, no, of course not. Of course I wouldn't. Why would you ask such a thing?

The young man's unease increases.

FRESHMAN
Well, I gotta get go —

ANON
— Do you think the others, your classmates, also took the lecture at face value? Without questioning it?

FRESHMAN
Ah, yeah, I guess so. With the skulls and all.

> **ANON**
> Good... That's good.

> **FRESHMAN**
> Yeah, okay, well, see you
> next time.

> **ANON**
> Yes. See you next time.

The young man walks off, shaking his head.

INT. STAIRS - DAY

DR. EVA LIE, carrying a number of books, is coming down the stairs. She is in her late 30s, slender, blonde and blue eyed, carrying herself with a certain European virtuous grace and femininity. Wearing little to no makeup, her innocent natural beauty shines, amplifying a fragile, aloof sensuality.

INT. CORRIDOR - DAY

The tattooed freshman, walking away from the auditorium, passes Eva, who is heading toward that lecture hall.

A passing **FRIEND**, a female faculty member, stops Eva before she can enter

Anon's auditorium, whispering to her:

> **FRIEND**
> I heard he's bald, with a
> grey beard.

Eva smiles.

> **EVA**
> Really? I heard the
> opposite.

INT. UNIVERSITY LECTURE AUDITORIUM - DAY

Anon is placing the last of the skulls
into his box as Eva enters. She looks
him over, pleased. In fact, she
unexpectedly finds herself unusually
drawn to him, in a way that she finds
surprising, sensing his gentle
confidence, his integrity, his
intelligence.

> **EVA**
> Dr. Anon?

> **ANON**
> Yes?

She places her books down upon the table
and extends a hand.

                    EVA
          Hi, I'm Dr. Lie, that's
          "Lie" as in not to tell
          the truth, although I
          always do. Eva Lie.
          Please call me Eva.

Anon shakes her hand, equally surprised,
quite taken by her natural beauty,
feminine mannerisms, and lovely,
although slight, Swedish accent.

                    ANON
          It's nice to meet you,
          Eva. You're lecturing in
          here next?

She nods.
                    EVA
          Ancient history.

Anon reaches for his box.

                    ANON
          Well, let me get my
          things out of your way.

Eva surprises herself by stepping in
front of him, blocking his exit.
Embarrassed, she rather quickly steps
back, but not completely.

> **EVA**
> Actually, I'm glad I
> happened to come down
> early, it gives me the
> opportunity to be one of
> the first to welcome you
> to the university.
> Welcome.

Despite her genuine warmth, and Anon's
attraction to her, his guarded
expression does not change much.

> **ANON**
> Oh. Thank you.

> **EVA**
> Do you like it so far?

> **ANON**
> Yes, yes I do.

> **EVA**
> That's good. They say
> there's nothing like a
> good first impression.

> **ANON**
> No, I guess not.

There is a growing subtle romantic
tension between them and it results in

an uncomfortable moment of silence. Eva
breaks it by motioning to his box of
skulls.

> **EVA**
> So, you um, teach
> anthropology? Human
> evolution?

This unexpectedly switches Anon back on
the path that he was pursuing with the
tattooed student:

> **ANON**
> Yes. — Did you know that
> over 50% of the populace
> disbelieves in human
> evolution?

> **EVA**
> Ah, no, I didn't know
> that.

> **ANON**
> Why do you think that is?

> **EVA**
> Religion perhaps?

> **ANON**
> You think there's a
> conflict? Between

religion and science?

                    EVA

I'm not sure. Maybe it's
that people don't like to
think of themselves as...
"glorified" apes.

                    ANON

Do you disbelieve in
evolution?

                    EVA

I'm not sure I want to
answer that.

                    ANON

Why?

                    EVA

Because you might not
like what you hear.

                    ANON

You do believe in human
evolution, don't you?

                    EVA

I really don't want to
start things off on a bad
note. I mean, if I were

to tell you "not really,"
or "perhaps not," or,
"I'm not sure," you,
being an anthropologist,
you'd probably react as
if I told you that I
believed the world was
flat. I don't want to
start things off badly.
I don't.

Anon pulls back, calming, yet
simultaneously stimulated by the
returning subtle romantic tension.

ANON
I apologize, I didn't
mean to make you feel
uncomfortable.

STUDENTS begin to enter the auditorium.
Anon picks up his box of skulls.

ANON
It was nice meeting you.

Eva nods and he leaves. She looks down,
blinking, thinking, and then she can't
help looking back up, to watch him as he
leaves.

INT. LONG CORRIDOR - DAY

Anon, carrying his box, glances about as he walks, looking at all of the student faces. He is still uncomfortable, ill at ease. He appears out of place, almost guilty of something.

Turning, he steps through a door labeled:

                FACULATY OFFICES
                    History
                   Sociology
                 Anthropology

INT. RECEPTION AREA / HALL BETWEEN OFFICES - DAY

Anon nods hello to the **RECEPTIONIST** and heads toward his office, where a **MAINTENANCE MAN** is finishing placing a nameplate, "Dr. David Anon," on the door.

                    ANON
            Sorry, excuse me.

INT. ANON'S OFFICE - DAY

Anon steps inside, carefully pulling the door closed. The room's walls are empty

of any decorations and a telephone is
the only object on his desk.

He drops his box on the desktop. Leaning
back against a wall, he remains
motionless for a moment, fighting some
unknown stress, thinking.

Lifting a hand, he nervously feels his
left side, beneath his upper arm.
Opening his suit jacket, he reveals a
concealed holster hanging under his left
arm. Something tubular and dark is
resting within it. Is it a gun? Anon
carefully pulls the object out, lifting
it into the light. It is not a gun. It
is a blue-black, prismatic crystal rod,
six-sided, a few inches in diameter, and
perhaps a foot long. Two rectangular
prongs are protruding from one of its
ends, making the rod resemble a large
skeleton key. Shimmering in the light,
it appears to be made of a polished,
futuristic, diamond-like glass. Somewhat
crude in shape, however, it does not
appear man made. In fact, it looks more
like some type of mineral oddity that
one might find in a subterranean cavern.

Holding this "skeleton key" tightly,
Anon stares at it as if it were of vital
importance.

EXT. UNIVERSITY CAMPUS - DAY

A large university campus centered within a city. Late in the day, waves of STUDENTS are moving along the numerous sidewalks. The surrounding streets are busy with traffic.

EXT. UNIVERSITY GROUNDS - DAY

Eva and her friend, the woman who had spoke to her in the hall, step out of a building and start walking toward the street.

> **FRIEND**
> So, what was he like?

> **EVA**
> I'm not sure.

> **FRIEND**
> Oh, Eva, you like him?

Eva is embarrassed.

> **EVA**
> Am I that transparent?

> **FRIEND**
> Well, what did he think of you? Tell me?

EVA

I'm not sure of that
either. Religion somehow
came up. And evolution.He
seemed so serious. It's
strange, I felt this
strong attraction to him,
but I also felt
uncomfortable, the way he
asked certain questions.

FRIEND

You mean he didn't show
you any of his southern
hospitality?

EVA

Southern hospitality?

FRIEND

Yeah, he's supposed to be
from North Carolina. Born
and raised in Charlotte.
Moved up here just two
weeks ago.

EVA

Are you certain?

FRIEND

Yeah, why?

> **EVA**
> He didn't have a southern
> accent. — Oh, there he
> is.

Thirty yards distant, Anon turns onto
the sidewalk, heading toward the street
and its crosswalk. (He did not notice
Eva and his back is now to her.)

> **FRIEND**
> Well, speak of the
> devil... — You want to
> catch up to him?

> **EVA**
> — No. No, slow down.

EXT. STEET INTERSECTION - DAY

Anon steps up to the edge of the
sidewalk as a black limousine pulls out
of traffic and parks on the opposite
side of the street. Anon focuses on the
limo, impatiently waiting for the light
to change so that he can cross the busy
intersection.

The limo's driver, the **PALE MAN**, dressed
in a dark suit and tie, rolls down his
tinted window, his eyes focusing on

Anon. Anon does not express the surprise
that should arise in any onlooker. The
driver's skin is dead white, his lips
are pale blue, and he has no eyebrows or
eyelashes. His thin, straight black hair
is covering a balding head and his razor
stubble appears to have grown back
unevenly, in patches, since he last
shaved. His dark, lifeless eyes are
sunken deep into their sockets and
although he does not appear to be
menacing, he is strangely and deeply
frightening.

EXT. UNIVERSITY GROUNDS - DAY

Eva and her friend are continuing
forward, slow. They see the limo but
cannot see its driver.

> **FRIEND**
> He's got a limo waiting
> for him?

EXT. STEET INTERSECTION - DAY

A darkly tinted window in the back of
the limo rolls down, revealing the
SLANTED EYED MAN. Because of interior
shadows, he can only be seen from his
eyebrows down. His eyebrows are entirely
white, despite his appearing no older

than his late forties.

His eyes are slanted, yet, oddly, in no
manner does his face appear Asian. His
face, a deep olive in complexion,
displays hubris and projects both a
noble bearing and formidable intellect.

Anon and the slanted eyed man make eye
contact. They know each other. The limo
is waiting for Anon.

Down the street: A car pulls out from
behind a truck, attempting to pass it.

INT. SMALL CAR - DAY

Now on the truck's left, the passing
DRIVER is unable to see Anon waiting to
cross the street, his vision obscured by
the truck.

EXT. STREET INTERSECTION - DAY

Eva and her friend are slowly walking up
behind Anon. Eva sees the opposing light
change from green to yellow.

> **EVA**
> Light's changing.

INT. SMALL CAR - DAY

The driver, rapidly approaching the intersection, sees the light change from yellow to red. He decides to run it and floors the accelerator.

EXT. INTERSECTION - DAY

Anon and the slanted eyed man are again looking at one another. The crosswalk sign changes from "DON'T WALK" to "WALK." Anon immediately steps off the curb, crossing the street.

INT. SMALL CAR - DAY

Flying past the truck, the driver sees Anon stepping directly in front of his car.

                    DRIVER
     Shit!

He slams on the breaks.

EXT. INTERSECTION - DAY

Car tires screech and Anon turns to face the breaking automobile. Unable to skid to a complete stop, the car bumps Anon, hard, knocking him to the street. The back of his head hits the pavement.

> **EVA**
> Oh my God!

Anon is lying flat on his back, his eyes blinking in a confused state of shock.

The slanted eyed man opens his door, about to go to Anon, but he stops as he sees all the **PEOPLE** rushing to the scene. He hesitates, then frowns, yanks the door shut, nods to the unusual driver, and the limo drives off.

Eva, squeezing through the gathering crowd, happens to notice the departing limo and its strange driver. At once, she expresses the shock that Anon had failed to display. At this moment, her friend bumps into her from behind and she lurches forward, her eyes dropping down to Anon. She kneels besides him.

> **EVA**
> Dr. Anon?

ANON'S P.O.V.: Anon sees Eva looking down at him. He can hear her clearly but he can barely hear the noise of the crowd.

> **EVA**
> Dr. Anon?

Her words echo is his head. Everything
surrounding her face fades to black.
Blurring slightly, her face slowly loses
color, becoming black and white.

ANON'S FOGGY BLACK AND WHITE VISIONS:

<u>In black and white</u>: Eva's face is in the
center of darkness. At first, it is the
face that had been looking down at Anon
but then it morphs into the face that
had first greeted him in the auditorium.
<u>Voices sound dreamlike</u>:

> **EVA**
> Dr. Anon?

Blurring, the face morphs into the
freshman student's.

> **FRESHMAN**
> Wow, great lecture
> Dr. Anon.

Blurring, the young man's face morphs
back into Eva's.

> **EVA**
> Dr. Anon?

Blurring again, Eva's face morphs back to the student's.

> FRESHMAN
> — great lecture Dr. Anon.

The face transforms once again, back into Eva's.

> EVA
> Dr. Anon?

The face blurs and remains blurred.

> FRESHMAN
> — Dr. Anon.

The voice echoes as the blurred face fades away. All is black.

Several silent moments and then a voice in the dark:

> DOCTOR (O.S.)
> Dr. Anon?

FADE IN:

INT. HOSPITAL ROOM - DAY

ANON'S P.O.V.: The world slowly brightens and comes into focus. Anon sees a **NURSE** and a young **DOCTOR** standing over him.

BACK TO: Anon is lying in a hospital bed. His eyeglasses have been removed, the back of his head is bandaged, and his right arm is in a cast from the elbow down.

>   DOCTOR
>   Well, it's good to see
>   you finally come around.
>   You were beginning to
>   worry us.

Anon lifts his left arm, reaching for his bandaged head, and sees that he is wearing a cast.

>   DOCTOR
>   No need to be alarmed.
>   Believe it or not your
>   injuries were
>   surprisingly minor,
>   considering the
>   nature of your accident.

The doctor looks into Anon's eyes with a penlight, observing pupil dilation.

> **DOCTOR** (CONTINUED)
> Besides the broken wrist,
> you have some badly
> bruised ribs and a slight
> concussion. You whacked
> your head pretty hard on
> the street. But, overall,
> I'd say you were pretty
> lucky. Very lucky. The
> doctor pulls the penlight
> away.

> **DOCTOR**
> How do you feel?

Anon is silent for a confused moment and
then:

> **ANON**
> I... I don't remember
> being in any accident.

INT. HOSPITAL WAITING ROOM - DAY

Eva is sitting rigid, concerned. Anon's
doctor enters and Eva moves to him.

> **EVA**
> Is he going to be all
> right?

                    DOCTOR
Well, we don't know
for sure.

                    EVA
But, I thought you said —

                    DOCTOR
— There's been an
unexpected complication.

                    EVA
What do you mean?

                    DOCTOR
Well, due to the blow
that he received to the
back of the head, he's
experiencing a state of
memory loss.
                    EVA
Memory loss?

The doctor leads Eva back to her seat,
sitting as well.

                    DOCTOR
Post-traumatic amnesia.
But it's an unusual case
because he's not
experiencing total memory
loss. He remembers his

name, the fact that he's
a teacher, and that he's
from North Carolina but
nothing else. He
remembers everything that
he's learned but nothing
that he's experienced.
Right now he's simply a
name without a past. Now,
in most cases, memory
usually returns in a few
days. But, if it doesn't
return inside of a week,
then, well, he may have
serious brain damage.

EVA

Oh God. Were you able to
contact his family?

DOCTOR

According to your
university, he has no
family.
    (A beat)
Would you like to see
him?

EVA

Oh, I don't know, I don't
really know him. I mean,
I only met him this

morning.

> **DOCTOR**
> This morning?

She nods.

> **DOCTOR**
> That would make you one
> of his most recent
> memories. Could you
> please come in to see
> him? Just to say hello.
> I'd like to see if he
> recognizes you.

She is not sure.

> **DOCTOR**
> It could help.

> **EVA**
> ... Okay. If it'll help.

INT. HOSPITAL ROOM - DAY

Anon is sitting up in bed, alert. He
notices his eyeglasses lying nearby. He
puts them on and becomes confused. He
takes them off and then puts them on
again, looking across the room.

ANON'S P.O.V.: Anon removes his glasses again. His vision remains unchanged. He can see equally as well with or without the spectacles.

BACK TO: The doctor and Eva enter.

> ANON
>
> Funny... I don't seem to need them... The lenses, they must be just plain glass.
>
> EVA
>
> Perhaps they were a fashion statement.

Anon puts down the glasses, reacting toward Eva as he did the first time they met, i.e., he is quite taken by her natural beauty and grace.

> DOCTOR
>
> David, do you recognize your visitor?

He does not.

> DOCTOR
>
> This is a colleague of yours, from the university.

                    ANON
          The university?

                    DOCTOR
          Where you started
          teaching.

                    ANON
          Teaching...

Anon strains but he cannot remember.

                    ANON
          ... I don't seem to
          remember you. I'm
          sorry...

Eva sees the confusion and helplessness
in his eyes. His serious demeanor and
self erected barrier of professionalism
no longer exist, replaced by frail human
vulnerability and commonality, which
nicely complement his look of decency
and quiet strength. She steps toward
him, extending a hand.

                    EVA
          Well then, allow me to
          reintroduce myself. After
          all, it's not very often
          that someone is given a

> second chance to make a
> first impression. My name
> is Dr. Eva Lie. Please
> call me Eva.

Anon reaches forward with his right
hand. Realizing that it is in a cast, he
smiles, genuinely, and switches hands,
awkwardly shaking with his left.

> **ANON**
> Sorry.

> **EVA**
> Oh, no, that's quite
> alright. Makes shaking
> hands
> > (MORE)

She attempts familiarity, using his
first name.

> **EVA** (CONTINUED)
> much more interesting.
> > (A beat)
> David.

An unsure smile lifts and drops on
Anon's face.

> **ANON**
> I um, I hear my name,

David, and, well, I know
it's my name, but for
some reason I'm just not
comfortable with it... It
doesn't feel right,
"David." I know
this is going to sound a
bit crazy but, would you
mind calling me by my
last name?

Eva experiences a moment of rejection
and then hope:

> **EVA**
> Dr. Anon? Or just Anon?

> **ANON**
> Just Anon. I realize it's
> a strange request but,
> well, I'd feel more
> comfortable if you called
> me Anon. I don't know
> why, I just would.

> **EVA**
> Well, Anon it is then.
> Anon. I like the name.

> **ANON**
> Thank you.

242

> **EVA**
> You know, you seem so
> much less professional
> than when we first met
> this morning. — In a good
> way. I mean, you seem
> more open. More like a
> real person. — Oh, I
> didn't mean it like that.
> Please don't take that
> the wrong way.

Anon's smile drops.

> **ANON**
> How can I? I don't
> remember this morning.

There is a brief, awkward moment of
silence.

> **DOCTOR**
> Well, I guess we'll leave
> you now. Let you get a
> good night's sleep.

> **ANON**
> I'll be staying here
> tonight?

The doctor nods.

Anon suddenly notices his holster, which is resting across the room, atop his folded clothes. He panics, jumps out of bed, and rushes to the holster.

> **DOCTOR**
> — What?

Anon scoops up the holster, looking to make sure the unusual key-like oddity is still within it. It is. He then clutches the holster to his chest, guarding it.

> **ANON**
> This - This is mine! —
> It's important. I — I
> need to keep it near me.
> Always. Close to me. I
> can't lose it. Can't risk
> that.

> **DOCTOR**
> Okay, okay, calm down.
> You can keep it with you.
> It's your property.
> Nobody's going to try to
> take it away from you.
> That's why it's here.
> It's yours.

The doctor guides Anon back to the bed as Eva watches, bewildered and concerned.

> **DOCTOR** (CONTINUED)
> Now I want you to get
> back into bed. Try to
> relax. Get a good sleep.

Anon slowly crawls into bed, holding
onto his holster as if his life depends
on possessing it. Half exposed, the
mysterious blue-black oddity sparkles in
the room's light.

> **EVA**
> Anon... What is that?

Anon, calms down by the sound of her
voice. He tries to remember.

> **ANON**
> ... I don't know. But I
> remember that, that it's
> important.
> (A beat)
> When will I be able to
> leave? I have to teach.

Eva and the doctor exchange glances.

> **ANON**
> It's very important that
> I teach. I remember that.

I'm supposed to teach.

                    DOCTOR
The most important thing
right now is for you to
get some rest. It's a
good sign that you're
beginning to remember
some things, but, we
don't need to rush this.
In a day or two you'll
most likely have regained
your memory completely.
Until then, I'd like to
keep you here, under
observation. Under our
care.

Confused, Anon looks first to Eva and
then to the doctor.

                    ANON
        Yes, alright, I
        understand.

                    DOCTOR
        Good.

The doctor is about to walk away.

                    ANON
        What day is it?

                    DOCTOR
          Tuesday.

                     ANON
          Tuesday... If I'm feeling
          better tomorrow, could I
          teach tomorrow? At the
          university? I have class
          on Wednesday. I remember
          that.

The doctor thinks for a long moment.

                    DOCTOR
          Perhaps. Placing you back
          into a familiar
          environment could prove
          beneficial. It's often
          used therapeutically.
          I'll consider it.
          Have a nurse go with you.

                     ANON
          Thank you.

The doctor moves with Eva toward the
door, as she appears reluctant to leave.

                      EVA
          Bye. Nice meeting you.
          Again.

They step out the door.

> **ANON**
> Bye.

The door closes and Anon is alone.

Slowly, he turns his attention to his glass-like key, straining to remember. Several moments pass.

EXT. SKY - NIGHT

The moon is nearly full.

INT. HOSPITAL HALL - NIGHT

The hospital is empty and quiet. A **LEAN NURSE** is walking down the hall.

INT. HOSPITAL ROOM - NIGHT

Anon is asleep, holding his unusual holster partially tucked beneath the blankets.

EXT. HOSPITAL - NIGHT

It is late and most of the building is dark.

EXT. STREET ALONGSIDE HOSPITAL - NIGHT

A black, two-door sedan, on older model, is driving toward the hospital. Oddly, its headlights are not on.

The car pulls into the hospital's back parking lot.

EXT. PARKING LOT - NIGHT

The sedan parks in the nearly empty lot.

INT. DARK SEDAN - NIGHT

A pale finger pushes in on a button, located where the automobile's ignition switch should be, and the engine stops. (An older car. No keys.)

EXT. PARKING LOT - NIGHT

The driver steps out of the sedan. It is the deathly pale man who had been driving the limo; who hand signaled to Anon. As before, he is dressed in a somber black suit, back tie, and a dull white shirt. Strangely, his clothing is unrealistically neat and wrinkle fee. Shadowed by the moonlight, he is a tall, grim, and eerie figure.

A passing stray **CAT** notices the man and the feline's hair stands on end. The cat's eyes flash an animal green and it hisses, scampering off.

Motionless, the pale man displays no hint of emotion as he walks toward the hospital. His movements are unusually slow and deliberate, as if his legs are having some difficulty following the orders given by his brain.

As this strange man proceeds along, his unblinking eyes catch the light of a passing car's headlights and momentarily shine green, like the cat's had.

INT. HOSPITAL CORRIDOR - NIGHT

The pale man comes up a set of stairs, entering the corridor, his grim face expressionless. Slowly and silently, he walks toward the distant nurses' station.

As the man passes a cart, on top of which is a coffee cup and a spoon, the spoon slowly curls up, bent by some supernatural, invisible force.

GLORIA and **PAM** (identified by their name tags) are the two nurses behind the

station. Gloria is putting a patient's
file away. Pam is paging through a late
edition newspaper, its headlines are of
the India-Pakistan War, the Taiwan
Conflict, and ongoing conflicts in the
Middle East.

The eerie man is slowly approaching
them.

The large, decorative desktop clock
resting atop the file cabinet suddenly
stops, its hands frozen in place. Gloria
looks up at the clock and notices the
reflection of the approaching man in its
glass facing.

> **GLORIA**
>
> Pam, can you take care of
> him?

> **PAM** (O.S.)
>
> Take care of who honey?

> **GLORIA**
>
> That

Gloria turns around to see an empty
hall.

> **GLORIA** (CONTINUED)
>
> man — ...

Gloria glances back at the clock face.
The reflection is gone as well.

> **GLORIA**
> I could have sworn...

> **PAM**
> They switch you to nights
> and you start seeing
> things?

> **GLORIA**
> No, I...
> > (A beat)
> I'll be right back.

Gloria puts her heavy key ring down on
the counter top and heads down the hall,
to where she thought she had seen the
approaching man.

She reaches the spot where the pale man
had been and she suddenly clutches
herself.

> **GLORIA**
> Oh — So cold. How'd it
> get so cold?

Gloria then gets a whiff of something
unpleasant.

> **GLORIA**
> Ugh — Smells... Smells
> like somebody died.

Frightened, she enters the room to her
left, investigating.

As she does so, the pale man reappears,
stepping out of one of the rooms that
Gloria had passed. Immediately, he
continues his silent walk toward the
nurses' station.

INT. PATIENTS' ROOM - NIGHT

Gloria is checking on the patients.

INT. HOSPITAL CORRIDOR - NIGHT

Black shoes walking silently down the
hall.

Pam turns a page. Suddenly, the bracelet
on her left wrist mysteriously buckles
and bends. She stares at it in
bewilderment. She then jerks upright and
clutches herself as she is hit by a
sudden freezing chill.

> **PAM**
> Ohh...

She next smells an offensive odor. She
looks about but the hall before her is
empty.

> **PAM**
> Gloria?

Gloria does not appear. Pam touches a
hand to the side of her head,
experiencing a sudden headache. She
calls out louder.

> **PAM**
> Gloria.

Out of Pam's line of sight, well behind
her, the mysterious man steps out of an
open closet and continues walking away
from her - having past her - approaching
the end of the corridor. He turns the
corner and disappears just as Gloria
pops back into the hall.

Gloria moves to Pam, holding a hand to
her left temple as well.

> **PAM**
> Did you smell that? What
> was that?

> **GLORIA**
> I don't know.

> PAM

Hey, you okay?

> GLORIA

I don't know. Suddenly I
don't feel too well.

> PAM

Yeah, me neither. Got a
splitting headache coming
on.

> GLORIA

Pam, did you do this to
my keys?

> PAM

Do what?

Gloria steps aside, allowing Pam to see
her keys. Lying atop the counter, all
the keys on her ring are bent and curled
up.

INT. HOSPITAL ROOM - NIGHT

Anon is still asleep, holding his
holster partially tucked beneath the
blankets.

Metal utensils resting atop a plate bend
and curl up.

The room's metal doorknob trembles,
turns, and the pale man enters. Almost
at once, Anon shudders as he is awakened
by the sudden intense cold and foul
smell that accompanies this man.

Anon sits up. He watches in amazement as
his eyeglasses, resting nearby, buckle
and bend, the lenses cracking. He then
notices a frightening, dark figure.

> **ANON**
> Who's there?

The strange man steps out of the
shadows, toward Anon. Anon sees his
visitor's dead white face and this time
he expresses shock and fear.

> **ANON**
> What do you want? Who are
> you?

The man steps up to a large metal table.
He touches it, lightly, and it vibrates
and supernaturally moves out of his way.

Keeping his sunken-in eyes on Anon, the
strange man seats himself in a wooden
chair. The man's voice, like his
expressionless face, is not malevolent,
but, dry and deep, it is frightening.

His speech, slow and deliberate, is completely devoid of emotion.

> **PALE MAN**
> ... Preliminary reports
> indicated that your
> injuries were minor.
> (A beat)
> ... They want to know...
> Why are you still here?

Anon is too confused and frightened to respond.

> **PALE MAN**
> ... How long will you be
> convalescing here?

> **ANON**
> I... I, don't know.

Several tense moments of silence.

> **PALE MAN**
> ... The Signature.
> (A beat)
> ... Do you have the
> Signature? ... Is it
> safe?

Anon glances down at his mysterious key-like rod. He makes a quick decision and,

shifting his body, conceals it entirely
beneath the blankets.

> **ANON**
> I — I don't understand. I
> don't know what you want.

The pale man slowly swings his head left
to right, looking over the room.

> **PALE MAN**
> ... Was it taken from
> you?

Anon lifts a hand to his left temple,
feeling ill.

> **ANON**
> Yes.

For the first time the strange man
expresses a slight reaction, narrowing
his eyes, predatorily. It is unexpected
and quite frightening.

> **ANON**
> — But I know where it is.
> I can get it back.

During the long, tense moment of
silence, Anon wonders if he made the
right choice in lying. Then, finally:

                    PALE MAN
          ... Will you require
          assistance?

                    ANON
          No, No. I won't require
          assistance.
                    (A beat)
          You want this thing...
          What is it?

The odd man stares at him for a silent
moment. Then, blinking slowly and
deliberately he speaks, his words coming
out slower.

                    PALE MAN
          ... My energy... is
          running low... ... I...
          will go now...

The man rises, slowly, his movements
unsteady. Anon just stares at him.
Moving to the door, the man touches the
knob, lightly, and it rattles and turns
by itself and the door swings open. The
man then turns back to Anon.

                    PALE MAN
          ... They... will be
          watching.

The man leaves, closing the door.

EXT. UNIVERSITY - DAY (RAINING)

It is a dreary, rainy day. STUDENTS, with umbrellas, dot the campus.

>   **ANON** (O.S.)
>   Many species of fauna and
>   flora alive today

INT. AUDITORIUM - DAY (RAINING)

Anon, the back of his head bandaged, is giving a lecture. Although his delivery is professional, he does not appear as confident nor is he as convincing as during his first lecture.(A NURSE is sitting inconspicuously off on the side of the lecture hall.)

>   **ANON** (CONTINUED)
>   are essentially identical
>   in appearance to their
>   ancestors and have
>   remained virtually
>   unchanged...
>   (A beat)
>   ... except for minimal
>   environmental variation
>   for millions of years.

Anon has his fossil skulls laid out on the table, positioned as they were at the end of his last lecture. He places a hand on the afarensis skull.

> **ANON**
>
> Why is it then that from afarensis to habilis there is a rapid and sudden change two and a half million years ago?
> (A beat)
> Remember, Darwin's theory of Natural Selection calls for continued, minute changes over long expanses of time... The Australopithecus line clearly fits this pattern.

He motions to the line of three Australopithecus skulls.

> **ANON** (CONTINUED)
>
> The slow, gradual transition is very readily apparent. Moving back into the forest, these creatures slowly became more and more ape-

like until they met
extinction. But...

Pausing, Anon focuses his eyes on the
line of skulls of the genus Homo.

> **ANON**
> But what about habilis?
>   (A beat)
> Do we see gradual,
> smooth, continuous
> evolution in this line?
> From habilis to modern
> Homo sapiens, yes, we
> do... But what about from
> afarensis to habilis?
>   (A beat)
> ... There appears to be a
> "missing link" between
> them... Doesn't there?

Anon falters slightly. He seems to be
realizing something that is deeply
troubling him. He forces himself to pull
his eyes away from the skulls.

> **ANON**
> How can we explain this?
> This problem of a missing
> link? How did something
> so...

Anon picks up the afarensis skull.

>   **ANON** (CONTINUED)
>   — "ape-like."

EXT. SAVANNA - DAY (EARLY)

Color is faded - Distant past is viewed

Close on the chimpanzee-like young
female afarensis as she curiously looks
over the animals gathered around the
water hole.

INT. AUDITORIUM - DAY (RAINING)

>   **ANON**
>   ...Give rise to something
>   so...

With his other hand he picks up the
habilis skull.

>   **ANON** (CONTINUED)
>   — "human."

EXT. SAVANNA - DAY

Color is faded - Distant past is viewed

Close on the first true **EARLY HUMAN**.
Although his face is still primitive,

his eyes hold an intelligence and an
awareness seen nowhere else in the
animal kingdom. Bringing down a strong
right hand, he strikes two rocks
together, creating a sharp cutting edge.
The broken off section of stone thuds to
the ground. (One of the rocks is stained
by blood.)

INT. AUDITORIUM - DAY (RAINING)

Anon slowly lowers the skulls, this time
asking himself the question aloud and
uncertain:

> **ANON**
> How did this happen..?

Something is obviously wrong with Anon.
The nurse looks concerned.

After a pause:

> **ANON**
> This is the question that
> Darwin was Unable to
> answer. He couldn't
> explain it...

He simply couldn't understand it. Anon
does not believe what he is about to
say, and it shows, but he pulls himself

together and delivers to the class the
textbook answer regardless.

                ANON (CONTINUED)
     Punctuated equilibrium.
     This is what modern
     science has added to
     Darwin's theory... A
     macro-mutation. Every now
     and then, a species
     mutates. Creating
     something very, very
     different. This is how
     habilis came to be. Two
     and a half million years
     ago an afarensis gave
     birth to something...
     very different.
     Because... Because of a
     mutation.
        (A beat)
     ... This is what was
     missing from Darwin's
     theory. It's what he
     couldn't understand. What
     he couldn't explain.
     Mutation.
        (A beat)
     A mutation..?

A few **STUDENTS** begins to whisper. The
nurse rises.

> ANON
> Please, e — excuse me...

Anon gathers himself and then exists the auditorium, visibly upset. The nurse follows.

INT. CORRIDOR - DAY (RAINING)

Anon is walking off.

The nurse appears, pursuing Anon. Eva, coming down a staircase, appears behind them.

> NURSE
> Dr. Anon? — Dr. Anon?

Anon stops, turning about.

> ANON
> I — I can't believe I'm
> teaching that, that lie.
> A mutation. Do you really
> believe that? That you're
> here because of some
> freak mutation that
> happened over two million
> years ago?

Anon is working himself up, he asks himself a question, aloud:

> **ANON** (CONTINUED)
> Are there species alive
> today that are
> in a some intermediate,
> mutated, transitional
> evolutionary stage? I
> can't seem to remember...

Eva moves closer.

> **NURSE**
> Dr. Anon —

> **ANON**
> — Well I - I don't
> believe it. I'm not sure
> why but I just don't.
> Something deep down in my
> gut, in my mind, is
> telling me that it's
> wrong. That it's a lie. I
> don't believe it. I don't
> believe I ever did...
> Feels good to say that.
> Wow.

Passing **STUDENTS** slow, stare, and start
to gather.

> **NURSE**
> Please try to calm
> yourself —

The nurse gently takes Anon's upper arm, unintentionally grabbing him near where he wears his holster beneath he suit jacket:

> ANON
>
> — No!

He yanks away from her in an uncharacteristically violent, desperate manner, clutching at he concealed holster.

> NURSE
>
> I think we should go back to the hospital.

> ANON
>
> No! I'm supposed to be here. Teaching!

Anon for the first time becomes aware of the gathering mob of **STUDENTS**. He also notices Eva, momentarily making eye contact with her, it seems to calm him, ground him somewhat, and he recovers most of his composure.

> ANON
>
> I sorry. I apologize for the scene.
> > (A beat)

> But I'm not going back
> there.

Anon walks off, quickly.

> ### NURSE
> ... Dr. Anon?

Eva is about to call out to Anon but
decides not to.

EXT. UNIVERSITY GROUNDS - DAY (RAINING)

Anon hurriedly steps out of a building,
frustrated, confused, and upset. He
realizes that he is without an umbrella
and considers stepping back inside when
he sees, stepping out of a distant
limousine, the strange man who had
visited him at the hospital.

The pale man is wearing a light coating
of make-up and what looks like lipstick.
It appears that he, or somebody, made an
effort to make his appearance less
attention drawing. A passing **COUPLE**,
however, cannot help but stare. The limo
drives off and the pale man opens an old
fashioned umbrella, dipping it to hide
his face.

Anon quickly ducks around a corner

before the strange man sees him.

EXT. SCIENCE BUILDING - DAY (RAINING)

Anon is jogging across the campus. He looks over his shoulder to see the pale man turning a corner far behind him.

Anon quickly ducks into the building he is passing: "NEWTON HALL"

INT. SCIENCE BLDG HALL - DAY (RAINING)

Anon peeks out a small window and watches the pale man enter the building that he had left moments ago.

Anon sighs in relief, leaning against the wall. He then happens to notice the hall's directory. A thought comes to him and he focuses on the: "GEOLOGY DEPARTMENT"

INT. GEOLOGY LABORATORY - DAY (RAINING)

Dr. **EDWARD** Shaffner, a down to earth bookworm of a man, is alone in the lab, peering through a microscope.

Anon knocks lightly on the door, entering, nervously feeling for the hidden holster that he is wearing.

> **ANON**
> Excuse me...

Edward turns to him and smiles.

> **EDWARD**
> Dr. Anon.

> **ANON**
> I know you?

Edward moves to him, shaking his hand.

> **EDWARD**
> Edward Shaffner. Ed. We
> were introduced when you
> first arrived.

Anon does not remember.

> **EDWARD**
> When you toured the
> university?

Anon decides to lie in order to avoid a
complicated explanation.

> **ANON**
> Oh, oh yes. Edward.
> Sorry, I've always had a
> problem remembering names
> and faces.

> **EDWARD**
> Ah, no need to apologize,
> with all the new faces
> you've met here I'm
> surprised you can
> remember your own name.

Anon forces a smile.

> **ANON**
> Yes, I'm surprised too.

Ed chuckles.

> **EDWARD**
> So, what can I do for
> you?

> **ANON**
> Well, "Ed," I was
> wondering, since we're
> colleges now, I was
> hoping that you might be
> able to help me out with
> something.

> **EDWARD**
> Sure, what?

> **ANON**
> Well, how can one tell if
> something is

a mineral, found
naturally in the earth,
or, or man-made?

                EDWARD
A visual examination
should suffice. But it
has to be done by
somebody who knows what
they're looking at.
        (Chuckles)
There're a lot of
minerals out there that
you'd swear nature could
never have produced.

Anon motions to a nearby display case,
on wheels, which contains an array of
exotic and strange looking crystalline
minerals. (The case is open.)

                ANON
Are all these here
"nature-made?"

                EDWARD
Yep. Fluorite, Barite,
Tourmaline, Beryl,
Uvarovite, — look at this
item of Gypsum.

Ed carefully lifts the item out of the

case. It is over two feet long, pearly white, silky, and curved like a tightly curled elephant's tusk.

> **EDWARD**
> Almost looks as if it was carved, doesn't it?

Anon focuses on the green prismatic rod lying in the case. It closely resembles his "key" in both size and shape, without, of course, the unusual key-like teeth.

> **ANON**
> What's this one?

Ed returns the specimen of Gypsum.

> **EDWARD**
> Quartz.

> **ANON**
> Is...

Anon reaches into his concealed holster and pulls out his mysterious key, which he now has wrapped up in a soft cloth.

> **ANON** (CONTINUED)
> ... this Quartz?

Anon unwraps the top portion of the key, leaving its unusual prongs concealed.

> **EDWARD**
> Nope. Color's wrong.

Ed visually examines the oddity.

> **EDWARD**
> Hexagonal prismatic
> crystals...
> Horizontally striated...

Ed takes Anon's hand and lifts the blue-black key up into the light. It sparkles, surprising Edward.

> **EDWARD**
> Wow... Index of
> refraction must be
> Adamantine. Near that of
> diamond.
> (A beat)
> With this brilliance,
> optical identification
> should be immediate
> but... I have no idea
> what it is.

> **ANON**
> Is it natural?

Ed shrugs, attempting to scratch Anon's
key with a fingernail but he cannot mark
its surface. He pulls a plastic file out
of his shirt pocket, and tries again.

> **EDWARD**
> I'm not sure but... all
> minerals have physical
> and chemical properties.

The file cannot scratch it.

> **EDWARD** (CONTINUED)
> Some are inherent and
> reliable... Such as
> degree of hardness.

Edward picks up one of the colorless
crystals, from the portable display
case, and using it against Anon's
oddity. The crystal cannot mark it.

> **EDWARD**
> Harder than Quartz?

Ed hesitates and then picks up a pale
blue crystal, using it, unsuccessfully.

> **EDWARD**
> ... Harder than Topaz?

Ed puts the Topaz back, puzzled.

> **EDWARD**
> It appears that you have
> something here harder
> than almost any common
> substance.

> **ANON**
> But... Look what happens
> when you squeeze it.

Anon wraps his left hand around the
exposed section of the key, closing his
fingers about its circumference. He then
squeezes, tightly.

> **ANON**
> It takes a moment.
> (A beat)
> I think it has something
> to do with body heat?
> Temperature?

Several silent moments pass and then
Anon removes his hand. Impressions of
his fingers are left indented into the
strange rod, as if it were made of clay.

Baffled, Ed pulls a fingernail down
across the key's indented surface,
easily creating a tiny trench.

EDWARD
Incredible...

Cooling, the key's interior pushes the
indentations outward, rapidly returning
its surface to its original shape and
hardness.

ANON
And it always returns to
its original shape.

EDWARD
But... Where'd you get
this?

ANON
... I'm afraid I can't
tell you that.

EDWARD
Well, until this little
magic trick, I was about
to guess that this was
one of nature's mix-ups.
A mineralogical imposter,
pseudo-morphs we call
them. The Earth rocks the
nursery, changes in
temperature, pressure,
what have you, and
sometimes you get

adaptation of the mineral
inside. Like your
Darwin's survival of the
fittest. But, no matter
what happens on the
inside, the new mineral
always retains its
original shape... Can't
change it by squeezing
it... And the way it
morphed...

Anon lowers the key, placing it atop a
nearby table. A small Geiger Counter
resting on the table begins to "click"
rapidly.

> **EDWARD**
> It's emitting
> radiation..?

Anon pulls his crystal away from the
Geiger Counter.

> **EDWARD**
> Now, that's not an ore
> and it's not uranium or
> thorium. What's going on
> here?

> **ANON**
> I wish I knew.

Edward possessively focuses his eyes on
Anon's oddity.

> **EDWARD**
> Sometimes, an invading
> molecule can act as an
> agent of change... The
> parting plane of a
> mineral is related to its
> atomic structure, a fresh
> fracture would show its
> true color. With a
> sample, I could test it
> for water infusion,
> fusibility, magnetism,
> electrical properties,
> specific gravity... I'd
> like to break it.

Anon reacts with strong emotion.

> **ANON**
> Break it? No, no. It,
> it's not supposed to be
> broken. Not now. Not yet.
>> (confused)
> Why do I feel that way?

> **EDWARD**
> What?

ANON
I, I'd better be going.

Anon spins about as JOHN, an elderly
professor, enters the lab. Startled,
Anon drops his crystal. Hitting the
floor, it unravels from its cloth and
its unusual prongs are exposed.

Recognition flashes across Edward's face
and he quickly picks it up. John also
recognizes it.

EDWARD
I didn't recognize it
without seeing the teeth.
How'd you get the museum
to lend it to you?

ANON
Museum? What museum?

EDWARD
You didn't get this from
Chapman?

Anon, confused, pulls his key away from
Ed.

ANON
I'm not sure. What is it?

Ed looks to John who is still staring at
the key, inquisitively, seriously.

                    EDWARD
          John?

                    JOHN
          It's an incredibly unique
          mineral anomaly. Or a
          fake. Dr. James Chapman,
          over at the Whitman,
          claims he dug it up about
          3 years ago. Shortly
          after announcing the
          find, he stated it was a
          fraud and locked it up.
          Wouldn't let anybody see
          it. Nobody.

                    EDWARD
          What are you doing with
          it?

Anon thinks and then:

                    ANON
          Returning it.

Anon leaves.

EXT. MUSEUM - DAY (RAINING)

Anon is still without an umbrella. He crosses a street and heads toward: "THE WHITMAN MUSEUM OF NATURAL HISTORY"

Anon enters the museum.

Across the street, a man lowers a newspaper, which he has been holding up in front of his face. It is the strange pale man.

INT. MUSEUM LOBBY - DAY (RAINING)

Anon is walking away from the ticket counter. He stops a passing **MUSEUM EMPLOYEE**. (An middle-aged woman.)

> ANON
> Excuse me, can you tell me where I can find Dr. James Chapman?

> **MUSEUM EMPLOYEE**
> Oh, I think I just saw him in the Paleontology Exhibit.

> ANON
> The Paleontology Exhibit?

> **MUSEUM EMPLOYEE**
> Yes, through that door
> and all the way back.

> **ANON**
> All the way back. Thank
> you.

> **MUSEUM EMPLOYEE**
> You're welcome.

Anon heads off in the direction
indicated.

INT. BIRD WILDLIFE EX. - DAY (RAINING)

Anon enters a hall exhibiting a
fantastic array of stuffed birds. He
proceeds toward the door at the far end
of the hall.

INT. PALEONTOLOGY EX. - DAY (RAINING)

Anon enters. The hall is filled with
fossils from all ages. Chapman is not
present, nor is anyone else.

Anon walks forward.

To his left he sees a large sheet of
cracked rock upon which are a half dozen
fossilized trilobites, frozen in place

upon what must have once been an ancient sea floor.

(Trilobites are an easily visually recognized but long extinct armored marine creature related to crustaceans.)

EXT. ANCIENT SEA FLOOR - DAY

Color is faded - Distant past is viewed

The same fossilized **TRILOBITES** are alive and moving about the bottom of a shallow sub-tropical sea in the company of **OTHERS** of their kind. They are strange, ancient creatures of a young, alien Earth.

An extinct shell covered **SQUID** jets by, picking off one of the trilobites. Moving in a school, the remaining trilobites all turn in one direction, taking on positions nearly identical to their fossilized remains in the Whitman Museum.

EXT. ANCIENT SEA - DAY

Color is faded - Distant past is viewed

A volcanic island explodes, spewing lava, ash, and debris into the surrounding sea.

EXT. ANCIENT SEA FLOOR - DAY

Color is faded - Distant past is viewed

A layer of ash and solidifying lava
smothers the trilobites, sealing their
doom.

INT. PALEONTOLOGY EX. - DAY (RAINING)

Continuing onward, Anon encounters a
flat slab of sandstone containing
impressions of sand grains, ripples, and
dozens of jellyfish the size of dinner
plates.

EXT. TROPICAL BEACH - NIGHT

Color is faded - Distant past is viewed

Beneath the strong moonlight thousands
of **GIANT JELLYFISH** quiver, stranded on a
lonely stretch of tropical beach.

INT. PALEONTOLOGY EX. - DAY (RAINING)

Still walking, Anon comes to a vertical
sheet of sedimentary rock containing the
partial fossilized remains of a
primitive armor plated fish, caught in

the act of swallowing another sea
creature.

EXT. TROPICAL SEA - DAY

Color is faded - Distant past is viewed

Thrashing its heavily armored body
through a shallow tropical sea, the same
fossilized **FISH** bites into a **SMALLER
INHABITANT** of the deep.

An instant later, a larger **CREATURE**
flashes by, violently ripping the
armored fish in two, swimming off with
its tail section. The armored fish, cut
in two, sinks to the bottom, its dinner
still in its mouth. It lands on the
sandy bottom, positioned identical to
the fossilized "photo" in the Whitman
Museum.

INT. PALEONTOLOGY EX. - DAY (RAINING)

Anon steps away, as if sensing the
brutality of the ancient ocean realm. He
turns to a nest of fossilized dinosaur
eggs, all of which are crushed. One,
displays the tiny skeleton of a hatching
occupant.

EXT. EDGE OF SWAMP - DAWN

<u>Color is faded - Distant past is viewed</u>

The world is carpeted by primordial ferns. The nest is undisturbed, its eggs uncrushed. The shell of one of the eggs cracks and a **BABY DINASAUR** peeks out, glimpsing the strange brutal world that it is being born into. There is a terrible sound behind it. The hatchling turns its eyes toward the sound.

INT. PALEONTOLOGY EX. - DAY (RAINING)

Anon turns his eyes to a fossil of a saber-toothed cat.

EXT. PREHISTORIC FOREST - NIGHT

<u>Color is faded - Distant past is viewed</u>

The **SABER-TOOTHED CAT** pounces upon the back of a large **HERBIVORE**, bringing the kicking animal crashing to the forest floor.

INT. PALEONTOLOGY EX. - DAY (RAINING)

Anon is staring at the carnivore's skull.

EXT. PREHISTORIC FOREST - NIGHT

Color is faded - Distant past is viewed

The cat sinks its claws into the kicking beast, securing its position on top of the creature.

INT. PALEONTOLOGY EX. - DAY (RAINING)

Anon is still staring at the skull.

EXT. PREHISTORIC FOREST - NIGHT

Color is faded - Distant past is viewed

The giant cat bites into its prey, pulling and tearing at its flesh with is sharp claws. The herbivore thrashes one final time and then becomes still. The saber-tooth snarls savagely, its eyes shimmering in the darkness.

>   **CHAPMAN** (O.S.)
>   "I wondered why

INT. PALEONTOLOGY EX. - DAY (RAINING)

Anon turns about to find himself facing **DR. JAMES CHAPMAN**. Graying, bearded, and wearing eyeglasses, he is the stereotypical image of an aging scientist.

>   **CHAPMAN** (CONTINUED)
>   such perfect fury had
>   been swept away, while
>   man, wide roaming dark
>   assassin of his kind, had
>   sprung up in the wake of
>   such perfected
>   instruments as these..."
>   — The thoughts of Loren
>   Eisely, paleontologist
>   and poet.

>   **ANON**
>   Profound thoughts.

Chapman extends a hand and they shake
hands.

>   **CHAPMAN**
>   I'm James Chapman, I was
>   told you were looking for
>   me.

>   **ANON**
>   Yes. My name is Anon. Dr.
>   David Anon. Anthropology.
>   I have something that I
>   believe you'll be
>   interested in. Anon
>   glances about to make

sure that they are alone
and then pulls out and
unwraps his mysterious
crystal key.

CHAPMAN
My God... There are two
of them?

ANON
Two of them?

INT. SAFE - DAY (RAINING)

All is black. The sound of a combination
lock being dialed echoes in the
blackness. There is a loud click and a
heavy metal door swings open, allowing
the light outside to flood into the
large, walk-in safe.

INT. CHAPMAN'S OFFICE - DAY (RAINING)

A sub-basement windowless office
decorated by stacks of books and
scattered fossils. Chapman pulls the
safe door open all the way, stepping
inside. Anon remains behind him.

INT. SAFE - DAY (RAINING)

Chapman walks deep into the safe and

kneels, reaching for a cloth-covered
object hidden away in a dark corner. His
forehead beads with perspiration. He is
a bit nervous, frightened.

>   **CHAPMAN**
>   They — They say that in
>   archaeology you never
>   really find what you set
>   out for. And... And that,
>   well, with the exception
>   of the occasional
>   surprise from Asia, maybe
>   Europe too, that there's
>   always something new
>   coming out of Africa.

Chapman rises, cradling the object,
heading back out of the safe.

INT. CHAPMAN'S OFFICE - DAY (RAINING)

>   **CHAPMAN** (CONTINUED)
>   ... I found both of these
>   statements to
>   ring very true.

Chapman steps back into the office,
placing the object upon a table.

>   **CHAPMAN**
>   Three years ago... That's

when I found it. In
Kenya.

Chapman unwraps the object, his hands
trembling. Within the cloth is a blue-
black rod nearly identical in size,
shape, and composition to Anon's
crystal, with the exception that this
one has three large prongs instead of
two.

EXT. AFRICAN RIVER BANK - DAY

<u>Color is faded - Distant past is viewed</u>

Looking up ahead, up high, perhaps at
some mountain, a male Australopithecus
afarensis, **THREE PRONG**, with an unusual
awareness in his eyes, is running,
frantically, down the muddy bank of a
shallow, drying river. Hanging around
his neck, by a thin rope of twisted
dried weeds and vines, is Chapman's
three-pronged "key."

INT. CHAPMAN'S OFFICE - DAY (RAINING)

Anon reaches down and carefully picks up
Chapman's key, lifting it up into the
light. Although it is considerably older
in appearance than Anon's, it sparkles
just the same.

EXT. AFRICAN RIVER BANK - DAY

<u>Color is faded - Distant past is viewed</u>

Three Prong is running for his life.
Behind him, chasing him, is a pack of
cackling, prehistoric **HYENAS**.

Bouncing about, the key-like rod hanging
about Three Prong's neck breaks loose
and falls to the muddy ground.

INT. CHAPMAN'S OFFICE - DAY (RAINING)

Anon is staring at Chapman's key, which
is sparkling in the light.

EXT. AFRICAN RIVER BANK - DAY

<u>Color is faded - Distant past is viewed</u>

Three Prong realizes that he has dropped
his key. He stops and turns about.
Sparkling in the sunlight, the key is
halfway between himself and the rapidly
approaching hyenas.

Three Prong then glances up ahead, like
before, up high, perhaps at some
mountain.

Turning back about, Three Prong runs

toward his crystal, knowingly risking almost certain death.

INT. CHAPMAN'S OFFICE - DAY (RAINING)

Continuing to stare at Chapman's key, Anon slowly begins to lower it, bringing it down out of the light.

EXT. AFRICAN RIVER BANK - DAY

Color is faded - Distant past is viewed

Racing toward his dropped rod, Three Prong trips and falls. The key is less than two feet away. He throws out a hairy arm, reaching for it. The hyenas tear into him.

INT. CHAPMAN'S OFFICE - DAY (RAINING)

Anon is continuing to lower Chapman's rod. It is reflecting less and less light.

EXT. AFRICAN RIVER BANK - DAY

Color is faded - Distant past is viewed

The hyenas are attempting to pull Three Prong in different directions. One sinks its teeth into an outstretched arm.

Another into a leg.

The blue-black rod is pressed down into
the mud by the talon of a landing
VULTURE.

Three Prong's death scream is strangely
sentient, chilling and it echoes out
over the land.

INT. CHAPMAN'S OFFICE - DAY (RAINING)

Anon placing Chapman's three pronged rod
back down upon its wrapping. Anon then
places his crystal rod beside it. There
is a moment of silence as both men
simply stare at one another.

> **CHAPMAN**
> I found it among the
> fossilized remains of a
> torn apart afarensis.
> Potassium-argon dating
> set the find at two and a
> half million years ago...
> You really don't know
> where yours came from?

> **ANON**
> No. Like I told you, I
> can't remember
> a thing.

      (A beat)
    Over at the university,
    they um, they
    said it was a "mineral
    anomaly."

Chapman slowly shakes his head.

         CHAPMAN
    Minerals contain only
    inorganic elements. I did
    a sort of biopsy on this.
    It contains carbon,
    hydrogen, oxygen...
    Typical of living things.
    — And not the result of
    some invasion of water,
    mind you, no, this isn't
    some geological
    trickster. No, this is
    clearly different.
    Unique.

         ANON
    But, if it contains
    organic chemicals... Then
    why didn't it fossilize?

Chapman slowly shrugs his shoulders.

         ANON
    What? Is it an artifact?

Are you saying that some
hominid made it?   .

Chapman, again, slowly shrugs his
shoulders.

ANON
I don't understand. Why
didn't you let anyone
examine it, study it? Try
to determine what it is.

Chapman becomes nervous again,
frightened.

CHAPMAN
Shortly after I announced
my finding it, I... I was
visited by... by someone.
I don't know who he was
but he, ah, he threatened
me. Said... "They"...
would kill my wife if I
didn't denounce what I
found. They, they kept
watching me. I was
frightened. Really
frightened. It's
difficult to explain. I
couldn't risk my wife's
safety. You see, I felt
the threat to be real.

And imminent.

> ### ANON
> This "person" who visited
> you. Did he, was his skin
> unusually pale?

Chapman's eyes light up with fear.

> ### CHAPMAN
> They... They know about
> you?

> ### ANON
> It looks that way. — But
> as to who "they" are, I
> don't have a clue.

> ### CHAPMAN
> I — I don't want any part
> of this. I don't want
> this starting all over
> again. I'm afraid I have
> to ask you to leave.

Chapman wraps up his three pronged
crystal and heads back toward the safe
with it.

> ### CHAPMAN (CONTINUED)
> So please, just take your
> "mineral anomaly" and
> leave.

                    ANON
          But —

                    CHAPMAN
          — Just, just go.
               (A beat)
          ...Please. Just go.

As Chapman places his crystal back in
the safe:

                    ANON
          This... "man" that came
          to visit me. He um, he
          referred to my crystal as
          a "Signature." Do you
          have any idea what he
          meant by that?

Chapman thinks for a second.

                    CHAPMAN
          No.
               (A beat)
          Look, I'm sorry but I
          can't get involved.

                    ANON
          ... I understand.

Anon picks up his crystal key and is
about to leave.

CHAPMAN

Wait.

Slowly, Chapman steps back into his
safe, pulling out small black box that
is resting near his wrapped crystal.
Chapman, with trembling hands, offers
the box to Anon.

CHAPMAN

In this box, there's a
collection of skull
fragments. One
individual. No
a complete skull, but,
well, enough. I found
them nearby, in the same
stratum as the crystal.
They're... They're
very... unusual. Maybe
the missing piece to the
puzzle... I don't know. I
never told anyone about
this. Kept it to myself.
Didn't pursue it. Didn't
want to know...

A moment of silence and then Anon takes
the box, frustrated, angry.

ANON

Just one question. Why

    didn't "they" try to take
    your crystal away from
    you?

Chapman, for a third time, simply shrugs
his shoulders.

Anon leaves with the black box.

EXT. MUSEUM - DAY (RAINING)

The sun is setting.

Anon exits the museum. (With Chapman's
black box.)

EXT. MUSEUM - DAY (RAINING)

Dead, unblinking, sunken-in eyes, are
watching Anon from <u>across the street</u>.
The pale man steps out of the shadows
and starts toward Anon. As he walks down
the sidewalk, a "NO PARKING" sign groans
and leans away from him as he passes it.

The pale man stops abruptly as he sees
Eva, with a bright umbrella, crossing
the street, moving toward Anon.

The strange man stands motionless,
staring at them, completely devoid of
expression. He tilts his head, as if

preparing to listen from an impossible distance.

EXT. MUSEUM - DAY (RAINING)

<u>In the front of the museum</u>: Eva steps up to Anon, they are both momentarily unsure of what to say to one another.

It starts to rain harder.

She steps close to him, covering the both of them with her large umbrella.

> **ANON**
> Thank you.

They look into each other's eyes, and then shy away, both feeling the same unusually strong attraction and romantic tension.

> **EVA**
> The way you left, I wanted to see how you were. I found out you might be here. You're leaving?

He nods yes.

> **EVA**
> That nurse is looking all
> over for you. Are you
> going back to the
> hospital?

> **ANON**
> No. I don't think so. Not
> after last night. I guess
> I'll be going home.

She decides to let the "Not after last
night" comment pass.

> **EVA**
> Are you going there now?

> **ANON**
> I don't know. In a way,
> I'm kind of afraid to. I
> don't know what it'll be
> like. What I'll find.

Anon glances about, nervously.

> **ANON** (CONTINUED)
> Ah, could we, could we
> talk someplace else? I
> don't feel comfortable
> standing around out in
> the open like this.

> **EVA**
> I don't understand.

Anon cracks a nervous smile.

> **ANON**
> Believe me, neither do I.

Eva sees, behind Anon, on the other side of the street, the pale man, standing beneath his dark umbrella.

> **EVA**
> Anon... I think that's
> the man who was driving
> that limo that was
> waiting for you. Right
> before your accident.

Anon turns about and freezes. The strange man focuses on Anon's black box, which Anon quickly conceals behind himself.

> **EVA**
> What? What's wrong?

> **ANON**
> I'm not sure...

> **EVA**
> Anon, are you in some

type of trouble?

> **ANON**
> I — I have to go. Sorry.

> **EVA**
> Anon?

Anon walks off, rapidly, and then he starts running. Eva, confused, looks back for the pale man but the man has vanished.

INT. PALEONTOLOGY EX. - DUSK (RAINING)

Black, wet shoes walking silently.

INT. CHAPMAN'S OFFICE - DUSK (RAINING)

Chapman is seated, slumping forward, lost in thought. Suddenly, the frames of his eyeglasses bend and tighten around his face. He yanks the glasses off, watching them curl up into a ball in his left hand.

Next, he shivers and covers his nose, stiffening in terror.

A dark, ominous shadow then slowly covers him. Ever so slowly, Chapman turns around to face the pale man.

> **PALE MAN**
> ... What did you give
> him?

> **CHAPMAN**
> I don't know what you're
> talking about.

The pale man simply stares at him with
his dead, unblinking eyes.

> **CHAPMAN**
> But, I didn't give him
> anything. Nothing.
> Nothing! — I swear. I'll
> show you the crystal,
> it's still in the safe.

The corpse-like man stops him with a
question.

> **PALE MAN**
> ... What was in... the
> box?

Chapman reaches for his left temple, in
pain.

> **PALE MAN**
> ... Do not... lie... to
> me.

EXT. TREE LINED STREET - DUSK

A taxi is driving down the wet street.

INT. TAXI CAB - DUSK

Anon is in the back of the cab, looking at his driver's license in his open wallet.

> **ANON**
> There, that's it, it's up ahead. You can pull over here. Let me out here.

EXT. TREE LINED STREET - DUSK

Anon gets out of the cab, his right foot stepping down onto the street.

INT. MUSEUM BASEMENT - DUSK

A gristly right foot, wearing a shoe, drops down upon the concrete floor of a dark basement. The section of the lower leg that is attached to the foot is burnt to a crisp, reduced to a greasy ash. Exposed, calcined bone is sizzling.

Directly above the foot is a smoldering hole in the ceiling.

INT. CHAPMAN'S OFFICE - DUSK

Surrounding the burnt hole in the floor are the remains of Chapman's body. A left hand and forearm, a blackened neck and head, and an ashy lump of burnt flesh. Strangely, the floor surrounding the hole, and Chapman's remains, is undamaged. (His remaining left hand is still holding his curled up eyeglasses.)

Pale fingers are punching a memorized number on a nearby phone. Slowly, the pale man places the phone against his ear. (In his other hand, he is holding Chapman's threepronged crystal, which is partially wrapped in its cloth.) A second passes.

> **PALE MAN**
> ... Chapman gave him a fossil. ... An important fossil.

EXT. ALLEY - DUSK

A black limousine is parked in the alley.

INT. LIMOUSINE - DUSK

The slanted eyed man listens for a

moment and then ends the call on his
cell phone. For the first time he can be
seen in his entirety. His forehead is a
number of inches higher than a normal
man's and his hair, like his eyebrows,
is white. His hubristically intelligent
face is etched with deep concern.

Seated next to this slanted eyed man are
two other **PALE MEN**. They have the same
unusual characteristics as the pale man
who had just made the phone call; the
same dead white skin, pale blue lips,
and unblinking, sunken, dead eyes.

EXT. TREE LINED STREET - NIGHT

Anon is walking up the sidewalk,
Chapman's black box tucked under an arm.

Anon stops before an attractive, four
story brick apartment building. He flips
open his wallet and matches the address
on his driver's license to the apartment
building. He lives in apartment 3 - B.

INT. THIRD FLOOR HALL - NIGHT

Anon comes up the stairs and moves to
his apartment door. He looks at the lock
on the door and then pulls out a key
ring with a single key on it.

> ANON
>> I guess this is "the"
>> key...

He sticks the key in the lock. It fits.

INT. ANON'S LIVING ROOM - NIGHT

Anon enters the dark apartment, keeping Chapman's box cradled in an arm.

He suddenly lifts his key, watching it curl up before his eyes, unable to understand whatever force is at work.

Anon then shudders, feeling an icy cold chill. It is then that he sees, seated, on the only piece of furniture in the room, a **FOURTH PALE MAN**. This man shares the same common characteristics and facial similarities as the other corpse-like men but he is completely bald. His sunken eyes are closed.

Anon just stares at the pale man, wondering if the strange man is asleep or, perhaps dead?

Anon covers his nose and slowly approaches the man. The man's chest is still. He does not appear to be breathing. Anon extends an index finger

and slowly presses in on the man's
wrinkle free suit. The pale man does not
react. Anon, pushes in again, this time
on the man's stomach.

The man's mouth drops opens and a breath
of stale air forces its way out. Anon
falls backward in fright.

The pale man's bald head slowly lifts
and his dead eyes open.

> **FOURTH PALE MAN**
> (Slow)
> ... W... h... a... t..?

Anon kicks frantically, backpedaling
until he finds himself pressed against
the door.

> **FOURTH PALE MAN**
> ... Wh... ere... have...
> you... been..? ... My...
> en... ergy... is... ...g
> ... o... n... n.. n.. n
> .. e...

The strange man's deep set eyes slowly
blink, once, and then close. Once again,
he appears dead. Anon sits motionless,
attempting to calm himself.

> ANON
> ... Are you dead now?

The pale man does not respond.

Anon rises, rubbing his left temple,
feeling ill.

> ANON
> You look dead.

Anon sums up his courage and take a step
toward the pale man.

> ANON
> You certainly smell dead.

Anon forces himself to take a second
step.

> ANON
> Please be dead.

Anon timidly pokes the man in the chest.
There is no response. Anon feels for a
pulse.

> ANON
> No pulse... So cold.
> (A beat)
> What the hell am I
> involved in..?

A moment passes and Anon then steps toward the kitchen.

INT. ANON'S KITCHEN - NIGHT

Anon opens the refrigerator. It is completely empty.

INT. ANON'S HALL - NIGHT

Anon walks down a short hall, moving toward a bedroom.

INT. ANON'S BEDROOM - NIGHT

Anon enters, finding the room completely empty. No bed.

He looks in the closet. Hanging neatly within are four suits, identical in style to what he is wearing but of different colors.

> **ANON**
> ... Guess I travel light.
> Am I on the run?

INT. ANON'S BATHROOM - NIGHT

Anon peeks inside.

                    ANON
Not even a roll of toilet paper...

INT. ANON'S LIVING ROOM - NIGHT

A cell phone starts ringing, loudly.
Anon searches his pockets, finds, and
pulls out his cell, and then just looks
at it, with trepidation. After several
more rings, Anon decides to answer it.

                    ANON
          Hello?

There is a second of silence and then
breathing, followed by the deep, dry
voice of the first pale man.

               PALE MAN (O.S.)
               (Filtered)
          ... Wait where you are.
          ... We are coming to
          collect you.

Anon closes the phone, disconnecting the
call.

                    ANON
          Collect me?

He glances at the seated corpse and then
runs to the door.

EXT. TREE LINED TREET - NIGHT

Anon is leaving his apartment building.
(With Chapman's box.) As he reaches the
sidewalk, he sees a black limousine
turning the corner, heading toward him.

Anon runs down the building's driveway.

EXT. BACK YARD - NIGHT

Anon, looking behind himself while
running, does not see a **FIFTH PALE MAN**
step out of the darkness, directly in
front of him. Anon turns his head
forward, gasps, and skids to a stop. The
pale man reaches out to grab him but the
man's movements are unusually slow and
Anon manages to avoid capture.

Anon runs off, coming to a high wooden
fence, cornered. He sees that the fifth
pale man is walking toward him, hands
outstretched, zombie-like.

Anon tucks Chapman's box under an arm
and climbs up the fence, kicking and
slipping.

Anon accidentally drops the black box.
The pale man is only yards distant and
closing. Anon drops back down to

retrieve the box.

Anon grabs Chapman's box, rises, and notices, behind the approaching fifth pale man, the slanted eyed man, standing out on the distant sidewalk with three other pale men. (The first pale man and the other two from the limo.)

Anon leaps up and grabs the fence top again, kicking his way up, this time with pale fingers fumbling over his thrashing legs.

EXT. OTHER SIDE OF FENCE - NIGHT

Anon flips over the fence, landing hard.

The fifth man in black begins banging, loudly, like a Frankenstein's monster on the other side of the fence. Anon runs off, disappearing into the darkness.

EXT. STREET - NIGHT

Anon is running down the street.

Headlights brighten the street as the limo starts down it.

Anon ducks into a side alley, hiding from sight. He catches a glimpse of the

profile of the strange pale man
(driving) as the limo passes.

Anon gets an idea. Searching his
pockets, he finds and pulls out a cell
phone, flipping it open and dialing
information.

> **ANON**
> Hello? Hello, yes, I need
> a phone
> number. Eva, Eva Lie.

EXT. EVA'S CONDO BUILDING - NIGHT

An attractive condominium building.

> **EVA** (O.S.)
> So, you have no idea who
> these men are?

INT. EVA'S LIVING ROOM - NIGHT

Eva and Anon are sitting together on a
couch. Chapman's black box is resting on
a coffee table. Anon's two-pronged key
and its holster are lying beside it.

> **EVA** (CONTINUED)
> (Referring to crystal)
> Or what this is?

                    ANON
          Absolutely no idea.
                (A beat)
          Chapman found the first
          crystal. I guess I must
          have found this second
          one. I just can't
          remember. But... I know
          it has something to do
          with the past, man's
          past.

Eva is silent for a moment, taking it
all in. Then, carefully:

                    EVA
          Anon, earlier today, I
          overheard what you said.
          To that nurse. Is it your
          memory loss, or are you
          suddenly having doubts,
          about human evolution?
          About what you're
          teaching?

Anon thinks for a long moment.

                    ANON
          I don't know. It seems as
          if, as if there's
          something missing.
          Something important.

> Something that I know,
> that I found out, but
> that I can't remember.
> Something that changed my
> view on what I'm
> teaching. But I'm not
> sure. It's confusing...
> (A beat)
> Why can't I remember?

She reaches out and with care adjusts
the bandage on the back of his head,
finding herself stroking his hair, and
tenderly touching the bruised side of
his face.

> **EVA**
> It'll be alright. When
> your memory returns,
> everything will become
> clear.

Anon is calmed by her soft, caring touch
but then he suddenly notices his
reflection in a mirror on the other side
of the room and jumps slightly,
startled. He rises and moves to the
mirror, visibly upset, staring at his
reflection, touching his own face.

> **ANON**
> Eva...

She moves to his side, concerned.

>   ANON
>   For a moment I, I — I
>   didn't recognize myself.
>   Not at first...

She does not understand, she struggles
to.

>   EVA
>   You're not wearing your
>   glasses. Maybe it's
>   because you're not
>   wearing your glasses.

>   ANON
>   No... I think it's more
>   than that. I somehow
>   look... I don't know,
>   younger, maybe? I look,
>   different than I feel.
>   Something's wrong... I
>   didn't recognize
>   myself...

>   EVA
>   Anon, maybe you should,
>   um, maybe you should let
>   me take you back to the
>   hospital. Until your
>   memory does returns.

ANON

No. They'd find me there.
Again.

EVA

Anon... These men that
you say are following
you, I know you said that
they threatened this
Chapman person, at the
museum, but they haven't
really threatened you in
any way, have they?

ANON

Eva, there was a dead man
in my apartment.

EVA

But, the police didn't
find a body...

ANON

Because they came looking
to "collect" me and
probably took him away
instead.

He turns to her.

                    ANON
          You don't believe me?

                    EVA
          I'm honestly not sure
          what to believe. She
          reaches out, taking his
          arms in her hands.

                    EVA
          I want to believe.

Anon pulls away and paces away from her,
frustrated, upset.

                    EVA
          Would you like a drink?

Anon sighs, frustrated.

                    ANON
          Yes. Yes, I think I
          would. Thank you.

                    EVA
          Scotch?

                    ANON
          Sure.

                    EVA
          Water? Ice?

He just shakes his head "no," thinking.
She is about to head off but stops.

> ### EVA
> Anon, what happened to
> your glasses?

Anon sighs again.

> ### ANON
> Oh, nothing you'd
> believe.

She hesitates and then steps into the
kitchen, which is open to the living
room and can be viewed in its entirety.
She pours two drinks, putting ice in
hers, and heads back with the glasses
and the bottle.

She then sits down next to Anon,
offering the drink while placing the
bottle of Scotch on the coffee table.

Anon takes the drink, hesitates, and
then empties the glass in one gulp. He
then reaches for Chapman's box but Eva
stops him, gently.

> ### EVA
> Anon, perhaps if we, if
> we took a short break

from all this, step away
from it for a little
while, think about
something else. Talk
about something else.

> ANON
> Like what?

> EVA
> Oh, I don't know,
> anything.

There is a moment of silence. Anon pours
himself another drink.

> ANON
> Okay... What's your
> favorite color?

She smiles.

> EVA
> Blue. And you?

Anon is about to answer but stops short,
almost amused.

> ANON
> I don't remember. Sorry.

He gulps down the rest of the drink and

begins to pour another. Eva, concerned, spots a book lying nearby and quickly picks it up.

> **EVA**
> Look, this might be
> interesting.

The book is titled: 'DICTIONARY OF SUBJECT QUOTATIONS" She flips through it.

> **EVA**
> Knowledge... Laughter...
> Madness... Man — Man.
>   (A beat/Reading)
> "The only animal that
> blushes — or needs to."
> Mark Twain.

> **ANON**
> Clever. But I seem to
> prefer this one, Man, "An
> ape with possibilities."
> Roy C.
> Andrews. Although this
> one's even better, "The
> cause for women's dislike
> for one another."

She laughs lightly, her tension slowly disappearing.

> **EVA**
> Oh no, I think this one's
> much better. Man, "The
> second strongest sex in
> the world."

Anon also relaxes somewhat, the alcohol
and conversation helping to ease his
mind.

> **ANON**
> This one's different.

She reads aloud what he is pointing to:

> **EVA**
> "A foundling in the
> cosmos, abandoned by the
> forces that created him."

She bobs her head, not really liking or
disliking it.

> **ANON**
> No? What about this one.
> "The greatest miracle and
> the greatest problem on
> this earth."

Eva shakes her head, spotting one that
she likes.

EVA

"The bad child of the universe."

ANON

"Nature's sole mistake."

EVA

Too pessimistic. "An earthly animal but worthy of Heaven." Saint Augustine. Now that's nicer but —

ANON

— But here's the one that suits us best. "Mankind is poised midway between the gods and the beasts." Plotinus. — Or, here, ever better, more succinct. "Half beast, half angel."

EVA

I don't think I like those two.

ANON

That's because you don't like to think of people as "glorified apes." —

Hey, I remember that. I
remember you telling me
that.

Eva smiles and Anon finds himself pulled
into her eyes.

ANON
But what I don't
understand is how I
couldn't remember you...

There eyes meet and their souls slowly
melt into one another.

EVA
Why is it when I see you,
when I'm with you, I
feel... The feeling, the
attraction it's so
strong. Since I first saw
you...

They close toward a kiss but Eva
hesitantly holds him back.

EVA
I've, this is so fast...
I've been alone for so
very long...

They hesitate and then kiss, sinking

down into the couch.

INT. EVA'S BEDROOM - NIGHT

Anon and Eva are lying together in bed.
Eva is asleep, Anon is not. He quietly
slips out of bed and pulls his pants on.

INT. EVA'S LIVING ROOM - NIGHT

Anon sits upon the couch, looking at
Chapman's mysterious box, and whispers
to himself:

> **ANON**
> The missing piece to the
> puzzle...

He opens the box. There are a dozen or
so fossilized skull fragments within it.
They are of many different sizes and
shapes and it would require a fair
amount of work and anatomical knowledge
to put them together.

Anon sits back, staring at the
fragments.

EXT. AFRICAN GRASSLAND - NIGHT

Color is faded - Distant past is viewed

An infinite number of stars are twinkling in the dark night sky and the red glow of flowing molten rock decorates a nearby volcanic mountaintop.

Standing together in the tall grass, a group of four Australopithecus afarensis males, all possessing an unusual awareness, are silently staring at one another, as if acknowledging some sort of mutually understood kinship or secret brotherhood. Each of the hominids has a blue-black crystal rod hanging around its neck, each with a different number of prongs, varying from one prong to four prongs Apparently, the teeth of their "keys," the prongs, symbolize their number in unity.

One of the males is Three Prong - who will meet his demise later by the hyenas - the one wearing Chapman's threepronged rod. Two of the other males are **ONE PRONG** and **TWO PRONG**. (One Prong is always only seen in profile; his left side.) The hominid possessing the crystal with the four prongs has a **GRAY STREAK** running through the hair on his head.

Parting company, the small group disperses, each key holder moving off in a different direction.

EXT. AFRICAN GRASSLAND - NIGHT

<u>Color is faded - Distant past is viewed</u>

Wading through the tall grass, Gray
Streak is making his way to a nearby
river. A group of ancient **ELEPHANTS** is
on the opposite bank, their gray hulking
bodies lighted by the moonlight.

Grey Streak steps up the riverbank and
moves into a small group of other
afarensis **CREATURES**. Walking up to one
of the females, he touches her
affectionately. She looks at him with
caring eyes, less aware than his. He
looks up at the stars. She does not. A
cloud is passing over the glowing moon.

EXT. EVA'S CONDO BUILDING - NIGHT

A cloud is passing over the glowing
moon.

The fourth pale man, the bald one who
had "died" in Anon's apartment, is now
alive and standing across the street,
staring up at the windows of Eva's
condominium.

The strange bald man lowers his dead,
unblinking eyes and slowly walks off,
disappearing into the darkness.

INT. EVA'S LIVING ROOM - NIGHT

Anon is asleep on the couch. His eyes
are moving rapidly beneath his closed
eyelids. He is dreaming.

Everything blurs and fades to absolute
darkness.

BEGINNING OF ANON'S GUILT DREAM

For several moments, all is dark. The
daytime sounds of moving automobiles and
chattering people slowly fades in but
only rises to the audible level of a
muffled background noise.

EXT. UNIVERSITY CAMPUS - DUSK

(ANON'S GUILT DREAM)

This dream is in black and white:

The darkness slowly blows away like
frightened smoke, revealing Anon, who is
walking across the campus. The
buildings, landscape, and **PEOPLE** are
blurred. Only the immediate foreground

has clarity.

Anon looks about nervously, appearing insecure and guilt ridden. Passing **STUDENTS** and **FACULTY** are all staring at him, as if he were on display, a strange untrustworthy animal imprisoned in a bar-less zoo.

Anon quickens his pace. The people start to follow him, pointing at him with long, accusing fingers.

EXT. STREET INTERSECTION - DUSK

<u>(ANON'S GUILT DREAM)</u>

<u>This dream continues in black and white:</u>

Anon, unable to escape his pursuers, turns to the street. Waiting on its other side is the black limousine.

Anon looks up at the traffic light. He will have to wait to cross.

Seated in the limo's driver's seat is the first pale man. He makes eye contact with Anon. His dead, sunk-in eyes are without eyelashes and framed by an eyebrowless dead white face.

The window in the back of the limo rolls
down revealing the slanted eyed man.

Suddenly, there is absolute silence.
Anon turns back to face the limo driver.

> **PALE MAN**
> ... Deceive.
> (A beat)
> ... Lie.

The strange corpse-like man grins,
horrifically — nightmarishly.

> **PALE MAN**
> ... Teach

Absolute silence again. The traffic
light changes from yellow to red, the
crosswalk changing from: "DON'T WALK" to
"WALK"

Anon starts toward the limousine, the
slanted eyed man waving him over.
Tires screech horribly. A car! It is
going to hit him!

A loud ringing noise.

INT. EVA'S LIVING ROOM - DAY

Anon lurches upright, awakening from his

nightmare. The telephone, on the coffee
table, is ringing. The answering machine
engages the call.

>   **EVA** (RECORDING)
>   Hello. I'm unable to take
>   your call right now so
>   please leave a message
>   after the tone.

There is a beep. Silence on the other
line. Then someone breathing, listening.
The caller then hangs up.

Anon searches for and pulls out his cell
phone. It is dead, in need of
recharging.

>   **ANON**
>   Eva?

She does not respond. He gets up,
looking for her.

>   **ANON**
>   Eva?

The condominium's doorknob rattles and
starts to turn. Anon spins about,
staring at the rattling, oddly turning
knob.

The door lurches open and Eva enters
with a newspaper tucked under an arm.
She sees that Anon is shaken.

> **EVA**
> Sorry, didn't mean to
> startle you. Lock sticks,
> need to jiggle it.

She looks at him in a very special way
and gives him a good-morning kiss. He is
stiff, suspicious.

> **EVA**
> What's wrong?

> **ANON**
> Where were you?

> **EVA**
> Just downstairs. To get
> the paper. Why?

He relaxes.

> **ANON**
> Oh, just jumpy I guess.

Eva drops the paper down onto the
countertop that separates the living
room from the open kitchen.

>   **EVA**
> Anon, I was thinking, how
> do you feel about
> hypnosis?

>   **ANON**
> Hypnosis?

>   **EVA**
> I was thinking it might
> be a way to Help you
> regain your memory. It's
> how a friend of mine
> quite smoking.

Anon unfolds the paper, opening it. His
face pales.

>   **ANON**
> Eva... Did you see this?

She moves to him as he reads the
headline aloud:

>   **ANON**
> Nobel laureate killed by
> unexplained fire...

He points to the photograph accompanying
the headline. It is of Dr. James
Chapman. His name is beneath his
picture.

> EVA
>> Dr. Chapman?

> ANON
>> Now do you believe me?
>>> (A beat)
>> They killed him. Made it
>> look like an accident.
>> Because he talked to me.
>> Because he had a crystal
>> like me.

She is speechless. Her eye drift over to
Anon's crystal and holster, which are
still resting besides Chapman's box. The
phone rings. She jumps.

> ANON
>> Somebody called when you
>> went out. Didn't leave a
>> message.

The answering machine picks up.

> EVA (RECORDING)
>> Hello. I'm unable to take
>> your call right now, so
>> please leave a message
>> after the tone.

There is a beep followed by a second of
silence, like before. Then there is the

breathing, and then, the voice of the
first pale man.

>   **PALE MAN** (O.S.)
>   (Filtered)
> ... Anon...
>   (A beat)
> ... They now understand
> your condition. ... But
> they need you to
> cooperate. ... Failure to
> cooperate... may result
> in additional
> incinerations...
>   (A beat)
> ... Stay... where you
> are. ... Both you... And
> Dr. Eva Lie.

The pale man hangs up. Anon and Eva are
silent for a second, frightened,
thinking.

>   **EVA**
> The police?

>   **ANON**
> What would we tell them?
> We still don't
> know what this is about.
> We don't even know who
> these people are.

> **EVA**
> But we have the call
> recorded. The threat.

She plays it back.

> **EVA** (RECORDING)
> Hello. I'm unable to take
> your call right now so
> please leave a message
> after the tone.

There is a beep and then static. Nothing
but hissing static.

> **EVA**
His voice, it didn't record.

> **ANON**
> No recording. Just like
> there was no body at my
> apartment. Now do you
> believe me? We've got to
> get out of here. Before
> they come to "collect"
> us.

> **EVA**
> But, where..?

Anon thinks while nervously dressing.

> ANON
> I have to regain my
> memory, right?
>   (A beat)
> Hypnosis?

She agrees.

> EVA
> Hypnosis.

EXT. BRICK BUILDING - DAY

A attractive three story building
housing offices of doctors, lawyers, and
other professionals.

INT. PSYCHIATRIST'S OFFICE - DAY

Anon, trying to relax, is sitting upon a
deep and comfortable brown leather
couch, in a dark, cozy, booklined
office. A folded blanket is resting near
him.

The door to the room is ajar and Eva and
the **PSYCHIATRIST** can be seen standing
together in the adjacent room. (Their
conversation cannot be made out.) A
large, powerful brown **DOBERMAN PINSCHER**
is sitting, at attention, near them.

INT. PSYCHIATRIST'S WAITING ROOM - DAY

Eva is holding Chapman's black box. The Doberman is watching her. The psychiatrist is a lean man with graying hair and a neatly trimmed goatee. His voice is intelligent, calm, and soothing.

> **PSYCHIATRIST**
> Do you know if the hospital tested him for collagen diseases? Or Amyloidosis? Sarcoidosis?

> **EVA**
> I'm not sure. I really don't know.

> **PSYCHIATRIST**
> What about alcoholism? Does he use tranquilizers or barbiturates?

> **EVA**
> I don't think so. All I know is that they treated his injuries and told me that he was suffering from post-traumatic amnesia.

PSYCHIATRIST
Because of the injury to
his head?

EVA
Yes.

PSYCHIATRIST
So, the diagnosis was
based solely on the
injuries that he
sustained from the
accident.

EVA
Yes, I guess so.

The psychiatrist peeks in at Anon.

PSYCHIATRIST
He seems to be healthy.
Alert.

EVA
I don't understand.

PSYCHIATRIST
Well, receiving a blow to
the head isn't the only
way to become amnesic.
Certain diseases and
toxic agents can also

cause amnesia. And post-traumatic amnesia is not the only type of amnesia. There are also purely psychiatric forms. Repression amnesia, hysterical amnesia. Maybe it was the trauma of the accident and not the visible, physical injury that induced the condition. Before he lost his memory, do you know, was he feeling guilty, frightened?

Eva thinks.

> **EVA**
> I don't know, maybe. Why?

> **PSYCHIATRIST**
> Well, the mind has a number of ways of protecting itself. A person's psychoneurotic motivation to dissociate himself from what he views as an intolerable situation in his personal life can result in the repression of painful or

guilt ridden memories.
This sometimes occurs
when a person feels that
he must for some reason
suppress many of his
natural impulses and
feelings. In some cases,
individuals have even
been known to assume new
identities in which they
can act out their
suppressed feelings.

> **EVA**
> So, you're saying that
> Anon's memory loss might
> not be due to his
> physical injury... but to
> some suppressed feelings
> of guilt or fear?

> **PSYCHIATRIST**
> It's possible.

> **EVA**
> But, do you think you can
> help him?

> **PSYCHIATRIST**
> I think so.
> (A beat)
> Why don't you take a

seat. It'll be a little
while. Oh, and pet
Sigmund. Petting a dog
has been proven to relax
people. Even if it's a
Doberman.

She puts on a smile and takes a seat,
keeping Chapman's box close to her. The
Doberman moves closer to her.
Hesitantly, she pats the dog on the head
and it surprisingly reacts
affectionately.

INT. PSYCHIATRIST'S OFFICE - DAY

The psychiatrist enters, closing the
door. He then pulls down the window
blinds, darkening the room.

> **PSYCHIATRIST**
> Well, Dr. Anon, are you
> feeling somewhat
> more relaxed now?

> **ANON**
> A little.

> **PSYCHIATRIST**
> Good. Now, before we
> begin, I'd like to point
> out to you that, although

> hypnosis is a very useful
> exploratory tool, there
> really isn't any way to
> predict in advance if
> anything useful will
> actually come of this.

Anon nods.

> **ANON**
> I was thinking. What if I
> can't be hypnotized?

The psychiatrist smiles slightly, taking
a seat near Anon.

> **PSYCHIATRIST**
> I don't think we'll have
> to worry about that.
> Although the degree of
> suggestibility varies
> greatly from person to
> person, most people can
> be hypnotized. The key is
> placing your trust in me.
> Do you think you can do
> that?

> **ANON**
> Yes.

PSYCHIATRIST
Good. Now, most
individuals feel cold
when reliving experiences
so I'd like you to wrap
that blanket around
yourself.

Anon does so.

PSYCHIATRIST
Now, please place your
feet comfortably upon the
floor and drop your hands
into your lap.

Anon does so.

PSYCHIATRIST
Keeping you head level, I
want you to raise only
your eyes and focus them
upon an imaginary spot on
the ceiling.

As Anon does this:

ANON
I thought... Aren't you
going to swing something
back and forth and tell
me to stare at it?

For the second time the psychiatrist
smiles slightly.

> **PSYCHIATRIST**
> The Chevreul Pendulum. I
> realize that it's become
> synonymous with hypnotism
> bit it's rarely used
> today as an induction
> method.

> **ANON**
> Oh.

> **PSYCHIATRIST**
> Do you have your
> imaginary spot?

> **ANON**
> Yes.

> **PSYCHIATRIST**
> Stare at it. Stare at it
> and concentrate only on
> my voice.
> > (A beat)
>
> I want you to begin to
> take slow, deep breaths.

Anon does so.

                    PSYCHIATRIST
With each breath you will
feel more and more
relaxed.
          (A beat)
Your face will relax.
          (A beat)
Your arms will relax.
          (A beat)
Your hands will relax.
          (A beat)
Your legs will relax.
          (A beat)
All the tension will
leave your body.

Relaxing, Anon is continuing his slow,
deep breathing.

              PSYCHIATRIST (CONTINUED)
          (A beat)
Now breath normally,
concentrating only on my
voice.

Breathing normally, Anon blinks his
eyes.

                    PSYCHIATRIST
Your eyes feel as if they
want to close.
          (A beat)

Let them close.

Blinking slowly, Anon allows his eyes to close.

> **PSYCHIATRIST**
> Good. Let your head fall
> forward.

Anon does.

> **PSYCHIATRIST**
> Now, I want you to
> imagine a descending
> staircase in the darkness
> of your mind. A deep,
> dark staircase.
>   (A beat)
> Soon, you will be
> descending these stairs.
> With each step that you
> take you will fall deeper
> and deeper into a
> hypnotic state.
>   (A beat)
> You will count each step
> aloud as you take it.
>   (A beat)
> Start down the stairs.

A second of silence and then:

                    ANON
                (Slow/Very relaxed)
        One...
                    (A beat)
        ... Two...
                    (A beat)
        ... Three...
                    (A beat)
        ... Four...
                    (A beat)
        ... Five...
                    (A beat)
        ... S.. s.. ss...

Silence.

                    PSYCHIATRIST
        You are now in a deep
        hypnotic state. The only
        voice that you hear is
        mine. When you awaken you
        will not remember any of
        this. Do you understand?

                    ANON
                (Slow/Labored)
        ... I... understand...

                PSYCHIATRIST
        Good.

The psychiatrist pushes down the record

buttons on a large tape recorder.

PSYCHIATRIST
Dr. Anon, together we
will now open your memory
and examine your past.
But first, I have a
question for you. Before
your accident, were you
experiencing feelings
of guilt? Of fear?

A short period of silence and then:

ANON
... Yes... Guilt...
Fear...

INT. PSYCHIATRIST'S WAITING ROOM - DAY

The Doberman is lying at Eva's feet. Eva
is staring at the closed door to the
psychiatrist's office.

After a moment, she turns her attention
to Chapman's black box, opening it,
looking in at the skull fragments. She
carefully sifts through them, looking
for matching pieces. It is difficult but
she finds three pieces that fit
together. Holding them in place, she
stares at them.

> **EVA**
> If only you could talk...

EXT. AFRICAN GRASSLAND - NIGHT (RAIN)

<u>Color is faded - Distant past is viewed</u>

Lightning flashes in the distance. A storm is rolling in, its forewarning drums of thunder announcing its arrival. Several Australopithecus afarensis **INDIVIDUALS** run for cover, disappearing into a small grove of trees.

On a flat rock, surrounded by a sea of tall grass, Gray Streak is helping his afarensis mate give birth. She is lying on her back and in great pain. A spider-webbing bolt of lightning brightens the sky over the field as the storm grows nearer.

Gray Streak's mate is frightened. He calms her by placing a palm on the side of her face; a human-like gesture. She cannot be moved, it is too late for that. She must give birth where she is. She strains.

A head appears. Gray Streak pulls out a newborn child. It is a boy. Strangely, it is not covered with anywhere near the

amount of hair that its parents are,
and, more noticeably, its forehead is
much higher. The child looks much more
human-like. Much like a Homo habilis,
not an infant afarensis. (Mutation?)

Her labor is not over. A second head
appears. Twins. A **BOY** and a **GIRL**.
Lightning explodes and thunder crackles.
It begins to RAIN. The large falling
droplets baptize the newborns; these
"different" children.

Reaching up and holding onto the crystal
rod hanging about his neck, Gray Streak
actually smiles, human-like,
uncharacteristic of an afarensis.
Looking heavenward, he then closes his
eyes, with deep satisfaction, content to
simply feel the rain on his face.

INT. PSYCHIATRIST'S WAITING ROOM - DAY

Eva's eyes are closed. Leaning back in
her seat, she is resting. The door to
the psychiatrist's office is still
closed.

INT. PSYCHIATRIST'S OFFICE - DAY

Anon is still in a deep, hypnotic state.

The psychiatrist is disturbed, his forehead beaded with perspiration. He presses the stop button on his tape recorder, his hand trembling as he does so.

> **PSYCHIATRIST**
> (Shaken)
> ... Anon.
> (A beat)
> I... I want you to um, walk back up your staircase now... Counting backward from five to one... with each step that you ascend.

After a brief moment of silence:

> **ANON**
> ... Five...

INT. PSYCHIATRIST'S WAITING ROOM - DAY

Eva's eyes are still closed. They open as the door opens and Anon and the psychiatrist step out. The Doberman rises.

Anon is tired, drained. The psychiatrist is nervous, frightened.

> **EVA**
> Well?

> **PSYCHIATRIST**
> (To Anon)
> Why don't you take a
> seat.
> (To Eva)
> ... Give me a few moments
> alone, in privacy. To
> review the session.
> I'll... I'll um, be out
> shortly.

The psychiatrist steps back into his
office, glancing back at Anon, oddly,
before closing the door.

> **EVA**
> What was that all about?

> **ANON**
> (Groggy)
> I don't know. I don't
> remember anything after
> he put me under.

INT. PSYCHIATRIST'S OFFICE - DAY

The psychiatrist locks his office's
heavy wooden door and then moves to a
small liquor cabinet and pours himself a

drink, a double, which he gulps down.

A curtain billows and the psychiatrist
sees that one of the room's large
windows is now open, displaying the fire
escape outside. He shivers, and turns
his nose away. It is then that he
notices the bald pale man, standing in
the shadows near the window.

> **PSYCHIATRIST**
> Oh no...

The unusual man steps forward, pulling
out a large, futuristic handgun.

> **FOURTH PALE MAN**
> ... Where is Anon?

The psychiatrist glances at the door to
his waiting room. The pale man sees
this. His dead eyes glance at the couch
and at the nearby tape recorder.

> **FOURTH PALE MAN**
> ... You treated Anon?

The psychiatrist does not know how to
respond. He reaches for his left temple,
feeling ill.

FOURTH PALE MAN
... You treated him?

PSYCHIATRIST
Yes, I did.

FOURTH PALE MAN
... You entered Anon's
mind?

The psychiatrist nods. There is a moment
of silence and then:

FOURTH PALE MAN
... You know about...
"Them?"

The psychiatrist hesitates and then
nods.

Immediately the pale man expresses his
only reaction thus far, a narrowing of
his eyes, predatorily. Simultaneously,
he lifts his unusual handgun. The hole
at the end of the weapon's barrel
automatically winds outward, widening to
a incredible diameter of over a foot
across.

FOURTH PALE MAN
... That knowledge is
forbidden.

The psychiatrist carefully picks up his desktop phone, punching in 911.

Stepping forward in his slow and deliberate walk, the pale man lightly touches his pale fingertips against the metal file cabinet that is in front of him. Vibrating, it rumbles out of his way.

INT. PSYCHIATRIST'S WAITING ROOM - DAY

Sigmund, the psychiatrist's Doberman, rises and moves to the office door, growling.

INT. PSYCHIATRIST'S OFFICE - DAY

The phone's other line is ringing. (The 911 call not yet answered.)

The pale man points his nightmarish weapon at the psychiatrist as the call is answered.

> **WOMAN** (O.S.)
> (Filtered)
> 911 emergency, operator
> 21, please state the
> nature of your emergency.

The interior of the weapon's barrel

ignites and glows a bright yellow-orange.

>   PSYCHIATRIST
>   ... 517 Baldwin...

INT. PSYCHIATRIST'S WAITING ROOM - DAY

The Doberman barks and starts scratching at the door. Eva and Anon step up to the dog.

>   EVA
>   Why's he acting like
>   that?

INT. PSYCHIATRIST'S OFFICE - DAY

The pale man steps up to the telephone, which is now lying on the desktop. Out of sight, somewhere down near the floor, there is a sizzling, frying sound.

>   WOMAN (O.S.)
>   (Filtered)
>   A unit is en route and
>   will be there shortly.

The pale man turns toward the door to the waiting room. The Doberman, on the other side, starts to bark louder, its hard nails scratching at the wood.

>   **WOMAN** (O.S. CONTINUED)
>   (Filtered)
>   Repeat, a nearby unit is
>   en route and
>   will be there at any
>   moment.

The pale man makes a decision and turns away from the door. Ripping the tape cassette from the psychiatrist's recorder, he heads toward the fire escape in his slow, deliberate walk.

EXT. FIRE ESCAPE - DAY

The pale man steps out onto the fire escape, pulling the window closed. He then motions with a finger and the window's metal lock, on the other side of the glass, magically twists, locking the window from the inside.

INT. PSYCHIATRIST'S WAITING ROOM - DAY

The Doberman whimpers and shuffles backward, reacting to a light blue smoke coming out from beneath the door.

>   **ANON**
>   Smells like electricity…

They both look at each other. Anon tries

the door but it is locked. They hear
police sirens approaching.

INT. PSYCHIATRIST'S OFFICE - DAY

On the floor, in the middle of the room,
is a large ashy lump of burnt flesh.
Surrounding it is a left arm, a right
hand, a right leg from the knee down,
and half of a smoldering skull.

All of the limbs are covered by their
blackened clothing. Protruding calcined
bones merge into the central lump of
greasy ash.

EXT. BRICK BUILDING - DAY

Several police cars, an ambulance, and a
fire truck are parked in front of the
building housing the psychiatrist's
office.

                    FIRE MARSHAL (O.S.)
          Spontaneous Human
          Combustion.

INT. PSYCHIATRIST'S WAITING ROOM - DAY

FIREMEN, **POLICEMEN**, and **MEDICAL
TECHNICIANS** are moving about the office
and waiting room. (The office door is

open.) Anon and Eva are talking to an alert, focused, and rapid talking **FIRE MARSHAL**. Sigmund is besides Eva, leaning against her.

>   **FIRE MARSHAL** (CONTINUED)
>   That's what it's called.
>   SHC for short. There's
>   been about 200 reported
>   cases. As he continued,
>   he looks in at the
>   victim's remains.

INT. PSYCHIATRIST'S OFFICE - DAY

Medical technicians are shoveling the psychiatrist's burnt remains into a body bag.

>   **FIRE MARSHAL** (CONTINUED)
>   Nobody understands it but
>   sometimes a person just
>   ignites. Just like that.
>   Woof! Up in smoke.
>   There's never any
>   apparent source of flame
>   but the person's always
>   fried to a crisp. It's
>   something that seems to
>   start in the torso. Limbs
>   are usually left intact.

INT. PSYCHIATRIST'S WAITING ROOM - DAY

> **FIRE MARSHAL** (CONTINUED)
> It's weird. — And to have
> two cases in the same
> week is even weirder.
> Human flesh isn't easy to
> ignite you know. It takes
> a hell of a lot of heat.
> Just think what it would
> take to make a T-bone
> steak disintegrate in a
> pan. And look...

He points into the office.

> **FIRE MARSHAL**
> No damage to the
> surrounding furniture.
> Only the burnt spot on
> the carpet.

Eva glances at Anon.

> **EVA**
> Do you think... Was it
> murder?

> **FIRE MARSHAL**
> Murder? He was in the
> room alone. The room
> locked from the inside.

                        EVA
            But, it's just that,
            well, it's so
            hard to believe, that a
            person can
            just burn up like that.

The technicians leave the office,
wheeling the body bag past them.

                    FIRE MARSHAL
            Yep... I know what you
            mean. Makes you wonder if
            it can happen to you.
            Incineration. And it's
            not something you can
            hide from if it's gonna
            happen. People've been
            burnt like this in bed,
            in the shower, believe it
            or not, in planes, on
            trains. Hell, this can
            get you anywhere.

                        EVA
            Anywhere?

                    FIRE MARSHAL
            Anywhere.

Anon and Eva look at each other.

EXT. COUNTRY ROAD - DAY

A car zooms by, driving away from the
sprawling city.

INT. EVA'S CAR - DAY

Eva is driving. Anon is riding passenger
and Sigmund, the Doberman, is in the
back seat.

> **EVA**
> So, we hide out until
> your memory returns? And
> we head north?

He nods.

> **ANON**
> Feels safe that way,
> north. I'm not sure why,
> it just does. Feels like
> the right direction to
> travel.

Sigmund barks, and Anon reaches back,
his touch very quickly calming the dog.

> **ANON**
> Maybe we shouldn't have
> taken him?

                    EVA
          I feel safer, having him
          with us.

Anon notices how tightly she is gripping
the steering wheel

                    ANON
          Would you like me to
          drive?

                    EVA
          No, I'm alright.

                    ANON
          Are you sure?

She nods.

                    EVA
          So, how far should we go?

                    ANON
I don't know. I guess until we're too
tired to go on, until we need to stop.

Another brief moment of silence,
followed by:

                    ANON
          Eva, I'm sorry I dragged
          you into this. It wasn't

my intention...

      EVA
You needed somebody.
    (A beat)
I wanted to be that
somebody. To be there for
you.

He just looks at her for a second.

      ANON
    Eva, last night, I want
    you to know That it was
    very special to me. As
    if... As if it gave my
    life meaning, as if it
    was the purpose of my
    life, to meet you, to be
    with you.

He takes her hand. There is a silent,
tender moment between them and then:

      EVA
That skull in Chapman's
box. I was thinking that
maybe you should put it
together.
    (A beat)
There's a roll of tape in
the glove compartment.

Anon keeps his eyes on her for a second and then:

> **ANON**
> Sounds like a good idea.

EXT. COUNTRY ROAD - DAY

Eva's car drives by, disappearing down the road.

EXT. TREE LINED HORIZON - DUSK

The sun has sunk low on the horizon.

INT. EVA'S CAR - DUSK

Eva is driving.

Anon has taped together the three skull fragments that Eva had temporarily pieced together earlier. Sigmund eyes the fossil, softly growling at it.

Anon picks up one of the larger fragments, examining it. He fits it into what he has assembled thus far.

EXT. AFRICAN GRASSLAND - DAY

Color is faded - Distant past is viewed

A **GROUP** of afarensis families is gathered together, sitting in the tall grass. Digging up roots, eating gathered fruits, and grooming one another, are silently going about their simple activities.

Gray Streak, his mate, and their two unusual children are among this group. (Gray Streak still has the crystal hanging around his neck.) The children, the **BOY** and **GIRL**, are older and the difference in their appearance is now much more apparent as they are strikingly much more "human" than their progenitors. Two Homo habilis children within an afarensis group?

The boy breaks a stick, shaping it into a digging "tool."

Grey Streak's children draw uneasy stares from the others, who recognize them as different. Two larger **MALES**, uncomfortable, cautiously approach Grey Streak's family. Their observation soon turns into aggression. Barring teeth, they begin to grunt and hiss at the family. Others soon join in, kicking dirt, throwing small sticks, and screeching at the "different" family. Next, hairy arms start swinging and Grey

Streak and his family are hit over and over. Huddled together, the family stumbles off, driven away, ostracized.

EXT. COUNTRY ROAD - DUSK

Eva's car drives by, disappearing down a lonely stretch of road.

INT. EVA'S CAR - DUSK

Having taped the fourth piece into place, Anon finds a fifth piece that fits.

EXT. AFRICAN GRASSLAND - NIGHT

Color is faded - Distant past is viewed

A nearby volcano, glowing against the night sky, is gently spewing molten rock and cinder. Grey Streak and his mate, carrying their unique children, are walking across a field of soft dark ash, laid down recently from the ongoing eruption.

Grey Streak's son plays with the crystal dangling about his father's neck.

Grey Streak turns his eyes heavenward, staring at the millions of twinkling stars.

Slowly, Grey Streak takes hold of his
mate's hand, holding it as they walk.
She does not fully understand the
meaning of the gesture but she accepts
it.

The family walks toward the horizon,
leaving their footprints behind in the
volcanic ash.

EXT. COUNTRY ROAD - DUSK

Eva's car drives toward the horizon,
leaving its tire tracks behind in a
stretch of mud that recently washed over
a section of the road.

INT. EVA'S CAR - DUSK

Anon fits another piece into place.

EXT. AFRICAN RIVER BANK - DAY

Color is faded - Distant past is viewed

Grey Streak's son, now in his early teen
years, is digging into the mud with a
branch that he has shaped into a shovel.
His twin sister is nearby, shaping a
branch into a digging tool of her own.

Grey Streak and his mate are watching their children. The mother's eyes are filled with curiosity and a lack of understanding, the father's with acknowledgement and pride.

The habilis boy strikes a buried nest of turtle eggs and starts to pull out the eggs, one by one.

His sister moves closer, watching. The soil in the hole is moist and it sticks to the boy's palms.

The habilis girl moves still closer, casting a shadow down over the hole. Her brother presses a palm upon her forehead and gently pushes her back, removing the shadow. He is surprised to see that he has left a print of his hand, in mud, pasted upon her forehead.

He creates a handprint on his own forehead. His sister smiles and they begin to paste handprint over each other's bodies.

Their mother has little understanding, nor appreciation of their discovery of art. Grey Streak does. His crystal rod sparkles in the bright sunlight.

The two habilis children laugh and run to the river's edge, washing their hands. They notice their reflections in the water and stare at themselves for several important moments.

The habilis boy then, for the first time, attempts to speak. The words come slowly.

> **BOY**
> Ka... Tama... Ka...
> Tama...

His sister attempts an imitation.

> **GIRL**
> Ka... Ka... Tama... Ka.

The boy sticks a hand into the water, rippling its surface, observing the undulating, concentric rings.

Grey Streak stares at the children. Tools, art, and language. Culture.

INT. EVA'S CAR - DUSK

Anon stares at the assembled fragments. A face is forming. It looks odd. The eyes appear as if they will turn out unusually large.

                    ANON
          ... Large cranium.

Eva glances at him but says nothing.

                    ANON
          Unusually large...

The Doberman, staring at the partially
assembled fossil, backs up, moving
deeper into the back seat.

                    EVA
          Sun's almost down. I
          guess we'll stop at the
          first place we see.

Anon nods and picks up another skull
fragment, turning it about to fit it
into place.

Anon suddenly stops as he notices
something out on the darkening horizon.
He watches what seems to be a falling
star. This "star," however, unexpectedly
turns away from impacting on the earth
and begins to move directly toward them
at an incredible speed, growing in both
brightness and size.

EXT. COUTNRY ROAD - DUSK

This "star" flashes toward Eva's car, growing nearer and nearer, quickly taking on the shape of a classic yet surreal 1950s style flying saucer with a large lump in its center, which is surrounded by windows. Its nearly featureless surface is shiny, the color of polished silver. A strange glow of ionized gas surrounds its hull.

INT. EVA'S CAR - DUSK

Approaching swiftly and silently, the saucer is about to flash over the automobile at an <u>extremely</u> low altitude. Anon stares at it in disbelief.

> **ANON**
> ... Eva...

She turns to him, totally unaware of the approaching saucer.

SWOOOSH! - The entire car shakes madly as the saucer zooms over it. Eva nearly loses control and crashes. Anon, having ducked, peeks over the dash to witness the saucer disappear over the distant horizon.

> ANON
>
> Oh wow...

Eva regains control of the car and immediately looks up to see what had passed over them but, of course, it is too late. She sees nothing.

> EVA
>
> — What? What was that? A plane?

Anon shakes his head and silently mouths the word "no."

> EVA
>
> Where'd it...

> ANON
>
> Eva... I think we're in real, real trouble.

> EVA
>
> What?

> ANON
>
> Real serious, serious trouble.

> EVA
>
> What are you talking about?

Sigmund growls. In the rear view mirror, Eva sees that a dark sedan is approaching them, unnaturally fast.

                    EVA
          Oh no...

                    ANON
          Oh no what?

                    EVA
          They found us.

Anon notices that she is looking in the rear view mirror and spins about. The car approaching them is being driven by the bald pale man. The car is now right behind them and will, within seconds, bang into them.

                    ANON
          Faster. Drive faster.

Eva floors it.

EXT. COUNTRY ROAD - DUSK

Eva's car accelerates down the road but the sedan gains at an unrealistic rate of speed.

BANG! - The sedan rams them from behind.

INT. EVA'S CAR - DUSK

Eva screams as she and Anon lurch forward.

> ANON
> Faster!

> EVA
> I can't go any faster!

EXT. COUNTRY ROAD - DUSK

The sedan is preparing to ram them again.

INT. DARK SEDAN - DUSK

The pale man's corpse-like face is rigid, expressionless.

EXT. COUNTRY ROAD - DUSK

BANG! - The bumpers smack.

INT. EVA'S CAR - DUSK

Sigmund falls to the floor.

Anon sees that the sedan is about to hit them again. Eva's foot has the gas pedal to the floor.

INT. DARK SEDAN - DUSK

The gas pedal is only partially down.
The pale man narrows his eyes,
predatorily, and floors it.

EXT. COUNTRY ROAD - DUSK

The sedan leaps forward as if powered by
some supernatural rocket engine.

INT. EVA'S CAR - DUSK

BANG! - Eva and Anon are thrown against
the dashboard and windshield.

EXT. COUNTRY ROAD - DUSK

The cars' bumpers are mashed together.
The sedan pushes Eva's car forward,
increasing its already terrific speed.

INT. DARK SEDAN - DUSK

The pale man's gas pedal is still
floored.

EXT. COUNTRY ROAD - DUSK

Eva's car is being pushed forward at a
constantly increasing speed.

INT. EVA'S CAR - DUSK

> **ANON**
> We — We have to slow
> down.

Eva comes to her senses and stomps both
feet down on the break.

EXT. COUNTRY ROAD - DUSK

Eva's car's tires lock and skid but the
automobile continues to rocket straight
ahead at an incredible, unrealistic
speed, propelled forward by the
supernatural sedan.

INT. DARK SEDAN - DUSK

The pale man's expressionless face is
grim, his dead eyes unblinking.

EXT. COUNTRY ROAD - DUSK

A short distance ahead of the two cars
the road divides, forking around a high
outcrop of rock.

INT. EVA'S CAR - DUSK

They see that the road forks and that
they are speeding straight ahead, toward

the rock outcropping.

Eva jerks the steering wheel to the right.

EXT. COUNTRY ROAD - DUSK

Eva's car swerves off to the right, skidding down the road.

The dark sedan barrels straight ahead.

INT. EVA'S CAR - DUSK

Eva and Anon hold on for their lives as their car spins and twists down the road.

INT. DARK SEDAN - DUSK
The sedan is about to hit the rocks. The pale man's face remains expressionless.

EXT. COUTRY ROAD - DUSK

The sedan crashes into the rock outcropping. Ricocheting, it flips, rolling over and over, tumbling past Eva's car, which is still skidding to a stop.

INT. EVA'S CAR - DUSK

Eva's car stops. They watch the sedan
roll by them and tumble off the road.

EXT. COUNTRY ROAD - DUSK

Tumbling off the road, the sedan flips
over and hits a stand of trees. There is
then a surreal near silence, the only
sound that of free spinning tires.

INT. EVA'S CAR - DUSK

Eva and Anon are staring out at the
upside-down sedan. Their car coughs and
the engine dies. They just look at one
another.

EXT. COUNTRY ROAD - DUSK

Eva and Anon get out of the car,
followed by Sigmund. They follow the
Doberman over to the turned over sedan.

They stop at the road's edge, looking
down at the wreck. Sigmund growls.

Unexpectedly, the driver's door is
kicked open and the pale man drops out.
Moving slowly and deliberately, he
feebly rises to his feet. He then

suddenly loses all of his strength and
drops into a seated position. His bald
head slumps forward and he becomes
motionless.

          EVA
     Is he dead?

          ANON
     No, I don't think so.

She doesn't understand.

          ANON
     This is the same one that
     "died" in my apartment.

Sigmund runs down to the motionless man.
Nearing the man, the dog stops abruptly,
shivering; the hairs on its back
standing on end. Sniffing the air,
Sigmund begins to bark loudly.

          EVA
     What do we do?
          (A beat)
     My car, do you think
     it'll start?

Anon looks at her car, up into the
darkening sky, and then down at the
mysterious pale man.

>   ANON
>   I think we need some
>   answers.

He starts down to the wreckage. Eva,
unsure, follows.

Anon steps up to Sigmund's side and
shivers. Eva reacts the same way.

>   EVA
>   What's that smell? And
>   that cold? So cold.

>   ANON
>   I'm not sure, but I think
>   it's part of him.

Eva steps closer and her bracelets and
rings tighten and buckle.

>   EVA
>   Ow!

The open car door groans and bends away
from the pale man.

>   ANON
>   I think that's part of
>   him too.

Anon picks up a broken branch and moves

closer to the "dead" man.

> ### ANON
> I don't think he's really
> alive. Not like us
> anyway. I think, I think
> he's some sort of living
> robot.

Anon prepares to poke the man with the
stick.

> ### EVA
> A living robot?

Anon pokes the man in the stomach. The
man's mouth drops open and a breath of
air gurgles its way out. Then slowly,
very slowly, the man's dead eyes open
half way. Eva prepares to run.

> ### ANON
> — No. I, I think it's
> okay.

The pale man is sitting there,
motionless, staring at them with his
half opened eyes.

> ### EVA
> When you say a living
> robot, do you mean

> like... like a
> Frankenstein's monster?

Anon nods and grabs the man's wrist.

> **EVA**
> So, he, he's made up of
> parts of dead bodies?

> **ANON**
> No, just a single body,
> reanimated. Sort of like
> a big rechargeable
> battery, I imagine. No
> pulse.

> **EVA**
> But, his eyes are open.
> He — He's looking at us.

> **ANON**
> I wonder if they're
> looking at us too.
> Through those eyes.

Anon sums up his courage and pokes the
man again.

> **ANON**
> Who are they? Where are
> they?

A silent moment and then the man's eyes widen. It is frightening.

> **FOURTH PALE MAN**
> Bro... ken... Hill...
>> (A beat)
> They... are at... Bro...
> k... en... ... H...
> ill...

> **ANON**
> Broken hill?
>> (A beat)
> Near or far?

The pale man does not answer.

> **ANON**
> Is it near or far?

A moment of silence and then:

> **FOURTH PALE MAN**
> ... N... e... a... r...
> r... r... r...

The man's eyes slowly close. The car's open door groans and the automobile's metal body crumples as if a giant invisible rolling pin is moving over it. Eva's jewelry breaks off and falls to the ground. The sign up on the road groans and bends completely over, its top touching the asphalt.

> ### ANON
> I guess they're always leaking energy... What was left in him must have just, well, been released. Shot out.
> (A beat)
> Inefficient.

There is a moment of silence between them.

> ### ANON
> Do you have a map?

> ### EVA
> Why?

> ### ANON
> I think we should try to find out what this is all about.

> ### EVA
> By going to Broken Hill?

He nods as he notices a bulge in the pale man' wrinkle free jacket. He pushes the jacket open, revealing a strange

weapon holstered at the man's side. It
is the unusual gun that had been used to
kill the psychiatrist.

> **ANON**
> Eva, they found us.
> They'll find us again.

Anon takes the gun.

> **ANON** (CONTINUED)
> Maybe, it's time we find
> them. If we can learn
> what we're up against,
> well, then we'll know
> what to do. We'll have a
> fighting chance.
> (A beat)
> I don't think we can run
> from them. I don't think
> we can actually get away
> from them.

> **EVA**
> What was it that flew
> over us?

He does not answer immediately.

> **ANON**
> A flying saucer. Believe
> it or not.

INT. EVA'S CAR - DUSK

The ignition key turns repeatedly.
Finally the car starts.

> **EVA**
> Oh, thank God.

Anon is looking over a map.

> **ANON**
> Broken Hill, Broken
> Hill... — Found it.

She looks at his pointing finger.

> **EVA**
> That's way out in the
> middle of nowhere. —
> It... It's a cemetery.
> It's labeled a cemetery.

> **ANON**
> We have to go. To find
> out what this is about.

Slowly, she puts the car into drive.

EXT. COUNTRY ROAD - DUSK

Eva's car slowly drives off.

EXT. GRAVEL ROAD - NIGHT

Eva's car is driving down a narrow gravel road located deep in the country.

INT. EVA'S CAR - NIGHT

Eva glances at the unusual gun taken from the pale man, which is lying between them.

> **EVA**
> Are you sure this is the right way?

> **ANON**
> According to the map.

She glances at the gas gauge. A quarter of a tank left.

> **EVA**
> How much further?

> **ANON**
> Three, four miles, maybe le — What's this?

There are several abandoned vehicles parked, haphazardly, in the road directly before them. Their hoods and doors are open.

EXT. GRAVEL ROAD - NIGHT

A United States mail jeep, an old pick-up truck, and a tow truck. All abandoned.

INT. EVA'S CAR - NIGHT

Eva's car's engine suddenly dies.

EXT. GRAVEL ROAD - NIGHT

Their car rolls to a stop near the other vehicles. The automobile's headlights dim and then go out.

INT. EVA'S CAR - NIGHT

> **EVA**
> What happened?

> **ANON**
> I don't know.

Eva tries to re-start the car. Nothing. Anon tries to beep the horn. Nothing.

> **ANON**
> I think the battery's dead.

> **EVA**
> It was a new battery.

EXT. GRAVEL ROAD - NIGHT

They get out of the car. Sigmund too.
Anon is carrying the map, Chapman's
black box, and the unusual gun.

> **EVA**
> Think their batteries
> died too?

Anon does not answer.

> **EVA**
> So, what now?

> **ANON**
> Walk, I guess.

> **EVA**
> To the cemetery?

> **ANON**
> To the cemetery.

Anon hands Eva the gun as a bribe. She
takes it. She also pulls Sigmund close
to her as she follows Anon off.

EXT. GRAVEL ROAD - NIGHT

Anon is leading Eva up a steep hill.
(Their car is nowhere in sight.) As they
move past a dark grove of trees, they
notice an old farmhouse up the road, to
their right. All the windows of its
first floor are boarded up and there are
no lights on within.

> **EVA**
> Think anybody lives
> there?

Anon shrugs and lengthens his strides,
heading toward the house.

> **ANON**
> No lights.

EXT. FARMHOUSE - NIGHT

They stop in front of the farmhouse.

There is an old, beat up tractor parked
in the center of the road. Its hood is
up, and its large tires are wedged by
huge clogs of wood. Although the tractor
is pointing up the hill, these blocks
are oddly positioned in front of its
tires, not behind them. Up the road,
over the hill, a nearby hilltop is

glowing a strange electric blue.

>   **ANON**
>   Let's see if anyone's
>   here.

They walk down the dirt path that leads
to the front door. Anon is about to ring
the doorbell when Sigmund growls. Behind
them, somebody steps out of the darkness
and cocks a gun.

>   **FARMER** (O.S.)
>   Turn around real slow
>   like.

They do. A tall, big boned **FARMER** is
holding a double barrel shotgun pointed
at them. He is roughly fifty years old,
has no eyebrows or eyelashes, and the
hair on the front of his head has been
burnt down to almost nothing. He looks
ill, pale. A large nail is hanging
around his neck, dangling from a long,
dirty string.

>   **FARMER** (CONTINUED)
>   And don't move one damn
>   inch. — And hold that
>   there pooch.

He notices the unusual gun that Eva is

holding.

>   **FARMER**
>   Hey, you got one a their
>   guns..?

He steps toward them. Holding the nail
that is dangling from his neck, he
sniffs the air. Relaxing, he grins ear
to ear.

>   **FARMER**
>   You're okay, aren't 'cha?
>   You're normal. — You come
>   from the city?

Anon and Eva do not know what to make of
the man. Missing eyebrows, etc., he
resembled the pale men.

>   **ANON**
>   Yes, we're from the city.

>   **FARMER**
>   — How are the cities? Are
>   they okay? Or did they
>   black them out too?

>   **ANON**
>   I'm afraid we don't
>   understand.

        FARMER
So, the cities are
okay... And here all
along we thought it was
an all out invasion.
Guess it's only happenin'
out here. You come out by
car?

        ANON
Engine died a couple
miles down the road.

        FARMER
A couple miles?

They nod.

        FARMER
So, it goes for a couple
miles... Well, least now
I know how far the damn
thing stretches. — Come-
on, let's get inside
where it's safe.

They do not move. He smiles, turning his
gun away.

        FARMER
Oh, shoot, you think I'm
one of them zombies,

don't 'cha? Heck, look.

He touches the nail that is hanging
around his neck.

> FARMER
>
> If it don't "bend," he's
> a "friend."

He laughs at his rhyme but stops when he
sees their unchanged expressions.

> FARMER
>
> What? Can't you see I'm
> normal, like you? Hell,
> you ain't a shiverin' are
> ya? And I don't smell
> like no dirty beetle, do
> I?

> ANON
>
> But, your eyebrows, your
> face.

> FARMER
>
> Oh, don't mind that.
> Happened last night. They
> almost got me with their
> Goddamn kugelblitz.

> ANON
>
> Kugelblitz?

>   **FARMER**
>   That's what my Grandpa
>   called it way back in WW
>   I. — Ball lightnin'.
>   That's how they get ya.
>   Don't you know nothin'?
>   Ain't you seen —

Sigmund barks. The farmer is instantly alert, spotting something out on the horizon.

>   **FARMER**
>   Oh Lordy, here they come
>   again.

Anon and Eva turn to see a bright shooting star abruptly pull out of its nosedive and begin to race toward them. Growing larger and brighter, it rapidly takes on the shape of the flying saucer seen earlier.

>   **FARMER**
>   We - we'd better get on
>   inside.

EXT. SKY - NIGHT

Up in the sky: A dark, circular hole winds open on the saucer's otherwise uniform underside and spheres of plasma begin to drop down over the countryside, as if the craft was on a bombing run. Four of the fireballs drop down toward the farmhouse. The orbs are an intense red in color, beach ball size, and as bright as 1,000-watt light bulbs.

Sizzling hot, the quartet of fiery balls immediately separate from one another. Moving with unpredictable vigor, they zip downward, darting about at high speeds, changing directions instantaneously.

EXT. FARMHOUSE - NIGHT

> **FARMER**
> — Fast! Inside!

The farmer charges into the farmhouse.

INT. FARMHOUSE FRONT HALL - NIGHT

Anon, Eva, and Sigmund follow the farmer in.

> **FARMER**
> — Frank! Hey Frank! — We got incoming!

EXT. FARMHOUSE - NIGHT

Zipping downward, one of the balls of plasma ricochets off a nearby telephone pole, scorching it in the process. Exuding a bluish mist, it starts to roll down the pole's power lines, tumbling toward the farmhouse. The heavy-duty plastic encasing the lines melts as it is rolled over, sending up inky, black smoke, and dripping down plastic goo.

At this same moment, another orb lands upon a fence. Dancing along the fence top, it makes its way toward the farmhouse, turning the wood to ash beneath it.

Bouncing off the ground, a third ball starts to drift toward a boarded up window.

The fourth ball is slowly dropping down toward the farmhouse's chimney.

INT. FARMHOUSE LIVING ROOM - NIGHT

The farmer leads them into the room.

              FARMER
    Frank!

FRANK, a lean, weathered, 50 year old, jumps into the room from the kitchen. He points his shotgun at Anon and Eva.

> **FARMER**
> — No, no! They're okay!

> **FRANK**
> — So then what the hell's all the yellin' about?

> **FARMER**
> They're

EXT. FARMHOUSE ROOF - NIGHT

The fourth ball of fire drops into the chimney.

> **FARMER** (O.S. CONTINUED)
> shellin' again! — We gotta

EXT. FARMHOUSE - NIGHT

The third glowing ball pushes itself into the house, squeezing between and burning through the boards crisscrossing a window's frame.

> **FARMER** (O.S. CONTINUED)
> get down inta the cellar!

INT. FARMHOUSE LIVING ROOM - NIGHT

          FRANK
     What? — An' leave the
     prisoner? — Hell no! I'm
     stayin' up here. He ain't
     getting' away on us
     again. No way! - No way!

          FARMER
     — But ya can't stay up
     here, you'll get fried!

Eva screams. Everyone spins about to
witness a red ball of light emerge from
one of the room's boarded up windows.
Rolling up the wall, the sphere starts
across the ceiling. As this happens, a
second ball bounces out of the
fireplace. This one, sizzling hot, zooms
straight at the farmer.

The farmer fires his shotgun, hitting
the thing dead on. Spinning about, the
ball drops into one of two large casks
of water, instantly bringing it to a
roaring boil.

EXT. FARMHOUSE - NIGHT

The other two balls, the one rolling
down the power lines and the one

bouncing down the fence, both enter the
house.

INT. FARMHOUSE LIVING ROOM - NIGHT

The ball rolling across the ceiling
drops down and chases after Frank, who
runs off, yelling. The sphere flashes
forward, missing the man. Zipping into
the kitchen, it bounces into an old iron
stove. There is a thunderous explosion
and the stove blows up, sending bits of
metal flying everywhere.

The other two balls of fire enter the
room, one bouncing across the floor and
the other rolling over a wall.

> **FARMER**
> Every man for himself!

He takes off, the two balls chasing
after him.

The fourth Kugelblitz rises up out of
the boiling water.

Frank ducks into the kitchen.

The fiery orb zips toward Anon and Eva.
Sigmund takes off, running into the
dinning room. Anon and Eva run after the

dog.

INT. FARMHOUSE DINING ROOM - NIGHT

Anon slams the door shut behind them.

INT. FARMHOUSE LIVING ROOM - NIGHT

Becoming pencil thin, the plasma squeezes through the keyhole.

INT. FARMHOUSE DINING ROOM - NIGHT

Coming out the keyhole, the plasma resumes its spherical shape.

Anon, Eva, and Sigmund run toward the room's other door.

INT. FARMHOUSE BACK HALL - NIGHT

The farmer yanks open a door and leaps forward.

INT. FARMHOUSE CELLAR STAIRS - NIGHT

The farmer tumbles, head over heels, down the stairs, the two balls of light giving chase; one rolling down the ceiling, the other bouncing down the wooden steps, scorching each one it touches.

INT. FARMHOUSE HALL - NIGHT

Frank is running. The door in front of
him flies open and Anon, Eva, and
Sigmund race through it, running down
the hall. Frank runs after them.
Bouncing out the door, the fiery ball
chases after them, bouncing and rolling,
eerily, down one of the walls.

INT. FARMHOUSE CELLAR - NIGHT

The farmer is crawling, frantically,
across the dirt floor, the two balls of
plasma bouncing after him.

One of the orbs dives toward the man's
back. The farmer rolls, leaping to his
feet. The Kugelblitz misses. Hitting the
floor, it implodes and disappears with
the sound of a thunder clap.

                    FARMER
          Ha!

Hovering, the remaining ball sizzles,
exudes a bluish mist, and then slowly
turns toward the farmer who scampers
off.

INT. FARMHOUSE LIVING ROOM - NIGHT

Anon, Eva, Frank, and Sigmund, are racing about the room. The Kugelblitz is ricocheting, madly, off the walls, ceiling, and floor.

INT. FARMHOUSE CELLAR BACK STAIRS - NIGHT

The farmer is running up the stone steps.

EXT. FARMHOUSE - NIGHT

The cellar's storm doors fly open and the farmer jumps out. He looks down to see the red ball coming up the stairs. He slams the doors shut.

INT. FARMHOUSE CELLAR BACK STAIRS - NIGHT

The ball bangs against the storm doors. Imploding, it crackles and flicks out in silence, like a lamp turning off. It then reappears, materializing out of nowhere, only to explode with a violent crackle of thunder.

INT. FARMHOUSE LIVING ROOM - NIGHT

Anon, Eva, Frank, and Sigmund, are still racing about the room.

Frank drops into the second giant cask of water, attempting to hide from the ricocheting orb. (The cask besides the one that is still boiling.)

EXT. FARMHOUSE - NIGHT

The farmer backs away from the storm door, looking up into the starlit sky. He sees the saucer flying off in the distance, continuing to drop its ball lightening down on the countryside.

Hearing everyone's yells, screams, and barks, the farmer spins back about.

INT. FARMHOUSE KITCHEN - NIGHT

Anon, Eva, and Sigmund, race into the kitchen. Eva slams the door shut behind them. In the other room, there is a loud splashing sound.

The kitchen's back door yanks open and the farmer rushes in, his shotgun held ready. He jumps over to the refrigerator, which is tied closed by an

entanglement of thick ropes, and then
turns to them.

> **FARMER**
> — Where's frank?

Eva is the first to notice the light
blue smoke that is drifting into the
room, coming from beneath the closed
door.

> **EVA**
> Oh...

The farmer rushes past them, opening the
door.

Frank is standing there, soaking wet.
Blue smoke is emanating from a dark,
circular spot burnt on the center of his
chest.

> **FARMER**
> Frank?

Frank stumbles into the room, dazed.

> **FRANK**
> I — I don't feel so good.
> Chest... it, it's
> burning.

Suddenly, Frank's torso ignites, right before their eyes. His body begins to burn red hot but with the absence of flames. He tries to scream but cannot make a sound. He drops to his knees.

FARMER
Frank!

The farmer jumps to the sink, furiously pushing and pulling the handle of the water pump.

FARMER
— Hold on frank! I'll put ya out!

Frank collapses, his body quickly being reduced to a lump of smelly soot.

Eva notices that, in the other room, the second large cask of water is bubbling; the Kugelblitz had gotten Frank in the water.

Anon stares at Frank's rapidly disintegrating body in utter shock. The farmer runs over with a bucket of water but all that remains is a right hand and forearm and a smoldering left leg.

               FARMER
Oh...
       (A beat)
Oh, Goddamn... They got
ya Frank. They got ya.

After a moment of silence:

               ANON
Ex — Excuse me but, who
are "they?"

               FARMER
Who are they? Sons of bitches, that's
who they are. Sons of bitches.

The farmer steps over to the
refrigerator. Besides being tied shut,
it is penetrated by numerous jagged,
silver dollar sized holes that have been
punched into it.

               FARMER
I, I wasn't sure if it
was dead this time so we
locked it up in here.

He starts untying a large knot in the
ropes.

               ANON
It?

> **FARMER**
> Yep, it. So hold that gun
> ready.

Anon picks up the farmer's shotgun and
does so.

The ropes slacken and fall to the floor.

> **FARMER**
> Okay, you heard of little
> green men? Well, two
> weeks ago, I caught me
> this big green man.

He opens the refrigerator door. Squished
in the refrigerator, sideways, in a
fetal position, is a dead looking **ALIEN
BEING**, garbed in a form fitting flight
suit type of uniform, which is torn and
shredded. A wide, metal collar encircles
the neckline, for a helmet attachment,
although there is no helmet.

The alien's large, fetal head has
pronounced cheekbones and is dominated
by a pair of wrap-around mongoloid eyes,
which are closed. It has no real ears or
nose, only small holes in their place,
and its mouth is simply a narrow slit.

The alien's hairless body is lean,

fragile, and long armed with eight fingered hands. Its unusual skin is rough, wrinkled, and lime in color, resembling, in a strange way, putty, appearing as if it can be molded by mere touch.

INT. EVA'S CAR - NIGHT

Dark shoes crunch over gravel, approaching Eva's abandoned car. It is the first, original pale man.

EXT. GRAVEL ROAD - NIGHT

The pale man turns to the slanted eyed man who is standing before their limousine, in the company of the other three pale men. The bald man, having been recovered from the wreck, is sitting, motionless, in the back of the limo. The limo, unlike the surrounding vehicles, has power, its strong engine humming eerily beneath its hood.

> **PALE MAN**
> ... They are here.

INT. FARMHOUSE KITCHEN - NIGHT

The farmer pulls the knot in the ropes tight, securing the refrigerator. Eva,

sitting nearby, has her unusual gun
pointed at the refrigerator. Chapman's
black box is on the table besides her.
Sigmund is seated near her.

Anon dumps the last shovel full of
Frank's remains into a large sack.

> ### EVA
> If, if it might be alive,
> won't it suffocate in
> there?

> ### FARMER
> That's what them there
> air holes are fer. But
> after what they just did
> ta Frank, I got a good
> mind ta go an' plug 'em
> up.

He picks up his shotgun and moves to
Anon.

> ### FARMER
> So, you just keep that
> fancy gun of yours a
> pointed right at that
> door. It tries to get
> out, kill it.

He takes the sack, containing Frank's

remains, from Anon.

> **FARMER**
> We'll be right back.

> **ANON**
> (To Eva)
> You going to be alright?

She nods. Anon takes a shovel from the farmer and follows him out the back door.

EXT. FARMHOUSE - NIGHT

Anon follows the farmer away from the house. The farmer's eyes are searching the sky.

> **FARMER**
> Hate ta leave her alone
> in there like that but I
> just want ta bury Frank
> righ way. What's left of
> him anyway. But, better
> this way, I guess, than
> to let them turn him into
> one of their zombies.
> That's how they do it, I
> think. They raise up the
> dead.

                    ANON
From Broken Hill
Cemetery?

                    FARMER
Yep. From the ol' Broken
Hill graveyard.

                    ANON
It's that glow over the
hill, isn't it?

                    FARMER
Yep, it's glowin' with
spirit light.

The farmer points off to a very large,
perfect circle of dead grass that has
been flattened to the ground in
swirling, counterclockwise direction.
The grass surrounding this "crop circle"
is green and normal.

                    FARMER
There. That's where I
seen 'em land. Shoot, at
first I thought they was
gonna mutilate my cattle.
— Like they talk about in
them magazines. But they
didn't touch 'em. That's
when I figured it must be

an invasion.

                    ANON
How come you didn't call
the authorities?

                    FARMER
Phones don't work none.
No power for two weeks
now. The green bastards
cut us off. We thought it
was all over, like I
said. Guess it's just
here.

The farmer stops, handing Anon the
shotgun. Taking the shovel, he starts
digging.

                    ANON
Is there any way to reach
the police by foot?

                    FARMER
No use goin' fer help.
Neighbors tried that.
Found 'em burned to a
crisp 'bout half a mile
from here. That's when
they almost got me. A
Goddamn Kugelblitz blew
up right over my head.

> Set my hair on fire,
> burnt my eyebrows off,
> hell, threw me ten feet
> through the air and
> knocked off both my
> shoes! Nope. Believe me,
> you don't wanna go
> trampin' around out
> there.

Anon looks at the sack holding Frank's remains.

                    ANON
          I see your point.

INT. FARMHOUSE KITCHEN - NIGHT

Eva is still pointing the alien gun at the refrigerator.

She has a thought an opens Chapman's box. Taking out the partially assembled fossil, she starts to put the rest of the fragments into place.

Piece by piece, it slowly begins to take shape. She notices that the back of the skull is spider-webbed with cracks, as if something had impacted upon it with great force.

Soon, there is only one very large piece left, which she slides into place. This final piece makes a tremendous difference. The incomplete fossil is of an extraterrestrial identical to the dead alien locked in the refrigerator. (The fossil is incomplete; most of the large cranium is missing but there is enough of it to draw this conclusion.)

EXT. AFRICAN SAVANNA - DAY

Color is faded - Distant past is viewed

An **ALIEN**, turns toward an afarensis female.

INT. FARMHOUSE KITCHEN - NIGHT

> **EVA**
> Oh my God...

She runs out the back door, gun in hand.

Sigmund is about to follow but suddenly stops and turnsback to the refrigerator, as if he were called out by name.

Sigmund then slowly moves to and sits down before the refrigerator, as if obeying commands that only he can hear.

The ropes stretch and the refrigerator door pushes open a few inches. Enormous, coal-black eyes open and stare out at the Doberman.

Sigmund appears to fall into a trance. His eyes unblinking, the dog begins to passively chew through the ropes tying the refrigerator door closed.

EXT. FARMHOUSE - NIGHT

Eva is running toward Anon and the farmer.

> **EVA**
> Anon!

> **FARMER**
> What's she doing outside?

> **EVA**
> Anon, the fossil, it's one of <u>them</u>.
> — One of the aliens. They were here before. In the past. And — And now they're back.

She stops before them.

FARMER
— What're you doing out
here?

EVA
That's what this is all
about. - Don't you see?
They didn't kill Chapman
because he had a crystal.
They killed him because
he gave you that fossil.

FARMER
— Gimme my gun!

The farmer grabs his shotgun from Anon
and starts back toward the house.

FARMER
Hell's bells! — Never
trust a woman!

EVA
And the psychiatrist.
They killed him because
he learned what you can't
remember.

Anon pulls out his holstered crystal.

ANON
So, they're not after me

> because of this
> "signature." They're
> after me because I know
> about them. Somehow I
> know what they're doing
> here. Somehow, I must
> have discovered their
> presence, here on Earth.
> That's what this is all
> about.

The farmer is almost to the house.

INT. KITCHEN - NIGHT

The Doberman's teeth bite down one last time and the ropes slacken and fall to the floor.

EXT. FARMHOUSE - NIGHT

The farmer runs up to the kitchen's back door. It flies open, knocking the farmer to the ground, as the alien leaps out, hunched over, cricket-like.

BLAST! - The farmer shoots both barrels up into the air as he falls.

The alien runs off, experiencing difficulty breathing, its semi-naked chest quivering like a panting dog. It movements are stiff, insect-like, but quite fast. It bounds off toward the glow coming from the other side of the hill.

As the farmer reloads:

> **FARMER**
> Shoot it! Shoot it! Don't let it get away!

Eva aims her unusual gun at the fleeing alien. Its barrel winds open to over a foot in diameter and ignites yelloworange.

> **ANON**
> — Wait!

She pulls the trigger.

WHAM! A fiery kugelblitz rifles out of the weapon, zipping toward the escaping extraterrestrial. And then, a strange thing happens. For some unknown reason, the glowing orb stops dead in its tracks just before hitting the alien. Spinning about, it then starts to wander about, looking for a new target.

> **FARMER**
> Oh shit!

The farmer scampers into the house.

The fiery ball turns toward Anon and Eva.

> ANON
>
> Oh no...

Eva drops her gun. The kugelblitz exudes a bluish mist and then flashes toward them.

> ANON
>
> Run!

They do so. The sphere is fast, however, and will overtake them. They duck and it zips over their heads.

The farmer sticks his head out the back door and Sigmund jumps outside, barking.

> FARMER
>
> Come-on! Get inside! Run! Run!

They start running back toward the house.

Stopping, slowly, the Kugelblitz wobbles as it painstakingly turns about.

Bouncing forward, it darts left to right as it gives pursuit.

They are almost to the house. Eva trips and falls. Anon pulls her to her feet. Sigmund is barking like crazy. The fiery ball is flashing toward them, about to overtake them.

Anon, out of desperation, shoves Eva forward. The farmer grabs her, yanking her into the house.

INT. FARMHOUSE KITCHEN - NIGHT

The farmer and Eva fall to the floor.

EXT. FARMHOUSE - NIGHT

The Doberman runs off.

Anon turns about just as the kugelblitz is about to hit him square in the chest. But, at the very last possible moment, it stops dead, mere inches from Anon's torso, just hovering there, bouncing a bit, wobbling. Anon just stares at it, perspiring, his suit blackening from the heat.

Slowly, ever so slowly, the fiery orb turns toward the direction taken by

Sigmund. Pulsating, it jerks left to right as it moves a few yards from Anon. Then, it implodes, disappearing with the sound of crackling thunder.

Eva and the farmer rush outside to find Anon standing there, confused. Sigmund runs over to Eva.

> **EVA**
> What happened?

> **ANON**
> I — I don't know. It just imploded... Maybe because I have this signature? Is that what it's for, for protection?

> **FARMER**
> There he goes.

They see the alien's strange silhouette disappear over the hilltop, highlighted by "spirit-light."

> **ANON**
> He's going up to Broken Hill.

The farmer stamps his foot in anger.

                    FARMER
          Ah shit! He's gonna go
          an' tell them all where
          we are. That we're hidin'
          out down here. Goddamn!
          It's gonna be raining
          ball lightning tonight. —
          We gotta go an' get him
          else we're good as dead.

Anon and Eva exchange worried glances.

                    FARMER
          Come-on.

EXT. GRAVEL ROAD - NIGHT

The farmer kicks out the blocks from in
front of the old tractor's rear tires.
Amazingly, the tractor groans as if
straining to move forward, up the hill.

The farmer runs to the front of the
tractor, where Anon, Eva, and Sigmund
are standing.

                    FARMER
          Get on, get in and hold
          them breaks down.

Anon glances into the open hood.

                        ANON
But, there's no battery —

                        FARMER
— Just go an' do it.

They get into the tractor, Anon pressing
down on the break.

                        ANON
        Okay.

The farmer kicks out the block in front
of one of the front tires. The tractor
twists in the road, groaning, straining
to lurch forward.

The farmer is about to hand his shotgun
in to Eva but he has second thoughts.
Giving her a dirty look, he tosses the
gun into the back.

The farmer kicks out the last block. The
tractor groans and starts sliding
forward, skidding uphill! The farmer
jumps inside.

                        FARMER
        Okay, let go of them
        breaks.

Anon does so and the tractor lurches

forward, its large wheels spinning. Five
miles per hour, ten miles per hour,
fifteen, twenty miles per hour. Anon and
Eva look to the farmer.

> **FARMER**
> Don't ask 'cause I don't
> know how it works. It
> just does.

The tractor jerks slightly to the right,
its giant rear tires splashing through a
stream that is flowing along the side of
the road, the water running uphill.

As they roll toward the top of the hill,
the surrounding foliage begins to
change. Tree limbs curve and bend in an
eerie way, attracted by some unseen
force to what lies on the other side of
the hill.

A layer of green moss appears, thin at
first but thickening into a smothering
blanket as they approach the hill's top.
The surrounding trees and fence posts
are draped with it.

They reach the hilltop, finding dark
objects littering the ground; dead birds
and the hollow shells of dried out
insects.

The tractor jerks about a few times as it is yanked over the hilltop.

EXT. OTHER SIDE OF THE HILL - NIGHT

There is a long, steep slope, and then, down below, Broken Hill. The cemetery contains strangely leaning tombstones, open graves, and ground level patches of luminous electrical activity. These ground-hugging clouds of supernatural fog are glowing a frightening yet beautiful electric blue. The surrounding hills are all glowing with this strange "spirit light."

The tractor, jerking over the top of the hill, quickly picks up speed, pulled faster and faster toward the center of the cemetery.

Anon presses down on the break. The tires lock but the tractor continues forward, its non-spinning tires digging trenches into the gravel road, which ends at the foot of the Broken Hill Cemetery.

> **FARMER**
> Jump!

They do so, tumbling down the road. The

tractor, picking up speed, twists as it
reaches the bottom of the hill. Sliding
over tombstones, it finally slams into
an old caretaker's house, which itself
is squishes up against a nearby
hillside, as if sent there by some
invisible mudslide.

Anon, Eva, the farmer, and Sigmund rise
to their feet. Standing, they find
themselves leaning forward, toward the
cemetery's center, at an unnatural,
gravity-warped angle. It seems
impossible that they are not falling
flat on their faces.

The farmer readies his shotgun and lifts
his chin, pointing it toward Broken Hill
Cemetery, which he heads off toward.
Anon, Eva, and Sigmund follow, taking
uncoordinated, unsure steps.

EXT. BROKEN HILL - NIGHT

They reach the bottom of the hill:
Broken Hill Cemetery.

                    ANON
          I've been here before...

                    EVA
          This must be where you

found that crystal. Found
out about them.

He is unsure:

> **ANON**
> Yes... It has to be...

They start through the cemetery. Many of
the graves have been disturbed, dug up.

They cautiously step into one of the
low-lying patches of luminous electrical
fog. It engulfs them, wrapping them in
clinging, electric blue garments.

> **FARMER**
> St. Elmo's fire. That's
> what this is. St. Elmo's
> fire.

Anon raises a hand above his head. His
fingertips spark and glow a luminous
blue. Eva runs a hand over her hair,
which sparkles.

> **ANON**
> This must be some type of
> electromagnetic hotspot.
> Large-scale discharge of
> terrestrial electricity
> into the atmosphere.

Eva looks down at her legs as she steps
forward, continuing to have difficulty
walking in her leaning forward stance.

> **EVA**
> But, how can this be
> possible?

> **ANON**
> I don't know, the Earth
> is a gigantic electrical
> machine but this...

> **FARMER**
> — There he is!

BLAM! — The farmer shoots. A dark figure
falls to the ground, ten yards distant.

> **FARMER**
> Got 'cha you son of a
> bitch!

They run toward the fallen body. As they
near it, they straighten in their
stance, that is, having reached the
cemetery's center, they are now standing
straight again, the gravity anomaly no
longer in effect.

As they step up to the body, they feel a
sudden chill and a reeking odor assaults

them. The farmer's nail, hanging around
his neck, bends and curls up. Lying at
their feet is the fifth pale man who had
chased Anon down his driveway. He is
lying on his side, motionless.

>   **EVA**
>   He's "dead?"

Anon shrugs.

The farmer kicks the pale man over, onto
his back. There is a large wound in his
chest but there is no blood and his eyes
are open, blinking slowly. He tries to
speak but only manages to exhale stale
air. Slowly, his eyes close. The
farmer's nail then knots up and his
gun's barrel groans, bending slightly.

>   **FARMER**
>   First time I ever killed
>   someone who was already
>   dead.

Anon kneels besides the downed pale man,
taping him. His dead eyes re-open.

>   **ANON**
>   You, you're from here?
>   From Broken Hill? They
>   dug you up?

FIFTH PALE MAN
No... o... o... o...

ANON
But, then, what are they
doing out here? The open
graves?

FIFTH PALE MAN
Arch.. ae.. ology...

ANON
Archaeology? But, where
are you from?

FIFTH PALE MAN
... The... P.. a..
s..t...

ANON
The past?

FIFTH PALE MAN
... Y.. e.. s.. s.. s..
s... Ke.. pt... al..
ive... to,.. scr.. ve...

The pale man's eyes start to close.

ANON
- No, wait, what about
"them?" Where are they

from? What are they doing
here?

The man's eyes close completely and he
becomes lifeless.

The Doberman growls, the hair on its
back standing on end. Next, they are all
assaulted by an icy chill and an
overpowering stink. Groaning loudly, the
farmer's shotgun curls up, twisting
itself into a useless knot of dark
metal.

Shadows then appear, covering them. They
slowly turn around to find three pale
men standing behind them. (The original
pale man and the two from the limo.)

Additional shadows appear as three more
PALE MEN emerge from the darkness. (One
of them is the bald pale man, recharged
and "alive" again.) With grim, dead
faces, these six pale men stare
emotionlessly at Anon, Eva, and the
farmer, whom they have surrounded.

The original pale man looks down at his
dead comrade. Slowly, his dead white
face wrinkles up. He is angry and it is
terrifying. He pulls a kugelblitz pistol
from his shoulder holster, and points it

at the farmer.

The gun's barrel immediately winds open
to a diameter in excess of twelve
inches, its interior igniting a fiery
orange-yellow. He starts to pull the
trigger.

> **SLANTED EYED MAN** (O.S.)
> No! Stop.

The pale man lowers his weapon.

The slanted eyed man steps forward, out
of the darkness, walking up to the pale
man. The Doberman growls once but then
meekly approaches the man. The man takes
a moment to affectionately pet the dog
before he looks down at the dead pale
man, expressing a moment of grief. He
then focuses a potent combination of
arrogance and compassion on Anon's
little group. The man's tone is
hubristically noble, compassionate yet
chastising.

> **SLANTED EYED MAN**
> You still bear the stamp
> of your lowly origin. Too
> much "ape" in your blood.

There is a noise behind the man, and Eva

gasps as they witness the escaped alien
appear. The slanted eyed man takes one
of the extraterrestrial's arms,
steadying the alien, who is taking
labored breaths from multiple lungs. The
Doberman moves to the alien's side,
affectionately licking one of its eight
fingered hands.

The alien looks at Anon, Eva, and the
farmer. Its large, wrap around eyes are
entrancing, like living pools,
reflecting a noble alien mind of
benevolent wisdom. In regards to
intellect, the alien appears as distant
from humans as humans are from apes.
Yet, an intellectual kinship of sorts is
visible, sending a clear message that
there is nothing to fear. Anon loses
himself in the alien's eyes. Eva's
fright vanishes completely. She speaks
to the alien:

                    EVA
          You were here before, in
          our past, weren't you?

The strange man answers for the alien.

                    SLANTED EYED MAN
          Long ago, your ancestors
          were confronted with

regression. Extinction.
But your kind displayed
promise. And so they
helped. This is their
way.
    (A beat)
And now they're here once
again. To again prevent
your extinction. You
haven't really changed.
Only in your destructive
ability. You once used
stone to kill...And now,
20,000 nuclear
warheads..?

Eva, Anon, and the farmer are silent.

      SLANTED EYED MAN
To them, you were apes
only yesterday. They
believe you require more
time. And further
assistance, to mature.
They're here to help,
once more.

      EVA
But, if they're here to
help, then, why are you
killing people?

                    SLANTED EYED MAN
        Once unleashed, these
        pallid automatons can
        prove challenging to
        control. Even in this
        artificially maintained
        state, Cro-Magnons have a
        proclivity for violence.

                    EVA
        Cro-Magnons? - As in
        cavemen?

Anon snaps out of it and looks at the
pale men.

                    ANON
        The first early humans in
        Europe... The Paleolithic
        cave painters; of 30,000
        years ago... "Kept alive
        to serve."
                (A beat)
        ... "They've" been
        visiting Earth,
        repeatedly. Monitoring
        us...

A hint of a smile from the slanted eyes
man.

EVA
And killing?

SLANTED EYED MAN
They don't want to kill.
But, like all living
creatures, they feel the
need to protect
themselves. These
ancient, hibernating
benefactors, these elders
of the universe, to
protect the secrecy of
their existence, yes,
they will kill. In order
to help you.

ANON
You keep saying, to help
us? How? How did they
help us? How are they
helping us?

There is a bright disturbance behind
them as the flying saucer from earlier
appears, rises up from behind the other
side of a nearby hill. It silently
glides toward them, hovering over the
graveyard.

The slanted eyed man looks respectfully
and affectionately at Anon.

                    SLANTED EYED MAN
          Anon... It's time to
          break your signature.

Eva turns to Anon who, confused, pulls
out his crystal, looking at it.

                    SLANTED EYED MAN
          Yes, break it.

                    EVA
          No, Anon don't. Don't
          trust him.

Anon is unsure.

                    SLANTED EYED MAN
          If you don't trust me,
          what do you genuinely
          want to do? What are your
          innermost feelings
          telling you to do?

Anon, guided by instinct, takes his
crystal rod in two hands and strains to
break it. It becomes soft in his grip
and, after a moment, snaps in half. A
luminous blue-green mist begins to
slowly drift up out of the broken
crystal. Oddly it does not disperse as a
gas normally would, but it remains more
or less concentrated.

Behind them, a transparent tube - an elevator of sorts - descends from the saucer, down to the ground. Two lime colored **ALIENS** with giant, wrap around eyes, step out of this elevator. They are wearing flight uniforms similar to the escaped alien's, but both creatures are wearing giant, fully transparent helmets over their large, fetal heads. (One of the two aliens is **RED MARK**, who has a large, very distinctive reddish birthmark on the right side of his face his face.)

Anon, in an unexpected instant of pure instinct, dips his nose over the broken crystal and inhales the glowing mist.

>   **ANON**
>   Why did I do that..?

And then it happens, slowly. Anon begins to change, his skin turning lime green in color. Anon, shocked, looks down at his wrinkling body, and remembers, finally, who he really is: Anon the extraterrestrial.

>   **EVA**
>   — What did you do to
>   him!?

                    SLANTED EYED MAN
          It was time for Anon to
          shed his disguise.

                    EVA
          Disguise..? He, he's one
          of.."them?"

The slanted eyed man simply nods.

                    EVA
          Oh, Anon...

Anon does not know what to say.

                    SLANTED EYED MAN
          He didn't know.
               (A beat)
          He had become one of you.
          Temporarily. In order to
          complete his mission. The
          accident, the memory
          loss, it was unexpected.
          For a short time, he
          truly was one of you.
          They thought they had
          lost him.

Eva steps before Anon, her eyes tearing.

                    EVA
          Anon...

(A beat)
I — I loved you.

Anon begins to experience difficulty
breathing as he continued to slowly
transform.

                    ANON
               (Alien voice)
          — I — loved - you...

Anon is surprised by the sound of his
voice, frightened by it. It is alien and
vibratory, incapable of being imitated
by human vocal cords. He delivers each
word with effort.

                    ANON
               (Alien voice)
          - Eva... — I — love -
          you...

Anon's soul is being torn asunder by the
shock of rediscovering his true identity
coupled with the strong emotions that
are swelling within him.

The alien with the distinctive
birthmark, Red Mark, gently takes Anon
by the arm.

> ### SLANTED EYED MAN
> I'm sorry, but he must go
> now.

Red Mark, the alien, guides Anon toward
the saucer's elevator.

Eva, leans into the farmer's arms,
crying.

The original pale man, slowly turns to
the slanted eyed man.

> ### SLANTED EYED MAN
> No. Let them live.
> There's been too much
> killing.
>> (To the Pale men)
> It's.... your "time" now.

The pale men pick up their shot kinsman
and orderly assemble before their
master, who waves to the original pale
man, who obeys by stepping away from the
group and falling in behind the slanted
eyed man.

> ### SLANTED EYED MAN
> Faithful yet... The
> present is not for the
> likes of you.

Almost hesitantly, he draws out a long
alien pistol that resembles a garden
weed sprayer, with a trigger instead of
the pumping mechanism.

SLANTED EYED MAN
You belong to the past.

The slanted eyed man, with sympathetic
regret, waves his alien pistol,
peacefully spraying the pale men with a
diaphanous alien vapor, which silently
and unceremoniously disintegrates them,
clothing and all, into harmless piles of
dust.

To answer Eva's look:

SLANTED EYED MAN
Do not grieve for them.
They had their time.

The original pale man displays a hint of
facial disturbance and afterthought.

Eva and the farmer turn their attention
to the saucer's elevator.

Anon looks back at Eva as he steps into
the elevator. Their eyes meet.

INT. SAUCER ELEVATOR - NIGHT

Anon (still slowly changing) is looking out at Eva, staring into her eyes. The aliens converse in their own language (Alien language to be created) their words <u>SUBTITLED</u>:

> **ANON**
> (In SUBTITLES)
> No. — I want to stay.

The alien, with the birthmark, responds, compassionately.

> **RED MARK**
> (In SUBTITLES)
> You know you cannot.

> **ANON**
> (In SUBTITLES)
> I need to stay. I love...

Red Mark's giant eyes fill with sympathy and understanding.

> **RED MARK**
> (In SUBTITLES)
> This is not our world.
> Remember Atha?

Anon nods, grieving.

RED MARK
(In SUBTITLES)
Always remember Atha...

They start to ascend, slowly, floating up toward the saucer.

EXT. BROKEN HILL - NIGHT

The farmer looks to the slanted eyed man.

FARMER
Aren't you a going with them?

SLANTED EYED MAN
No. My place is here. It is now my time.

Eva looks at the man's abnormally high forehead and has an epiphany.

EVA
The way they helped us in the past... The way they're helping us now... You're...

He nods.

            EVA
And Anon's mission,
I'm... I'm...

Looking at her stomach, he nods again.

            EVA
Oh, no, please no...

            FARMER
What? I don't get it?

            EVA
I — I'm pregnant...
        (A beat)
... Glorified apes. "Half
beast... half angel."
That's what we are. ...
That's all we really
are...

The saucer's elevator retracts and the
craft silently lifts high up into the
sky, traveling straight up. Gliding off
like a slow moving star, it heads toward
the horizon.

            SLANTED EYED MAN
Long ago, when Earth was
young, they destroyed
their own planet. War.
Only these few survived.

> They've since genetically
> eliminated all aggressive
> traits within themselves.
> But they are so few in
> number. And only male.
>   (A beat)
> They adopted Earth, your
> kind, and the other known
> worlds. In order to live
> on in some way... by
> proxy. And, to prevent
> others from suffering
> their fate.
>   (A beat)
> You've been blessed.

With the saucer's departure, the
supernatural "spiritlight" slowly
vanishes and the cemetery returns to
normal.

EXT. FARMHOUSE - NIGHT
Everything is silent.

INT. KITCHEN - NIGHT

The assembled, incomplete fossilized
alien skull is resting on the kitchen
table. The spider web fracture, on the
back of the skull, remains a puzzle.

EXT. AFRICAN GRASSLAND - DAY

Color is faded - Distant past is viewed

Prehistoric herbivores and carnivores scatter as a flying saucer descends down toward the savanna. Hovering, the saucer maintains its position several stories above the grassland. (The saucer is the same saucer from Broken Hill Cemetery.)

A group of two **AFARENSIS FAMILIES** point excitedly up at the saucer. The children of the group are **HABILIS BOYS** and **GIRLS**. The two adult afarensis males, One Prong and Two Prong (as seen in an earlier prehistoric flashback) have their signature crystals hanging about their necks.

One Prong starts to walk off toward the saucer but stops as he sees Two Prong hesitating to follow, unwilling to leave his family.

One Prong goes back and gently takes Two Prong by the arm, pulling his away. But Two Prong resists, reaching out to touch his afarensis mate. One Prong pulls Two Prong close and whispers to him for some time.

Two Prong eventually composes himself
and allows One Prong to guide him away.
Walking off toward the saucer, they
leave their families behind.

EXT. AFRICAN RIVER BANK - DAY

<u>Color is faded - Distant past is viewed</u>

The male afarensis, Three Prong, with
Chapman's threepronged crystal hanging
about his neck, lowers his cupped hands
into the river to get a drink. He
notices a strange reflection in the
water and looks up to see the distant
flying saucer, hovering in place.

He starts running down the riverbank,
toward the saucer, which he is looking
up at.

A pack of prehistoric hyenas race over a
small hill and leap down onto the river
bank, giving chase to Three Prong who
starts to run for his life.

Looking up into the sky, Three Prong
strains to run faster, Chapman's key-
like rod bouncing about wildly. (<u>The
same as shown in the earlier prehistoric
flashback but now what he is looking at,
the saucer, is shown</u>.)

The key-like rod breaks loose and falls to the muddy ground.

Three Prong realizes that he has dropped his key. He stops and turns about. Sparkling in the sunlight, the key is halfway between himself and the rapidly approaching hyenas.

Three Prong then glances up at the distant saucer. Turning back about, Three Prong runs toward his crystal, knowingly risking almost certain death.

Three Prong trips and falls. The key is less than two feet away. He throws out a hairy arm, reaching for it. The hyenas tear into him.

The hyenas are attempting to pull Three Prong in different directions. One sinks its teeth into an outstretched arm. Another into a leg.

The blue-black rod is pressed down into the mud by the talon of a landing vulture.

Three Prong's sentient death scream is chilling and it echoes out over the land.

EXT. AFRICAN SAVANNA - DAY

<u>Color is faded – Distant past is viewed</u>

Grey Streak leads his mate and daughter out of a small clump of trees, drawn by the sound of stampeding hooves. He sees the saucer.

He turns to his afarensis mate, looking at her with caring eyes. He then looks back toward the hovering saucer. He sees the two other crystal bearing afarensis males (One Prong leading Two Prong) moving toward the saucer's descending elevator.

The form of a helmeted lime colored **ALIEN** is within the elevator, floating down toward the grassland.

Grey Streak takes his crystal, squeezes it, and snaps it in half. He then inhales the luminous gas emanating from it. Slowly, he starts to change into a lime colored extraterrestrial. His afarensis mate and habilis daughter cower in fear at he transforms.

Grey Streak, his skull swelling, turns to his mate. He loves her, and his daughter, and he suddenly does not want to leave his new family. He steps toward them, his arms outstretched. His habilis mate screams. He attempts to calm her, experiencing difficulty breathing in Earth's atmosphere.

GREY STREAK
(Alien voice)
— Eve...

At this moment, Grey Streak's habilis son comes out of the trees and sees an 'alien' approaching his sister. He picks up a large stone and charges the creature.

WACK! - He hits his alien father from behind, shattering the back of his skull. Grey Streak drops to the ground, dead, but continuing to transform.

Further out on the savanna: One Prong and Two Prong see Grey Streak fall to the ground; struck down. Expressing grief and hesitation, they step into the elevator. The aliens converse in their own language (Alien language to be created) their words SUBTITLED:

TWO PRONG
(In SUBTITLES)
Atha...

One Prong turns to Two Prong, for the
first time his right side can be seen.
The right side of his face is decorated
by a very distinctive birthmark. One
Prong is Red Mark

> **ONE PRONG / RED MARK**
> (In SUBTITLES)
> Atha is no more...
> (A beat)
> Always remember, Anon, we
> do not belong here.

Two Prong is Anon.

The alien standing besides them places a
comforting hand on Anon's shoulder.
Grief swelling in his large, wrap-around
eyes, he slowly activates a mechanism
and they float upward.

Down below: Grey Streak's habilis son is
standing over his father's alien body,
holding the blood stained stone. He
watches the saucer lift upward and then
flash off like a star in daylight.

Slowly, the animals move back onto the
vacated area of savanna.

The habilis boy eyes the carnivores and
then looks at the rock he is still

holding. He sees something inside it. He picks up a second rock.

<u>As seen in an earlier prehistoric flashback</u>: The first true early human. Although his face is still primitive, his eyes hold an intelligence and an awareness seen nowhere else in the animal kingdom. Bringing down a strong right hand, he strikes two rocks together, creating a sharp cutting edge. The broken off section of stone thuds to the ground. (One of the rocks is stained by blood.)

EXT. SAVANNA - DAY

<u>Color is faded - Distant past is viewed</u>

A small band of Homo habilis **YOUTHS** venture out onto the savanna.

> **ANON** (V.O.)
> Homo habilis. Handy man.
> First of the genus Homo,
> habilis possessed a
> substantially larger
> brain, rudimentary
> speech, the beginning of
> culture, and the ability
> to look into a stone and
> see the tool inside it.

>   Habilis dared to go out
>   onto the savanna. This is
>   your single most
>   important ancestor.

A large **SABER TOOTHED CAT** is facing the
sun, the yellow orb's reflection
mirrored in the carnivore's dark eyes.

EXT. SAVANNA - DAY

Color is faded - Distant past is viewed

Flashing over the savanna, the saucer
slips toward the distant horizon.

INT. SAUCER - DAY

Color is faded - Distant past is viewed

The interior of the saucer is dominated
by one enormous domed flight control
center, surrounded by approximately two
dozen elevator size, frost covered
chambers that line the circumference of
craft's slanted inner wall.

The spacecraft is being piloted by a
single **OLD ALIEN** who is wearing an
elaborate transparent helmet, flying the
ship by thought. Approximately two-dozen
OTHER ALIENS are present. A few are

quietly moving about, performing various
tasks. Most are silently making their
way to the elevator size chambers,
lining the surrounding wall. Climbing
into these frosty booths, the aliens are
sealing themselves into deep, cryogenic
freeze. Into hibernation.

The alien from the saucer's elevator is
walking with One Prong, who breaks his
signature. Inhaling its mist, he slowly
begins to transform into his true
extraterrestrial form.

Two Prong, Anon, still in his afarensis
form, is walking behind them,
heartbroken and grief stricken. He
breaks his signature, inhales its gas,
and then peers out one of the saucer's
huge rear windows, viewing ancient Earth
from a great height. There are clouds
and then the curvature of the planet
becomes visible.

EXT. PLANET EARTH

<u>Color is faded - Distant past is viewed</u>

The alien saucer leaves Earth's
atmosphere. Flying off into outer space,
it slowly disappears into a distant star
field.

EXT. FARMLAND - NIGHT

Gliding over farmland, the saucer slips toward the distant horizon.

INT. SAUCER - NIGHT

Two **ALIEN BEINGS** are helping the rescued alien (from the farmhouse) into a crystalline chamber, for medical treatment.

Anon, the alien, is following Red Mark to the saucer's flight control center, which is identical to that seen in the prehistoric flashback. Most of the aliens are preparing for icy hibernation in deep cryogenic freeze.

Anon, confused by his emotions, drifts away from the others. He looks out one of the saucer's huge rear windows, imagining, for a moment, that he sees Eva's face reflected in the portal. He hears Red Mark's voice in his mind:

> **RED MARK** (V.O.)
> (In SUBTITLES)
> This is not our world.
> (A beat)
> Always remember Atha...

He then hears Eva:

> **EVA** (V.O.)
> I - I loved you.

Anon looks to one of several spherical pods sunk into the ship's aft hull. Thinking, he moves to a huge orb containing several golf-ball size crystal spheres, blueblack in color. He takes one, clandestinely hiding it within his large alien hands.

Anon then moves to the back wall, pausing near a spherical pod. Emitting a visible stream of mental energy, he operates the pod's control console with his mind. Anon then slips inside the pod and it jettisons.

EXT. FARMLAND - NIGHT

The pod jets away from the saucer, plowing through the glow of ionized gas surrounding the ship's hull.

EXT. GRAVEL ROAD - NIGHT

The slanted eyed man is leading the original pale man toward a limo. He notices the escape pod, shining brightly, as it flashes down toward

Earth.

The original pale man witnesses this as well and narrows his sunken eyes.

INT. SAUCER - NIGHT

Red Mark and a few other aliens are gathered about the jettisoned escape pod, speaking in their alien tongue.

EXT. FIELD - NIGHT

The escape pod lands in a field. Anon crawls out of it and immediately it dissolves behind him, creating a strange crop circle.

Anon, still in alien form, staggers away from the dissolving pod and drops to his knees, finding it difficult to breath. He ingests the golf ball size sphere and doubles over in pain, slowly, ever so slowly, changing back into Anon the human.

Vomiting, he then scoops up what solidifies into a signature rod.

Anon rises, looking up into the sky. The saucer, shinning like a star, slows as it glides toward the horizon.

Anon staggers off.

EXT. COUNTRY ROAD - NIGHT

An old pick-up truck is driving down the road. Anon stumbles out of a cornfield, his clothing all torn up, stepping in front of the truck, stopping it. He moves to the **DRIVER**.

> **ANON**
> I, I need your help. Can you take me to the nearest town. I have to find someone.

ENDING CREDITS BEGIN and continue until **ENDING CREDITS END**.

FADE OUT

Brief notes for TV series follow:

Notes for TV series:

* These last two scenes of the movie can
be filmed both with the actor from the
film and with several other actors in
the event that the film's actor is
unable or unwilling to commit to a
sequel or television series. Anon's new
appearance can be easily explained as
the inability of the alien technology to
produce the same exact human disguise.
This could actually add some additional
drama to the television series, as Eva
will not recognize the new Anon.

* In the TV series Anon will always be
just missing Eva, as the men in black
come closer and closer to catching him.

* The creation of new "pale men" will be
shown in the sequel or TV series, now
that the slanted eyed man will need
assistance tracking down escaped Anon.
This will be part of the unveiling of
the secrets behind the pale men. Also
featured will be the personal history
(through flashbacks) of the surviving,
original pale man.

* The origin of the slanted eyed man
will also be unveiled.

* A voyage to the alien's home planet will also be featured.

The screenwriter has many other ideas for the proposed TV series and can present them to interested parties.

www.ingramcontent.com/pod-product-compliance
Lightning Source LLC
Chambersburg PA
CBHW051533250626
47157CB00001B/23